# H(

# Time

# Erica Lee

## Dedication

Dedicated to anyone who has struggled to come out or may still be struggling now. Your feelings are valid and you are important. If you're now out and proud, congratulations. I hope you smile a little deeper every day because of that fact. If you're still in the closet, take your time. Come out when you feel comfortable and when you're ready and just know that this community will be waiting for you with open arms.

# Table of Contents

# Chapter 1: Bailey

"Okay, you two. Get together." Tears came to my mom's eyes as she snapped pictures of my sister and me.

I rolled my eyes playfully at my mom, then looked toward my mama. "Could you please get her under control?"

Mama put an arm around Mom's waist and smiled at her lovingly, then shared the same look with me and my sister. "Take it easy on her, sweetheart. She's probably just thinking about the fact that at this time next year, you'll be going off to college, and Sophia will be starting kindergarten." With that, her eyes started to tear up as well.

I shook my head and bent down so I could be on Sophia's level. "Ready for your second year of preschool, kiddo?"

She put her hands on her hips, sassy as always. "Mom said I'm not allowed to wear my princess dress today, so I'm stuck wearing this." She dramatically pointed to the shorts and T-shirt she was wearing.

I laughed as I leaned in to give her a kiss on the cheek. "Well, for what it's worth, I think you look like a princess even without the dress." I put my mouth next to her ear like I was going to tell her a secret, but said it loud enough for everyone to hear. "You should have asked Mama. She's the pushover."

My mama kicked my foot with hers as I stood up. "I am *not* a pushover."

"You keep telling yourself that," I said as she pulled me into her arms.

She hugged me tightly and kissed my forehead. "How are you a senior in high school? It seems like just yesterday that I saw you sitting on the back of that U-Haul... Nevermind. I need to stop. I'm going to cry again."

Another set of arms wrapped around me from behind, and a much smaller set of arms wrapped around my leg. "Aw. A nice family hug," my mom cooed.

I wiggled away, laughing as everyone tried to fight to keep me in the hug. "I need to leave for school, or I'm going to be late. I still have to pick up Wyatt."

I turned and waved to my family one last time before getting into my car. My family was far from ordinary. My mom was biologically my aunt but raised me from the time I was born. My mama was my mom's college girlfriend who she reunited with eight years ago when we moved to Bellman. That's how I ended up with a sibling who was barely starting school when I was finishing. I wouldn't change it for the world though. I adored my family. Even the four-year-old little girl with too much sass for any of us to handle.

I smiled as I thought about the past eight years in Bellman. They had definitely been good to me, and it looked like my senior year was going to be the best year yet. Somehow I had snagged the position of both class president and captain of the track and field team. I also had a good group of friends, especially my best friend, who was now running toward my car, his brown shaggy hair blowing in the wind.

"What's up, Bails?" Wyatt asked as he jumped into my car. "Excited to be seniors?"

He stuck his fist out toward me, but I just stared at it and shook my head, a slight smile parting my lips. "You're such a dork."

Wyatt moved his hand and ran it through his hair, a wide smile lighting up his face almost as much as his blue eyes did. "That needs to stay between us."

"So, you don't want me to tell the whole school how you cried the first time we watched Frozen?"

Wyatt's grin grew wider as he tried, and failed, to ruffle my hair. "Only if you want me to tell everyone that their class president still sleeps with a stuffed animal."

I glared at him quickly before looking back toward the road. "Hey, Adi is special. You know my mama bought me that Teddy on the first birthday she was in my life."

"And you know that Elsa embracing her true identity and singing *Let It Go* is special to me."

Out of the corner of my eye, I saw Wyatt turn to face me more fully, his smile now more of a shit eating grin. "Speaking of which, is this the year?"

I lifted an eyebrow as I continued to stare out at the road. "Is this the year for what?"

"The year we both finally get a boyfriend or a girlfriend."

I shook my head. Leave it to my bisexual best friend to be convinced I was *also* bisexual. "Well, you might get a boyfriend or a girlfriend. While I would only be looking for a boyfriend, it's not going to happen. I'm going to be way too busy this year. Dating can wait until college."

"Never say never," Wyatt said smugly.

"Never say never to dating or…" I let my voice trail off, knowing Wyatt would know exactly what I was asking.

"Never say never to dating *and* never say never to *whom* you'll be dating."

I turned into the school parking lot, parked my car, then turned toward Wyatt, arms crossed. "Why are you so convinced that I'm bi? And please don't say it's because I have two moms."

Wyatt put his hand up to his chest as if he was offended. "Ew. As if. Gay parents don't make you gay. What makes you gay is how you reacted to kissing Tina Blake in that game of spin the bottle in eighth grade."

I thought back on that night. Years later, I could still remember that kiss, but contrary to what Wyatt believed, it wasn't because it was with a girl. It was because it was my first kiss ever. I was shocked when Tina wasted no time pulling me into her and wasn't shy about deepening the kiss, her tongue parting my lips in a way that made me forget everyone else in the room. It was an amazing kiss and made me realize just how much I loved kissing. Hence, why I've had many kisses since that one, all with guys. Some better than others, but all satisfying. Sure, Tina's kiss was the best, but that didn't mean anything. I liked guys. They were fun and hot, and even though I had yet to date someone seriously, I could see myself dating a guy. I had plenty of crushes on guys through the years. Sure, I could also appreciate a good-looking girl, and the softness of a feminine touch admittedly warmed me up inside, but it wasn't what I was looking for.

I forced myself from these thoughts and shoved Wyatt. "Whatever, dude. It was one kiss."

"One kiss that still has you blushing." Wyatt wiggled his eyebrows, and I shoved him again.

I pulled my schedule out of my pocket and stared down at it. "Please tell me your schedule changed and you have *Weightlifting* third period on A days now."

"I could tell you that, but I'd be lying. I think they split up the sections based on who does Fall and Winter sports. I have it second period on B days with Chloe, Audrey, Lily, and Jake."

"And you have first lunch everyday?"

"Yes, but that just means I eat at an ungodly hour. It's nothing to be jealous of."

"An ungodly hour *with* Audrey, Jake, and Ben. I have yet to find someone with the same lunch as me."

Wyatt patted me on the knee. "You're friends with, like, *the whole school.* I'm sure you'll find people to eat with."

I stuck out my bottom lip. "But it won't be with my besties."

"Cheer up, buttercup. This is *our* year." Wyatt grabbed my cheeks and blew me a kiss, before unbuckling his seatbelt and opening his door. Before getting out, he turned toward me one more time. "I'll see you in fourth period. I can't wait to hear all about your lunch with your new besties."

I dramatically grabbed his hand. "You know you're the only bestie for me."

"I better be, bitch." Wyatt winked at me, then pulled his hand away. "Now let me go or we're going to be late."

I watched as he walked in one entrance of the school, and I headed toward another, closer to my locker and homeroom.

As soon as I walked into homeroom, I heard my name being shouted from across the room and looked up to see my friend, Chloe, waving her hands at me. "Bailey! Get your ass over here, girl."

Chloe's dark skin and long jet-black hair were absolutely stunning. Being from a small town in Central Pennsylvania where diversity unfortunately wasn't our strong suit, she was destined not to blend in. But even without that, she wouldn't have. Chloe Douglas was born to stand out. She was outspoken, opinionated in the most hilarious way possible, and the life of every party. She was also my closest friend after Wyatt and the person I had known the longest since we lived in the same neighborhood when I first moved to Bellman.

"How's it going, Chloe?" I asked once I reached her.

"Better now that you're here," Chloe said while draping an arm over my shoulder. "I feel like I haven't seen you in forever."

I laughed at her dramatics. "Pretty sure you just saw me Friday at Ben's party."

Chloe rolled her eyes and pulled me closer to her. "Yeah, but my ball and chain was there so I was a little preoccupied."

"Yeah, preoccupied with making out with him on the couch. How would Jackson feel if he heard you calling him your ball and chain?"

Chloe dropped her arm from around my shoulder and sat down at her desk. "He knows I call him that and doesn't care. Also, I had to make good use of my time on Friday night. Now that school has started, we'll barely see each other, especially this fall between my soccer schedule and his football schedule."

Chloe's boyfriend, Jackson, was the quarterback of our rival football team. When they first started dating sophomore year, I thought she just liked the drama it caused, but the two of them really were perfect together. His cool quietness mellowed out her wild outspokenness.

"Hey, good practice for if you guys end up at different colleges, right?" I asked as I sat down at the desk beside hers.

Chloe pushed out her bottom lip. "I don't even want to *think* about that." A smile returned to her face as she reached out to nudge my shoulder. "How about we instead talk about whether or not this will be the year Miss Popularity finally lets her guard down and dates someone?"

I rolled my eyes. "What's up with you and Wyatt? You're both pushing to get me coupled up. Are you trying to get rid of me?"

"On the contrary, dear friend. Jackson has a bunch of hot, single friends. If you dated one of them, we could go on double dates all the time."

"Nice try, but I'm going to be way too busy this year to date."

Chloe lifted her nose in the air, feigning importance. "Of course. Saving the senior class one homecoming, prom, and spirit week at a time."

I reached out and slapped her arm playfully. "Hey, that's not *all* I do as president. I also figure out the best fundraisers for us so we can go on a kickass senior trip."

"And as vice president, Ben throws kickass parties just in case the kickass senior trip doesn't pan out."

"As vice president, Ben just sits around and looks pretty, but that's okay. He's very good at it."

Chloe lifted one eyebrow, her smile growing even wider. "You think Ben's pretty, huh? There's a romance for the storybooks—class president and vice president."

I shook my head, scrunching my nose up in disgust. "Ew, no. Ben and I have been friends almost as long as you and me. Remember when we went to homecoming freshman year, then made out at the bonfire afterward? It was like kissing my brother."

"Technically, you can't say that since you don't have a brother."

"Fine. It was like kissing Wyatt. He's practically my brother."

Chloe threw a hand over her chest. "Have you? You know, kissed Wyatt?"

"Ew, no. I know I've kissed a lot of guys, but that's where I draw the line."

Chloe looked away from me to stare down at her phone lying on her desk. "Too bad. You guys would be cute too."

I was about to argue with her, when I caught sight of someone walking into the room just before the late bell rang. She had long dirty blonde hair, perfectly tanned skin, and legs that went on for days. She was wearing large black rimmed glasses that only certain people could pull off, and she was certainly one of them. I watched as she walked across the classroom, her demeanor nervous and unsure, and said something to our homeroom teacher before taking a seat in the front of the room.

I tapped on Chloe's desk, pulling her attention away from her phone, and nodded my head toward the girl. "Who's that? I've never seen her before."

Chloe followed the direction of my nod and squinted her eyes. "No idea. She must be new." I felt Chloe's eyes on me as I continued to stare at the girl, unable to remove my eyes for some reason. "What's up with you? Measuring up the new girl? Afraid she might give you a run for your money as homecoming queen? She *is* hot, and she's got that whole mysteriousness going for her. But don't worry. You're a shoo-in."

I forced my eyes away from the new girl and looked at Chloe instead. "I'm not worried about being homecoming queen. I could honestly care less, and I don't know why you're so convinced I'm going to win."

Chloe scoffed. "Because you're by far the most popular girl at this school. You've got looks, smarts, and you're a hell of a lot of fun. Not to mention, you're going to lead the track team to another district championship this year, and on top of all of that, you're like the nicest person ever."

I could feel myself blushing at her compliments. "I'm not *that* great."

Chloe stuck her pointer finger in the air. "And also humble. Like I said, shoo-in."

I laughed and shook my head at her, then couldn't keep my eyes from drifting back up to where the new girl was sitting. For some reason, she had me fascinated. I wanted to know more about her. Maybe Chloe was right. Maybe it was the mysteriousness to her. This was a small town where everyone knew everyone else, so a fresh face was sure to turn some heads. There was also the question of why she would move her senior year. I know some job relocations are kind of unavoidable, but don't most parents do everything they can to keep their kids from having to start all over their senior year? I would have killed my moms if they did that to me. Not that I ever had to worry about that. My moms were obsessed with Bellman. Nothing was ever going to get them out of this town.

I was shaken from my thoughts by the feeling of someone's foot kicking against mine. I looked up to see Chloe staring down at me, a strange smirk on her face. "You gonna go to class or just sit here daydreaming all day?"

I shook my head and jumped to my feet, knocking my knee on the edge of the desk on the way up and gaining the attention of the new girl. She gave me a small, shy smile before turning around to walk out of the room. Although it was strangely difficult, I forced my eyes away from her and picked up my backpack, then smiled at Chloe, trying to hide the tension I was feeling throughout my body for some reason. "We have English together first period, right?"

Chloe laughed softly. "Um, yeah. I literally just said that. What's up with you today? Did you drink too much on Friday night?"

I forced out a strained laugh and shrugged. "I think I'm still just in summer mode."

Chloe put her arm back around my shoulder as we started to walk out of the classroom together. "Well, snap out of it, girl. It's time for the best year of our lives."

\*\*\*

By third period, I already felt like I was dragging. Only having four classes a day meant the not-so-fun classes dragged on *forever* and English and History definitely qualified as not-fun in my books. At least my third period would switch between Weightlifting and Gym every day. Now, if only I could find some friends in those classes, it would be perfect since these were the people I would be eating lunch with.

As I walked into the locker room, I looked around for some familiar faces. Of course, they were *all* familiar. This was Bellman. I said hello to a few of the younger girls from the track team and decided I would spend lunch with them if there was no one I hung out with from my own class.

When I was done changing, I headed over to the weight room and took another look around. I nodded my head at Coach Dominic who was the track coach at Bellman and also one of the gym and weight lifting teachers.

He waved his hand, motioning for me to come over. "There's my superstar," he said excitedly as he placed a firm hand on my shoulder. "Ready for your senior year?"

I tossed him a wide grin. "So ready."

He squeezed my shoulder one time before letting his hand drop. "Perfect. I'm going to have you following a different weightlifting routine than the rest of the class so we can get you in perfect sprinting shape for the spring." He looked around the room as if he was searching for someone. "If it's okay, I picked out your partner for you. She's new this year and is going to be a sprinter on the team with you."

His face lit up as his eyes landed on someone across the room. I followed his gaze and found myself looking right at the new girl from my homeroom. She gave me the same shy smile she had earlier, causing a strange sensation to spread throughout my body.

"Emma!" Coach Dominic's voice split through the small weight room, causing me to jump in surprise. He waved his hand to motion the blonde over just as he had done to me. When she was standing beside us, he looked between the two of us. "Emma West, I'd like you to meet Bailey Caldwell. Bailey is in your class and a fellow sprinter on the team." His eyes left Emma's to focus on me. "Now, Bailey, I can count on you to make Emma feel welcome, right? Show her the ropes of Bellman?"

I nodded my head, unable to remove my eyes from Emma to look at Coach. "Of course, sir. I'll be sure to give her a nice Bellman welcome." My smile grew as I continued to stare at Emma, whose blue eyes were just as focused on me. I was so mesmerized, I almost didn't notice Coach slipping away from us. Realizing how awkward we were acting, I cleared my throat and reached out a hand. "I'm Bailey. I… umm… You were wearing glasses earlier." *What the hell was wrong with me? Why was I suddenly tongue-tied?*

Emma looked toward the ground, the slightest hint of red coming to her cheeks, then took my hand in hers. "Emma West. I just moved here from Texas. My glasses are really just for helping me focus and for looks if I'm being honest."

Feeling some of my confidence return, I lifted an inquisitive eyebrow. "Texas, huh? I'm surprised I don't hear an accent."

Emma shrugged. "That's because I grew up in northern California. I moved to Texas in middle school. My Dad is a pastor so we are kind of at the mercy of the Methodist Church."

A pastor's daughter. I hoped that didn't mean she would have a problem with my family. For the most part, my moms and I hadn't run into any trouble in Bellman. I knew there were a few people who disagreed with their *alternative lifestyle*, but most of them kept it to themselves, the majority of the town being very accepting.

"Please don't give me that look," Emma groaned. "I promise I'm not some crazy pastor's kid who is going to try to save you from a life of sin."

"What if I told you I have two moms?" I asked before I could overthink it. Might as well know from the beginning if this was a friendship that was destined to fail.

Emma gulped, her eyes darting away from mine. "You… You have two moms?" Not exactly the reaction I was hoping for.

I crossed my arms in front of my chest and glared at her. "I do. Do you have a problem with that?"

Emma's eyes met mine again and a look of embarrassment surfaced on her face. "Oh God, no. Not at all. I'm sorry. You just took me by surprise. I promise I don't have a problem with it. I actually think it's cool. Like, really cool. I've never met someone with two moms before." She put her face in her hands, then shyly brought her eyes back to mine. "Sorry, I don't know why I'm rambling. I sound like an idiot."

I chuckled as she stumbled over her words, finding it strangely endearing. "You're fine. No reason to be embarrassed. As long as you're cool with my family, then we're cool."

Emma blew out a breath. "That's good, because I could definitely use a friend. Going from eight classes a day to four is a lot to get used to. Also, I've never lifted a weight in my life, so I'm going to need a lot of help in here."

"Well, Emma West, I have a feeling we are going to be good friends." And I meant it. I couldn't explain it, but there was something about this girl that felt different. Like I could immediately tell she was going to be a big part of my life. It wasn't a question of whether or not we would be friends. No. It was bigger than that. It was like we were *meant* to be friends, and the feeling brewing inside of me was both exciting and unsettling all at once, and I couldn't explain it.

After Weightlifting class, we went to the cafeteria together and took a seat at a table with a few other girls from the track team. I introduced Emma and she easily fit in with the rest of the group. I found myself getting lost in her a few times throughout the meal. I was fascinated by the pastor's daughter from California and Texas who acted like the idea of having two moms was a completely foreign concept.

When lunch ended, I was weirdly disappointed. Even more so than I would normally be. I should have been excited for my fourth period class. It was a chemistry class taught by my favorite science teacher, and Wyatt was in the class with me.

I suppressed a sigh as I said goodbye to my lunchmates and headed to my last class of the day. When I walked into the room, Wyatt waved his hands excitedly.

I sat down at the desk next to him and he wrinkled his eyebrows as he studied me. "You look weird."

"Um, thanks?" I responded sarcastically.

Wyatt rolled his eyes and patted my hand. "I didn't say you looked bad. Just weird. Contemplative almost. Like you're thinking about something." He wiggled his eyebrows. "Or someone."

His words caused my mind to flash right back to that dirty blonde hair and those captivating blue eyes. But why? Why couldn't I get Emma out of my mind?

I shook these thoughts out of my head and smiled at Wyatt. "You're crazy. I'm not thinking about anything. Just tired from the first day of school."

A heavy feeling settled in my gut when I realized I had just lied to my best friend for the first time ever. This was going to be a weird year.

# Chapter 2: Emma

"What a weird day," I mumbled as I threw myself onto my bed and stared up at the ceiling.

Keep a low profile. That was my plan for this year. Make some friends, but slip under the radar for the most part. Befriending the girl who I quickly learned was the most popular student at the school certainly wasn't part of the plan. What else wasn't part of the plan were the feelings I got when she looked at me. I *couldn't* feel this way.

It was hard not to though. Between her jet-black hair and those dark eyes, Bailey Caldwell was gorgeous. And that voice…

I groaned as I rolled over and shoved my face into my pillow. I told myself I was done having these feelings. Nothing good came from having these feelings. Case in point being the fact that I was stuck starting over during my senior year. Not only was I at a different school, but in a completely different part of the country. Pennsylvania was nothing like California or Texas. Granted, after everything that happened, the change was nice, but the feelings I vowed to leave behind were creeping back in.

They were feelings I had denied my whole life. My whole life until my ex-boyfriend, whom I had dated for a year and a half, hooked up with my best friend just two days after we broke up, and I was more heartbroken over her than him. It wasn't the betrayal that had broken my heart. It was the fact that she had sex with him. She and I were two of the only people in our friend group who hadn't had sex yet and hearing about her having sex had made me sick. It wasn't because it was my ex-boyfriend. I tried to tell myself that at first, but I knew the truth. I had known the truth for a long time. I had a giant crush on my best friend, and even though I wouldn't have ever been brave enough to act on it, the thought of her with anyone else crushed me.

That's when I made the big mistake. I had always been close to my youth pastor, so when I asked to speak to her in confidence, I believed it would stay between us. When I sat down with her in the empty church and worked up the courage to ask how to know if you're gay, I didn't expect her response to be, "No one is actually gay. Homosexuality is just the devil's temptation." I also didn't expect her to stick her nose up at me and ask me to leave. I certainly didn't expect for her to tell not only my parents but also the church staff and most of the congregation about my question.

When my parents sat me down and asked me about it, I could barely look them in the eye, unable to handle the disappointment on their faces. That's when I decided lying was my only option. I told them I was asking for a friend and this lie caused my dad to physically blow out a breath of relief.

My lie wasn't good enough for the church though. They claimed my dad's reappointment was because the church in Pennsylvania needed him, but I knew it was more than that.

My parents and I never talked about the real reason and they never brought up my question again, all of us happy to avoid the topic. And that's exactly what I planned on doing forever. I had denied it for almost eighteen years already. What was the rest of my life? I could probably find a nice guy and be happy. I had been happy enough with my ex. Sure, I hated kissing him and the whole reason we broke up was because I refused to have sex with him, but I could probably learn to like those things.

I sighed as my mind drifted back to Bailey. It was so easy with girls. I didn't have to force myself to think or feel a certain way. It was the complete opposite. I couldn't stop the thoughts, no matter how much I tried. My only hope was that once Bailey and I became closer friends, I could shake these feelings. I just had to get over the initial shock of how good looking she was.

I was pulled from my thoughts of Bailey's smile by the sound of a knock on my door. I sat up when my dad walked into the room.

"How was your first day of school, kiddo?" he asked as he sat next to me on the bed.

"It was fine. Everyone seems really nice."

"That's wonderful," he answered a bit too enthusiastically. "Make any friends?"

I shrugged, trying to feign nonchalance. "I met some girls from the track team. They're cool."

My dad stared at me, clearly waiting to hear more, then chuckled when he realized that was all I was going to say. "Don't want to share with your old man? I get it."

I studied his brown hair that was now turning gray and wondered when that happened. I didn't remember him having much gray before, and I couldn't help but wonder if that had to do with the stress I had caused him. "There's not much to share. It's my senior year. I'm not really expecting to make friends for life this late in the game."

My dad sighed and rubbed at his forehead, making me feel guilty about my comment. This wasn't his fault. It was mine, and we all knew that, even if no one would speak it out loud. He forced a smile and patted me on the knee. "You don't know that. Now that Fall is coming, the church youth group is going to start meeting more regularly again. You can make friends through that."

I groaned internally. I had no interest in being part of the youth group given my experiences with my old youth pastor. "I was thinking maybe I could skip out on being part of the youth group this year. It's one year, then I'm off to college. Is it really worth it?"

"You're the pastor's daughter. It would look bad if you didn't go." My dad gave me a knowing smile and ruffled my hair. "This is a new town. A fresh start for all of us." I knew what he was getting at. I could hear the words he wasn't saying. *This isn't the old youth group. This isn't the old church. No one knows about your question.*

\*\*\*

"Fresh start. It's a fresh start," I whispered to myself as I walked from my house to the church, which was practically in our backyard, just a week and a half later on my way to youth group.

"Emma! So great to see you," the youth pastor, Mrs. Green, shouted as soon as I walked through the doors.

As someone who looked to be around my parents' age, she was much older than any youth pastor of the churches we had been part of before. She motioned for me to come over and put her arm around a boy who I recognized from seeing in church and Sunday School the past month, although we had never been formally introduced. Objectively, I could tell he was very good looking. He was tall and muscular with sandy blonde hair and blue eyes that most girls would swoon over. As I came closer and his smile grew, I noticed small dimples forming on his cheeks.

"Emma, this is my youngest son, Elijah," Mrs. Green said proudly. "He's a sophomore at Bellman this year."

Elijah reached his hand out to me and wrapped mine in a firm, but warm, handshake.
"It's nice to meet you, Emma. How are you enjoying Bellman so far?"

His question made my mind immediately go to Bailey. I had found out she wasn't only in my Weightlifting class, but also the gym class that rotated every other day with Weightlifting, meaning I had third period with her every day. Third period and lunch. She had easily taken me under her wing and made me feel welcome, introducing me to more people and teaching me about life in Bellman. She had even suggested that we exchange phone numbers in case I had any questions for her. I hadn't actually texted her yet, but I spent many nights trying to think of an excuse to do it, then chickening out.

My thoughts were interrupted by the sound of a throat clearing, and I focused back on Elijah, standing in front of me with a patient smile on his face. Somehow I had missed Mrs. Green slipping away from us. "Sorry. Bellman is… Bellman is good. Very welcoming."

"Do anything exciting yet?" He looked around with a smirk on his face. "You know, aside from this super hopping youth group?"

His joke made me laugh as I shook my head. "Can't say I have."

Elijah lifted an eyebrow. "What do you say we change that? This Friday, after the football game, there's a party at Ben Perry's house. One of my buddies from the soccer team invited me." I hesitated momentarily and the smile dropped from Elijah's face. "Unless, of course, you're super against drinking. In that case, I never mentioned this." He looked past me at his mom, who was now trying to call everyone together for our lesson.

I gave him a reassuring smile. "Just because I'm a pastor's kid doesn't mean I'm boring. A party sounds fun."

Elijah blew out a breath, his smile growing even more. "Perfect. Why don't you give me your phone number so I can give you more details when we're not at church with my mom?"

***

Before I knew it, Friday had come and I was heading to the football game with Elijah. Since giving him my phone number just two days earlier, we had texted pretty nonstop and I was learning he was both sweet and funny. As soon as we started making our way toward the student section of the bleachers, a guy with brown hair stood and began waving his hands in our direction. "Yo, Little E! Up here!"

Elijah put a hand on my back and pointed toward the guy, who was now jumping up and down. "That's Wyatt. We're on the soccer team together."

He nodded his head toward Wyatt to acknowledge that he saw him, causing Wyatt to sit back down. As soon as he was sitting, I caught sight of who was sitting beside him. There's no way I could miss that black hair that I had spent so much time thinking about this past week. Bailey turned toward us, smiling her big trademark smile when her eyes met mine and causing my body to completely betray me. I smiled back, then shut my eyes trying to focus on the feeling of Elijah's hand on my back rather than the butterflies in my stomach. *Get control of yourself, Emma.*

Before I knew it, we were taking a seat right next to Wyatt and Bailey. I was happy when Elijah sat next to Wyatt, giving me some space from Bailey. It's not that I didn't want to be near her. In fact, that was exactly the problem. How much I wanted to be near her. Even having two people between us seemed like too much.

Wyatt slapped Elijah on the back as he smiled widely at him. "Little E. What's up, bro?"

Elijah rolled his eyes. "How many times have we been over this, man? I'm bigger than you."

"Doesn't matter. You're still just a sophomore. Not a big bad senior like me." Wyatt moved his eyes from Elijah over to me and reached out his hand. "I'm Wyatt. You must be new. You definitely don't look like you could be a freshman."

"I'm Emma. I just moved here a little over a month ago. I'm a senior too."

"No shit," Wyatt said with a laugh. He pointed his thumb at Bailey. "This is my bestie, Bailey. She's a senior too."

I looked at Bailey who was already staring at me with those big dark eyes and hoped my face wasn't turning red. "Oh, I know. We actually have third period together every day."

"Sure do. Emma does track, so she's been eating lunch with me and some of the other track girls."

Wyatt looked between the two of us, the wide boyish grin never leaving his face. "So that's why you haven't been complaining about lunch." He playfully patted Bailey on the knee. "You made a lunch buddy. How nice."

I swore I saw Bailey's face turn the slightest hint of red under the lights of the stadium, but I wasn't sure what part of what Wyatt had said had embarrassed her. All I knew was how cute it made her look and how angry I was at myself for even thinking about that. I was happy when the game started, serving as a distraction from Bailey.

A few minutes before halftime, Elijah put his hand on my shoulder and squeezed it gently. "I'm going to hit up the concession stand before it gets too busy. Can I get you anything?"

The fact that he only asked me wasn't lost on me, and I wasn't sure how to feel about the extra attention. "Oh, um, maybe just a coke. I'm not too hungry. I ate with my parents before the game."

Elijah squeezed my shoulder one more time, then stood and headed down the bleachers. When he was out of sight, Wyatt leaned over and elbowed me playfully. "My boy likes you."

"Wh-What?" I stuttered, not sure what else to say.

"Elijah. He definitely likes you. I can tell." He stared at me as if he was waiting for me to say something, then wiggled his eyebrows. "So... what do you think?"

"What do you mean?"

Wyatt laughed loudly as if I had just said something incredibly funny. "Do you like him? I know you're new and still adjusting to everything, but he's cute, right?"

I looked toward Bailey, but she seemed to be too into the football game to hear the current conversation. I forced my eyes away from her and stared out onto the football field. Wyatt was right. Elijah was cute. He was also really easy to talk to and seemed to be much more of a gentleman than my ex-boyfriend. Not to mention, his mom being the youth pastor. My parents would love it if I ended up with a guy like that. "I'm not really sure," I answered honestly. "I haven't really thought about it." *True.* "He's definitely good looking." *Also true.*

Wyatt smirked and elbowed me in the side again. "Oh yeah. You two are totally crushing on each other. How sweet." He turned away from me to focus on Bailey. "What do you think, Bails? Wouldn't Elijah and Emma make a cute couple? Even their names sound cute together."

Bailey rolled her eyes at Wyatt and shoved him. "I think you are too obsessed with playing matchmaker all the time."

Wyatt laughed again. "Is it so bad that I want my friends to be happy? Gotta let me set someone up. Clearly, you're not going to let me do it for you."

"You're single?" I asked much too quickly. I hoped it wasn't obvious how much I wanted to know the answer to that.

Bailey nodded her head. "I am. I have way too much going on to have a boyfriend this year."

"Plus, she's already made out with just about every guy in our grade," Wyatt added.

"Whatever. I have not. I never made out with you."

Their joking caused a heavy feeling to settle in my gut. I hated hearing about Bailey making out with a bunch of guys. What I hated even more was the fact that it bothered me. Why should it? She was my friend. That's all she was ever going to be. That's all I wanted her to be.

Luckily, the conversation was interrupted by Elijah returning. He handed me my soda then looked between the three of us. "So, what did I miss?"

"Nothing too exciting," Wyatt said with a wink.

Elijah gave me a confused look, but I simply shrugged in return. I spent the rest of the game overly invested in what was happening on the field. The heavy feeling wouldn't leave my gut, no matter how much I tried to focus on anything else.

Near the end of the game, Elijah leaned into me to get my attention and gave me a concerned look. "You okay? You've been quiet."

I nodded my head, swallowing hard and trying to will away the pit in my stomach. "I'm good. Just getting a little bit chilly."

Elijah quickly removed his varsity jacket and draped it around my shoulders. "There you go. Is that better?"

His jacket warmed me up and so did his kindness. He really was sweet, and I enjoyed the smell of his cologne wafting from his jacket. Maybe Wyatt was right. Maybe I did like Elijah, or at least was starting to. This was good. It was comfortable. Yep. Exactly how it was supposed to feel. I leaned into him and gave him a warm smile. "Much better. Thank you."

When the game came to an end, Elijah and I both stood and he rested his hand against my back again. "So, we'll see you two at Ben's?" he asked Wyatt and Bailey.

Wyatt nodded enthusiastically. "You know it. Wouldn't miss it."

About twenty minutes later, we pulled up to Ben's house, which was outside of town. His house was at the top of a long hill, making it secluded from any neighbors. When we walked in, I was surprised to see how much alcohol there was and wondered where he got it all. As if reading my mind,

Elijah leaned close to whisper in my ear. "Ben has two older brothers who get all the alcohol for him. His parents are almost never home on the weekends, but even if they were, they wouldn't really care."

I nodded my head, trying to understand what it would be like to have parents like that. I'm pretty sure my mom and dad realized that I drank, but it wasn't something that we talked about, and I always had a curfew unless I was staying over at a friends house. There's no way they would ever allow something like this to happen in their house.

Elijah pointed to the keg across the room. "Want a beer?"

I nodded my head and he quickly went over and filled up two cups, then brought them back to where I was standing and handed one to me.

"Elijah!" someone yelled from behind a long table set up in the kitchen. "Come play beer pong."

He turned to me. "What do you say? Want to be my partner?"

I shook my head and laughed. "Trust me. You don't want that. I'm awful at beer pong. I'd rather just watch."

"I'll be your partner, buddy," Wyatt said as he came out of nowhere and wrapped an arm around Elijah's shoulder. He smiled at Wyatt, then looked at me. "That is as long as Emma doesn't care."

Before I could answer, I felt an arm slip around my waist. The touch was soft and warm and made me want to close my eyes and breathe it in.

"She'll be fine. We need some girl time anyway," Bailey said cheerfully.

Before I knew what was happening, she was taking me around the house and introducing me to everyone. My mind flashed back to my goal of laying low this year and I cringed when I realized what was currently happening was anything but that. I took a deep breath to try to steady myself.

Bailey must have noticed, because she leaned in close to whisper to me, causing the intoxicating scent of her perfume to overtake my senses and make me forget everything around us. "I know this is all a bit much. Sorry. What do you say we get some fresh air?"

I nodded and followed her out of the house to a very large backyard. We walked past the few people who were hanging out outside, getting far enough away that they were just distant voices, before Bailey sat down and motioned for me to join her.

"So, what do you think of Bellman so far?" she asked, her eyes focused on me in a way that told me she actually cared about my answer.

"It's nice. Moving somewhere new at the beginning of senior year isn't ideal, but everyone at Bellman has been very welcoming."

Bailey continued to stare at me as she nodded her head in understanding. "Do you miss Texas? I'm sure you left a lot of friends behind. That had to be hard."

I thought back on the end of my time in Texas and the little bit of relief I felt to be leaving. While it was scary to start over so late, I also couldn't imagine what it would have been like to stay. Most of my friends went to my church, which meant that they all knew about what had happened. I didn't know how they felt about it, because I didn't give myself a chance to find out. I hadn't really talked to any of them since moving. It seemed better that way.

"I needed to get out of there." As soon as the words were out of my mouth, I cringed at my own honesty. Why did I just say that? I never even admitted that to my parents.

"Did something happen?" Bailey asked softly, a sincerity in her voice that sent a shiver down my spine.

"It's stupid. You don't want to hear about it."

Bailey scooted a little closer to me and wrapped an arm around my waist. "If it's important to you, it's not stupid." She studied my face like she was trying to see beyond what I was saying. "You don't have to tell me, but if you want to talk about it, I'm a great listener."

I closed my eyes and tried to ignore the warmth that overtook my whole body with one touch from her. *Stop. She's your friend.* I let out a breath as I continued to scold myself, then tried to shrug nonchalantly. "My boyfriend and I broke up and then that weekend he had sex with my best friend."

Bailey winced at my words. "Ouch. That sucks. How long were you guys together?"

"About a year and a half." I looked out in the distance as I continued to talk, unable to look Bailey in the eyes. "He and I were never going to last. I didn't love him and seeing as how he was easily able to replace me, I would say he didn't love me either. It was just… disappointing. I guess it hurts more that my friend would do that. Is that… is that weird?"

"Of course not. It's a shitty thing to do. I would never do anything like that to one of my friends." Bailey pulled me even tighter up against her. "But enough talk about the past. Let's talk about something happier. Have you thought about where you want to go to college?"

I shook my head. "Things have been so crazy, I haven't even really thought about it. All of the colleges I originally had in mind were on the west coast, but I can't imagine being that far away from my parents, so I kind of need to start over. What about you?"

"Don't judge me," Bailey said with a laugh, scrunching up her nose in a way that would make it impossible to judge anything she had to say. "I'm actually pretty sure I'm going to go to Bell U. Super lame, I know. Bellman High School *and* Bellman University? Talk about not branching out."

"There's nothing wrong with that. My dad was so excited to find out he was being relocated to a college town because my parents want me to stay close to home and you don't really get any closer than ten minutes down the road. They even insisted on doing a family walk through campus the day after we moved here. It's really pretty. Why do you want to go there?"

"There's a lot of reasons. Their track team is awesome and I like the fact that they are a Division II program, which means it's serious without being crazy. The track coach is also a family friend. I've known her from the time I moved here because my Uncle Bo works at the college with her."

"When did you move here?" I asked before she could say anything else. For some reason, I had just assumed she always lived here.

"Eight years ago. It feels like I've lived here forever though. The first nine years of my life were pretty good, but I felt like life really started for my mom and I once we came to Bellman."

I didn't miss the fact that she said mom instead of moms and I wanted to ask her about it, but didn't want to seem too nosy. As if reading my mind, Bailey laughed, causing her body to rock against mine in a way I wished I didn't enjoy so much. "You can ask. I can see the wheels turning in your head. I know what you're thinking. My mama wasn't always in my life. She married my mom about two years after we moved here."

"So, did she adopt you?"

Bailey's eyes lit up as a wide grin spread across her face. "She did." She removed her eyes from mine to look out into the distance and added a little more quietly, "Technically both of my moms adopted me. It always sounds crazy when I say it out loud, but my mom is biologically my aunt. From what I know, which isn't much, my biological mom was a mess. She got pregnant with me when she was a teenager and had no interest in being a mom."

I studied Bailey's face, which still had a smile even as she looked like she was miles away. Without thinking, I put my arm around her back as well, forcing our bodies even closer together. "Bailey, I'm so…"

Bailey shook her head and looked back at me. "Please don't say you're sorry. I love my family. My moms are amazing. Ariana, my biological mom, was never really in my life. Before we moved to Bellman, she would show up every once in a while for a few days or a few months at a time, but I barely even remember her. She was never my mom. But anyway, enough of my dramatic life story. This is a party. Don't wanna kill the mood."

"I don't mind. I think it's cool that you're comfortable talking about it."

"If I'm being completely honest, it's not something I talk about with a ton of people. Not that I try to hide it. I just don't think my family tree is anyone's business. You're just really easy to talk to."

The way her voice dropped as she said the last sentence made my heart race. "So, track is the reason you want to go to Bellman?" I asked, trying to change the subject and hoping Bailey didn't notice the slight crack in my voice.

"One of the reasons. Both of my moms are Bell U alums. They were college sweethearts, and even though neither of them will ever admit this, I'm pretty sure my birth is the reason they broke up the first time. I'm not one of those people who lives in a bubble and thinks that Bellman is the only town that exists, but it *is* the town where my moms fell in love and also where they fell in love all over again. It's the town that gave me my family. I can't imagine wanting to be anywhere else." She laughed and added, "Plus, I have a four-year-old sister. She might be a little diva, but I don't want to miss out on watching her grow up."

I wanted to ask her so many more questions. I wanted to know all about her life and her dreams. Unfortunately, before I could, Elijah's loud voice interrupted us. "There you are. I was wondering where you ran off to." He sat down and put an arm around my shoulder, replacing the arm that Bailey had just pulled away from me. "Sorry to leave you for so long. Wyatt and I kept winning."

"Not to worry. I kept her entertained," Bailey said as she stood to her feet. "I'm going to go see what Wyatt is getting himself up to now that he's done playing beer pong. Thanks for the talk, Emma."

I watched Bailey walk away, trying not to think about how much I wished she wouldn't. I forced my eyes back to Elijah and couldn't stop the smile that came to my face when I saw the wide grin on his.

Elijah cleared his throat and scooted closer to me. "So, I wanted to ask you something. It might be a little soon, but I figured why not. If you're going to turn me down, I might as well get it over with now. Anyway, I was just wondering if there is any chance you would want to go to the movies with me next weekend? No pressure. It doesn't have to mean anything. I just think you're really cool and would love to get to know you better."

I ran his question through my mind, fighting with myself over how I felt about it. *He said no pressure. Maybe it won't go anywhere. Maybe it will. That wouldn't be so bad, would it? Elijah is cool. He's cute, especially right now with that nervous look on his face. If I didn't like him, I wouldn't find that endearing, right?* Okay. I was making way too big of a deal out of this. It was just a movie. It was fun and easy. It was natural. Natural in the way a relationship should be without questions and doubt and wonders of what everyone else will think if they find out about it.

"I would love to go to the movies with you," I answered so cheerfully that I almost believed it myself.

# Chapter 3: Bailey

"Elijah asked me to go to the movies with him on Saturday," Emma mentioned nonchalantly as we added more weights to the bench press.

It wasn't what I was expecting to hear at that moment, causing me to drop the weight I was holding in my hands and luckily jumping out of the way before it hit my foot. I guess I shouldn't have been surprised after how cozy the two of them seemed to be at the football game and the party afterwards. I wasn't sure why I was having the reaction I was, as though she had just told me bad news rather than something exciting.

"That's great," I said with much less enthusiasm than I meant to. "So, I take it you said yes?"

Emma nodded her head slowly. "I did. Of course I did. Elijah is a good guy. I mean, he is, right?"

For whatever reason, right now, it didn't feel like he was. Right now, it felt like he was the enemy, but why? Worry for my friend? Overprotectiveness of the new girl? "I'm not super close to him. He has a different core group of friends since he's in a different grade. Wyatt thinks he's really cool though."

"Yeah. He is cool." She seemed hesitant for a moment, but then a small smile parted her lips.

It was a nice smile. One that made me forget feeling weird about Elijah. Honestly, it was a smile that made me forget just about everything. *What the hell?* I cleared my throat and forced myself to look away. "So, I take it you're going to the soccer game tonight?"

"Soccer game? Oh. I didn't really think about it."

"I'm going. We should go together." *Together.* Why did that word suddenly feel weird rolling off my tongue?

Emma's small smile blossomed into one that took over her whole face. "That sounds great."

\*\*\*

"Do you do any sports aside from track?" Emma asked as we sat down on the bleachers at the soccer game.

"Nope. I played basketball in middle school, but I absolutely sucked. I prefer sports that don't require hand-eye coordination. What about you?"

"Same. Just track. I played soccer when I lived in California, but stopped once I moved to Texas and joined the middle school track team. Track is my true love."

I laughed and elbowed her in the side. "Don't let Elijah hear you saying that."

At the mention of his name, Emma's body immediately went rigid. "Oh, it's not like that with him. We're just friends right now. I mean, we could be more, but it's not anything serious."

Even though I felt bad for stressing her out, I also felt a weird sense of relief. "I was just messing with you, don't worry. There's no pressure. If you don't like Elijah, it's no big."

"I do like him," Emma answered quickly. She took a deep breath, closing her eyes as she blew it back out. "Sorry. I guess I just didn't expect..." She paused and stared at me, a look I couldn't place settling on her face. "I didn't expect to fall for someone here."

With those words, something passed between us. I couldn't define what it was, but it was like nothing I had ever felt before. We both sat in silence for what could have been seconds or minutes just staring into each other's eyes. I didn't know why it was happening, but I also couldn't tear myself away. It was like a magnetic force keeping us there. I jumped when the sound of a whistle brought my attention back to the real world.

The game started and we were silent, both of us seemingly enraptured in what was happening on the field. When I finally found the courage to look back at her, something about the way the sun hit Emma's hair while a small smile played on her lips, caused her face to glow in a way that was absolutely breathtaking. *Wait. Where the hell did that thought come from?* I shook my head and focused back on the game. *Weird.*

When halftime started and there was no game to hold our attention, we went back to small talk, which led into us talking through most of the second half and only partially paying attention to the game. The game ended with Bellman winning 3-0 and after we made our way down the bleachers, a very excited Elijah and Wyatt were there to greet us. Wyatt wrapped me in a big sweaty hug and spun me around.

When he finally put me back on the ground, I scrunched up my nose and wiped the sweat from my arms. "You're gross, and you smell bad. But good game. I'm proud of you." I looked to Emma and Elijah who were standing close, but not touching. "You had an awesome game too, Elijah."

Elijah's already wide grin, grew even more. "Thank you so much, Bailey." He hesitantly reached out and put an arm around Emma's waist, smiling down at her when she scooted closer to him. "I'm so happy you guys came."

I quickly looked away and focused my eyes back on Wyatt. "You better go into the locker room and take a shower. You're not getting into my car smelling like that."

"I should probably do that too." Elijah removed his arm from Emma's waist and took a step away from her, a slight blush overtaking his face. "Do you need a ride home, Emma?"

Emma shook her head. "I have my car here, but thank you."

Elijah nodded his head slowly, not doing a very good job of hiding his disappointment. "Well, I'll see you ladies later. Thanks again for coming. I'll text you when I get home, Emma."

Once the guys were gone, Emma smiled brightly at me, causing my stomach to do something strange that I couldn't explain. "Do you want me to wait with you until Wyatt comes out?"

"You don't have to. He takes forever. Quite the diva." I looked toward my feet as I kicked a stone between them. "Unless you wanted to see Elijah again."

"I… I should actually probably head home. My parents are going to be expecting me for dinner."

Before I could even respond, Emma had turned around and was walking across the parking lot toward her car. I kept my eyes on her until she disappeared from view, shaking myself from whatever weird spell I was under.

Just a few minutes later, Wyatt walked back out of the school and did a spin in front of me. "Better?"

"Much! Let's go."

Once we were in the car, I contemplated whether I wanted to say something to Wyatt about Elijah and Emma's date. It wasn't any of my business, but I couldn't help the discontent I felt over it. "So," I said while tapping my fingers on the middle console. "What's the deal with Elijah? Emma told me he asked her on a date."

"Oh yeah! Elijah told me that when we went to shower. That's awesome."

I bit at my lip, an unusual heaviness settling in my stomach. "Is it though? I mean, what are his expectations? Emma is new, and he jumped at the opportunity to ask her out. They barely even know each other."

Wyatt chuckled as he studied my face, a look of confusion on his own. "That's kind of the point of hanging out—to get to know each other."

I rolled my eyes, partly at the situation and partly because I was still unsure why I was so annoyed about this. "And the movies are a place to get to know someone? More like a dark place to hook up."

Wyatt laughed again. "You would know. When was the last time you went on a date to the movies and didn't spend the whole time making out?"

I opened my mouth to argue, then closed it when I realized I couldn't.

"What's really going on, Bailey?" Wyatt asked.

I stared straight ahead, more focused on the road than I needed to be, to avoid my best friend's mixture of confusion and concern. The truth was, I had no idea what was going on. "Nothing is going on. I just don't know if I like it."

"I get it," Wyatt said with a chuckle. "You just made a new friend and you're afraid if she gets a boyfriend, she won't want to spend time with you anymore."

I gripped the steering wheel tighter. Was he right? Was I just jealous that someone else was going to get time with her? But why? It's not like I even knew her that well. I was never like this with any of my friends in the past. "Maybe you're right. Chloe's already barely around anymore. You keep talking about finding yourself someone. Maybe I'm worried about losing my friends and being the only lame single one."

Wyatt patted me on the knee. "First of all, you could never lose me. I'll forever let you be my third wheel if you need to be. Second, you could never be lame, no matter how single you are." I could feel his eyes still burning into me for a few seconds before he added, "What do you say we hang out on Saturday night? Friend date?"

I shook my head. "We're having a family day on Saturday. You can come if you want to though. My moms have been asking about you."

"Hanging out with all my favorite women? Count me in!"

"Technically, it won't be all women. My grandpa and Uncle Bo will be there too."

"Even better!"

*** 

By the time Saturday rolled around, I wasn't feeling any better about Emma's date. In fact, if anything, I was feeling worse. For whatever reason, I couldn't shake the feeling that there was something off about her and Elijah. Something that just didn't fit. It didn't sit well with me.

I pulled out my phone and stared down at her contact information, contemplating whether to text her for the first time. I took a deep breath and pushed on the message button. As I stared at the blank screen, I realized I had no idea what I wanted to say. Why was I being so weird? Why was it so hard to text one of my friends? My fingers hovered for another few seconds, before I started to type, erasing and rewriting a bunch of times until I had written a message I was happy with. *Excited for your big date tonight?*

I anxiously waited for her reply, but after five minutes, it still hadn't come. I blew out a breath and put my phone on my nightstand, then lay back on my bed and forced my eyes closed. After a few minutes, I jumped up to the sound of a vibration from my phone. I quickly grabbed it and smiled when I saw Emma's name on the screen.

*More like extremely nervous. I haven't been on a date since I first started going out with my ex-boyfriend.*

I let my fingers hover again, before I started to type out my reply. *You'll be fine. Just be yourself, and he'd be crazy not to like you.*

This time, Emma's reply came much more quickly. *Do you really think so?*

*I know so. You're smart and funny, not to mention beautiful.* I cringed after I pressed send. Was that too much? No. Of course not. Why would it be? I always said stuff like that to my friends. God, I was acting weird.

Still, I couldn't shake my anxiety as minutes passed and Emma still didn't text me back. I considered sending another text explaining what I had said or taking it back all together, but that seemed even more crazy. Luckily, a knock came on my door just in time to be a welcome distraction.

My mom's voice floated through the door. "Hey, sweetheart, your grandparents are here."

I hopped out of bed and left my phone in the room, figuring I would think about it less if I didn't have it attached to me. As soon as I got downstairs, my grandma ran over to me with arms open wide and wrapped me in a tight hug. "How is my favorite senior doing? Are you getting taller? I think you've gotten even taller since I saw you last week."

I kissed her cheek and pulled back. "You say that every time you see me."

"I've gotten taller, Grammy," Sophia said proudly as she came to stand beside us, pushing up onto her tiptoes to appear even bigger.

My grandma bent down and took Sophia in her arms, just as she had done to me. "You sure have, sweetheart. Watch out. Soon you'll be as tall as your sister."

Sophia pushed out of my grandma's arms and jumped up and down. "Look, Bailey, I'm as tall as you."

When she stopped jumping, I put a hand on her head and ruffled her hair. "Almost, pipsqueak."

Just then, my grandpa walked over to join us. He picked Sophia up in one arm and wrapped the other one around me. "How are my two favorite girls?"

"That's so unfair. I thought I was your favorite girl," mama said with a scoff.

Grandpa shrugged. "You used to be before you brought these two cuties into my life."

A knock on the front door grabbed all of our attention, and my Uncle Bo came through the door holding a diaper bag in one hand and his daughter's car seat, which she was asleep in, in the other hand. My Aunt Kylie came in behind him, not holding anything, but looking like she had just run a marathon.

"Why didn't anyone tell me having a baby was so much work?" she asked with a huff.

My grandpa laughed as he squeezed her shoulder. "We all told you it was, sweetheart."

Aunt Kylie rolled her eyes. "She's two months old. You'd think she'd be sleeping through the night by now."

"Actually, no one thinks that," Grandma chimed in.

Kylie sighed, a slight smile parting her lips. "I'm too old for this. No one should have a baby at thirty-four. She's lucky she's cute."

Mama pushed her sister's shoulder playfully. "I was thirty-five when I got pregnant. No complaining."

"The only one who should be complaining is me," my Uncle Bo said with a laugh. "I'm going to be the oldest dad at all the school events."

My grandpa reached out and delicately extracted my cousin, Vivian, from her car seat, placing a gentle kiss on her face before cuddling her close. "No one can complain about such a sweet little girl. Another one of Grandpa's favorites."

Uncle Bo put his hand down firmly on my grandpa's shoulder. "We've gotten ourselves very outnumbered, haven't we?"

"We have, but I wouldn't have it any other way," my grandpa cooed, still unable to take his eyes off of Vivian.

"Me either," Bo said softly as he stared down at his daughter.

I looked around at my family and thought about how lucky I was. Every time we were together, I couldn't help but reflect on what a blessing it was to be part of this family. Moving to Bellman hadn't just brought a fresh start for my mom and me. It also brought me my mama and my whole extended family, a group of people I now couldn't imagine my life without.

Thinking about moving to Bellman made my mind flash to Emma. I knew things had been tough on her before she moved, so I hoped this would be the fresh start she needed as well. A sick feeling came back to my stomach as thoughts of Emma reminded me of my phone up in my room harboring an embarrassing unanswered text. I was itching to run up and see if she had responded, but I forced my attention back to my family instead.

It turned out that while my mind was wandering, Wyatt had arrived and was now making his way around to all of my family members—laughing with my grandpa and uncle, spinning my little sister in circles, giving hugs to my moms, aunt, and grandma. It was too bad he was like a brother to me because he would have made the perfect boyfriend. But I could never possibly see him that way. Even my moms referred to him as the son they always wanted. He was family, and I was lucky to have him.

"What's up, Bails?" he asked as he finally made his way over to me. "You're awfully quiet today."

"Kind of hard to get a word in between you and the rest of my family," I joked, hoping he wouldn't catch on to the fact that I was lying.

Luckily, he simply shrugged and followed the rest of my family into the family room, where we spent most of the day playing board games and talking until it was time for Grandpa to make dinner.

The closer it got to the time of Emma's date, the more unsettled I felt and the less I could ignore the nagging in my brain telling me to go check my phone. I excused myself at the same time my grandpa did and made a beeline for my bedroom. I gawked at the phone as if I forgot how to use it. My fingers slowly wrapped around it like I thought it might burn me. When I saw Emma's name on the screen telling me she had finally responded to my text about an hour ago, I hesitated to open it. My stomach did flips as my finger tapped the text alert. Was I completely losing it? Why was I acting like this? I closed my eyes and took a deep breath, before finally looking down at the text.

*Sorry for not answering sooner. Things have been crazy today. I really appreciate it though. That was sweet of you to say. Wish me luck. T minus 2 hours until Elijah picks me up.*

*Good luck,* I typed before tossing my phone back onto the bed.

I sighed as I threw myself onto it as well. I was about to roll over and shove my face into my pillow when there was a knock at my door. Before I could even sit up, Wyatt walked in and sat beside me on the bed.

"I let it slide all week and most of today, but there's something going on with you that you're not telling me. I thought we told each other everything, Bails."

The sad look on his face made my guilt double. I wanted to tell him, but even I didn't know what was going on with me. "I wish I knew what to tell you, Wy. I can't explain what's going on with me. Ever since Emma told me about her date with Elijah, I've just felt off. I'm overthinking everything and I'm at the point where I feel almost sick over it. I have no idea what's going on."

Wyatt furrowed his eyebrows as he sat there and seemed to contemplate my words. "If I didn't know any better, I'd say..." He paused and a smirk took over his face. "I knew it."

"You knew what?" *What the hell was there to know and why didn't I know it?*

"You *are* bisexual. Girl, you have a crush on Emma. I don't know why I didn't realize this sooner. You always did have a thing for blondes."

A crush? On Emma? No, absolutely not. His assumption couldn't be more wrong. That didn't even make sense. I liked guys. I had no question that I liked guys. "You're crazy. I've always had a thing for blonde *guys*."

Wyatt patted my knee as if he was a father lecturing his daughter. "Yes, sweetheart, that's what it means to be bisexual. You like both guys *and* girls."

I shook my head. "No. Just because I might be jealous doesn't mean I like her. I've never felt like this with a guy or a girl. I've definitely had crushes in the past. I know I have."

"And I'm not doubting that. But maybe you never liked any of those people *as much* as you like Emma. Maybe she's different."

He was right about that. Emma *was* different. There was something about her that was so very different than all of my other friends. There was a depth to her that I hadn't seen in anyone else before, like there was so much below the surface that she wasn't showing me. So much I wanted to explore and find out. That didn't mean I liked her though. I couldn't like her. If I liked her, I became a cliche—the girl with two moms who also likes girls. I could only imagine the field day the few bigots in the town would have with that one. Shaking their heads and sighing as they said what a shame it was that their lifestyle had led me astray. No. Wyatt had to be wrong.

"I… I don't think you're right this time," I said quietly, looking down at the bed to avoid eye contact with my best friend who knew me better than anyone in the world—including myself.

"I think I am, Bails, and, just for the record, I'm sorry about any encouragement I gave either of them to go for each other. If I had known, I would have never done that. The last thing I want is for you to get hurt."

I smiled as I finally looked back up at Wyatt. "I'm fine, Wy. I really don't think this is a crush, and even if it was, there's no reason to keep Emma from dating. She's obviously straight."

"Well, for what it's worth, I support you no matter what. I mean obviously being bisexual besties would be awesome, but I just want you to be happy."

"I am happy, Wyatt. Seriously. I'm okay." I lifted my nose and sniffed as the smell of my grandpa's cooking wafted into my room. "I'll be even happier when I have some of that food. Should we go see if dinner is almost ready?"

I stood and walked toward the door before Wyatt could question me anymore. I knew he meant well, but this wasn't what I wanted to talk about right now. When we walked into the kitchen, I wrapped my arms around my grandpa where he was standing at the stove stirring his special spaghetti sauce. "Smells so good."

"Figured I should make the favorite of one of my favorites. Chicken Parmigiana is still your favorite meal, right? You haven't grown out of that?"

"I could never grow out of chicken parmigiana, and yours is my favorite."

"Ouch. All this time I thought your Uncle Bo's was your favorite," my uncle joked as he went to the refrigerator and pulled out a beer.

"I wouldn't know. I don't think you've made me chicken parm since I was about ten."

I gave him a challenging look and he simply shrugged in response. "Maybe someday, kid. Maybe someday." He chuckled and walked back out of the room with his beer in hand.

"Sweetheart, could you tell everyone that dinner is going to be ready in about fifteen minutes?" Grandpa asked without turning around from the stove.

I looked toward the clock hanging in the kitchen and felt a lump form in my throat when I saw what time it was. 6:00. A half hour until Elijah would be picking Emma up for their date. I wondered how it would go. Would he bring her flowers? Shake her dad's hand? Hug her mom? Would they hold hands at the movies? Maybe more?

"Sweetheart?" My grandpa's voice interrupted my thoughts. "Are you okay?"

I cleared my throat and tried to shake all of these thoughts from my head. "I'm good. Just a little bit hungry."

But as I made my way to the living room to tell my family about dinner, I didn't feel hungry at all. Instead, I felt sick to my stomach. I didn't know how I was going to eat when all I could think about was Emma's date and how it was going. Wyatt was wrong though. This didn't mean I liked her. I was just worried about my friend. Right? I groaned to myself as I slumped onto a chair in the living room. It was going to be a long night.

# Chapter 4: Emma

I jumped when I heard the doorbell ring downstairs, knowing it had to be Elijah. I picked up my phone to see that it was exactly 6:30. He was right on time. Points for being punctual. Instead of heading downstairs, I looked at myself in the mirror one last time, then opened my texts from Bailey for what had to be the thousandth time today. There wasn't much to see, mostly because I didn't know what to say after she sent me a text calling me beautiful, and I had spent all day contemplating how to reply. Bailey thought I was beautiful. *Bailey Caldwell* thought *Emma West* was beautiful. Simple, plain Emma. I couldn't believe it, but then again why was I thinking into it so much? Girls told each other they were beautiful all the time. This wasn't anything new. It just felt different coming from Bailey. I knew exactly why it did, but I refused to acknowledge it. Tonight I had my first date with Elijah. My first date with a guy who was sweet and caring and extremely good looking. This was good. This was exactly what I needed.

"Honey?" my mom said as she poked her head into my bathroom. "Elijah is here." She walked the rest of the way into the bathroom and put her hands on my shoulders, what looked like tears forming at the corners of her eyes. "Look at you. All grown up. I'm so proud of you."

What was she proud of me for? Going on a date with a guy? I looked toward my feet as I felt a blush overtake my face. "Thanks, Mom. I guess I better get going."

My mom moved her hands to both of my cheeks and forced me to look at her. "You look great, sweetheart. I'm sure Elijah is going to agree."

I shrugged and pulled away from her, then followed her out of the bathroom and downstairs to where Elijah was waiting by the door talking to my dad. His hair was nicely styled and he was wearing jeans and a button up shirt that looked way too nice to wear to the movies. I looked down at my own clothes - tight jeans and a black long sleeve shirt -

and worried I might not have dressed up enough for the occasion. Elijah's eyes told me a different story though. When he looked at me, they lit up and a smile grew across his face, causing his dimples to stand out even more than usual.

"Wow, Emma, you look really beautiful," he said as he continued to stare at me.

It was nice to hear him say that. It didn't make me cringe or wish I was somewhere else. It wasn't off putting. It made me happy. That had to be a good sign, right? If I didn't like him, it might feel weird for him to compliment me, and it didn't at all.

Once I was standing beside him, Elijah took his eyes off of me to look back at my dad. "I was thinking about taking Emma to get dessert after the movie if she wanted to. Would that be okay with you, sir?"

Instead of answering, my dad addressed me instead. "Quite the gentleman you have here, Em." He winked at me, then turned back to Elijah, whose face was now bright red. "That's fine with me. Just don't get her back too late. I can't have the two of you falling asleep during my sermon tomorrow."

Elijah nodded his head intently. "Wouldn't dream of it, sir. Thank you. Ready to go, Emma?"

He opened the door for me, then walked out close behind me. When we got to his car, he opened that door for me as well. We were both quiet for most of the drive, except for the sound of Elijah clearing his throat every few minutes as if he wanted to say something, but kept deciding not to. "Sorry, I've been so quiet," he finally spoke as he pulled into a parking spot at the movie theater. "I'm just really nervous."

"That's fine. You don't have to be nervous though. It's just me."

Without answering, Elijah hopped out of the car and quickly ran around to open my door before I could do it myself. I put my hands in my pockets as I followed him into the theater where he bought both of our tickets and some snacks. We settled into our seats and within a few minutes the movie was starting. About halfway through the movie, I noticed that Elijah had started to fidget with his hands. He looked down at his own hands, which were moving over his lap, then tried to discreetly look at mine, one of which was resting on the armrest between the two of us. He did this a few more times before reaching out and grabbing my hand. His hand was sweaty, but his grip was solid. Holding his hand felt safe. It felt comfortable.

We continued to hold hands when the movie ended as we made our way out of the theater and across the parking lot to Applebees. Elijah only dropped my hand once we took a seat on opposite sides of the booth we were seated at. I took this opportunity to wipe my sweaty palm off on my jeans, feeling the slightest bit relieved to have a break. "So, what were you thinking?" I asked as I stared down at the menu.

"Maybe we could share the Triple Chocolate Meltdown?" Elijah asked, sounding unsure and nervous.

Just the thought of the oozing chocolate cake made my stomach rumble. "That sounds great. It's one of my favorites."

"I kind of figured since you told me you had a soft spot for all things chocolate." Elijah's face turned red as if he was worried he had said too much.

"You're right. You sure do know the way to a girl's heart," I said to reassure him.

We spent most of our time at the restaurant talking about school and how I was adjusting and obsessing over just how good the Triple Chocolate Meltdown was. It was fun. Elijah was silly and easy to talk to. Things were comfortable between us. I didn't even mind how sweaty his hand was when he took mine as we walked to the car or the fact that he insisted on holding it the whole drive home.

When we pulled into my driveway, I was surprised when he turned his car off and immediately jumped out so he could walk me to the door. I couldn't remember a time my ex-boyfriend had ever done that. He much preferred making out in his car until I finally pushed him away and insisted I had to get inside. The thought made my stomach drop. This was the end of the night. Did Elijah expect a kiss? Was I ready for that? Even asking the question seemed silly. I was a senior in high school. Kissing a guy after a date wasn't some foreign concept. If anything, it was expected. Just a normal part of dating.

When we reached the front door, Elijah put his hands in his pockets and swayed back and forth on his feet as though he was nervous. "I had a really good time tonight," he said shyly.

I looked from Elijah to the door and then back to him. "I did too. Thank you for asking me."

I watched as he pulled his hands from his pockets and took a few steps closer to me, unsure if the feeling in the pit of my stomach was excitement or nerves. Soon, he was standing just inches from me and he reached his arms out and pulled me into a hug. His hug was both strong and warm. Just like holding his hand, being wrapped in his arms felt safe. I let myself relax into his embrace, enjoying the smell of his cologne as it invaded my nostrils.

After a few seconds we both pulled back, but Elijah kept his hands resting on my arms. "Well, goodnight, Emma."

Before I could fully comprehend what was happening, he was leaning toward me again, but this time it was his lips that were closing in on mine. I closed my eyes as I waited for him to come in the rest of the way. The kiss was… well, it was a kiss. Exactly what I've come to expect from kissing another person. It was quick. Elijah didn't try to force his tongue into my mouth which I greatly appreciated. It was good. Yep, it was good.

Elijah's smile took over his whole face as he pulled away from me. "Goodnight, Emma" he repeated once more before turning and practically skipping back to his car.

I was happy to find the house was dark and quiet once I got inside, telling me that my parents had already gone to bed. I went right up to my room and immediately opened my texts from Bailey, staring down at the good luck text she had sent me hours earlier. I looked at the time and figured she was probably still awake. The nice thing to do would be to text her about the date since she had texted me earlier. I lay down on my bed and began typing out a text that I quickly erased. I tried a few more times until I typed something I was somewhat satisfied with.

*Date went well. Thanks for wishing me luck!* Send.

Within less than a minute, I got a text in return. I blinked in surprise, not expecting her to get back to me so quickly. *I'm really happy to hear that! You deserve it.*

Did I though? I felt like such a fake. A fraud. Someone who was just playing the part she was supposed to play. I looked back on the date again. Everything was comfortable with Elijah. The hand holding, the kiss, it felt the way it was supposed to feel, or at least how I assumed it was supposed to feel. The whole fireworks and butterflies thing had to be a Hollywood fabrication. Plus, we had fun. We laughed together, talked like old friends. Maybe I wasn't a fraud. Just because I questioned my feelings in the past didn't mean I wasn't able to feel these things. Maybe I had just been waiting for the right person. There's no reason Elijah couldn't be that person.

*How was your night?* I sent back to Bailey before I could overthink it.

*It was great. We had a family day. Wyatt was here too. My grandpa made my favorite meal!*

I could picture Bailey typing out that text with a big smile stretching across her face, and the thought brought a smile to mine as well. *And what would that be?*

*Chicken Parm! Duh! Is there anything better?*

I sighed softly as I typed out my reply. *Just chocolate.* Hoping the conversation wouldn't come to an end, I followed that up with another text. *So, what are you doing tomorrow?*

Luckily, I didn't have to wait long for Bailey's reply to come through. *A chocolate girl, huh? :) I told my little sister I would take her skating.*

Of course she did. Because not only was Bailey the most popular girl in the school, but she also was close to her family. I was pretty sure she was pretty much perfect. And right now, she was texting me. Just that thought made my stomach flip in a weird way I hadn't experienced before. It continued the flipping feeling as I re-read her text, my eyes stuck on the smiley face. I was so distracted by that, I almost didn't realize another text had come through from her.

*What about you? If you're not doing anything, you're welcome to come with us?*

Now the flipping was out of control. Was this a weird reaction to eating chocolate cake late at night? Deep down, I knew it wasn't, but I pushed that thought away. *What time? I have church tomorrow. Normally I'm back home around 12:30.*

*How about 1:00? Is that too early? We can push it back if it is.*

*1:00 is perfect.*

*Awesome! If you give me your address, we can pick you up.*

I quickly typed out my address and sent it over to her and was satisfied when her response came back just as quickly. *Perfect. Right on the way! I'm tired though, so I'm going to go to bed. Goodnight Emma :)*

There it was again. That stupid smiley that had my heart beating extra fast for some reason. I set my phone on my nightstand, then jumped when I heard my text tone go off again. I fumbled with it for a second then breathed out when I saw the text was from Elijah.

*Made it home! Tonight was great :) Thank you so much.*

I typed out a reply to tell him that I agreed and would see him at church the next day, then put the phone back on my nightstand. I needed to go to sleep so I could be well-rested for skating the next day.

***

"Hey, Em, wait up," Elijah shouted as he ran after me as I walked out of the second church service of the day.

I slowed down and waited for him to fall into step with me. Running after me had apparently gotten him out of breath and it was cute to watch him struggle to get his words out.

"Just thought I would walk you home if that's okay."

"Oh. Yeah. Sure. That would be great."

Elijah smiled and took my hand as if it was the most natural thing in the world. Admittedly, it *did* feel pretty natural with him. Our hands fit well together even if his did kind of overtake mine. When we arrived at my house, I could tell Elijah was waiting for something.

"I would invite you in, but I don't think my parents would be too happy if they came home to find me alone with a boy." Wouldn't they though? It was a *boy* and that boy was Elijah.

Elijah's face dropped for a second telling me that he *was* expecting an invitation, but he quickly recovered. "Oh. Of course. That makes sense. I'll see you later, Em."

I leaned in and gave him a quick hug before anything else could happen. A kiss on the doorstep after a date was one thing. Kissing after church seemed kind of strange and unnecessary.

"Bye, Elijah," I said before ducking inside of my house.

I looked at the clock and realized I had just under a half hour until Bailey would be here to pick me up. I quickly changed out of my church clothes and opted for capris and a V-neck T-shirt that I threw a sweatshirt over. I must have looked in the mirror about ten times, making slight adjustments to my hair and the little bit of makeup I was wearing with every single pass.

The half hour flew by and before I knew it, there was a knock at my door. I checked my reflection one more time, then made my way downstairs. When I opened the door, my breath caught in my throat. Bailey was wearing tight black jeans and a white T-shirt with a black leather jacket over top of it. The outfit made her dark eyes stand out even more and her black hair was slightly curled, falling perfectly down her back. She was holding the hand of a little girl whose brightly colored outfit was in deep contrast to hers. Forgetting how to speak, I stared at the two of them like a complete idiot.

The little girl tilted her head and smiled up at me. "I'm Sophia. Are you Emma?"

"I am," I answered when I finally found my voice. "Sophia is a very pretty name. It sounds like the name of a princess."

Sophia excitedly nodded her head. "Yep. Just like Sophia the First. She's my favorite princess, after Elsa."

"Well, of course, who doesn't love Elsa?" I laughed as the little girl giggled shyly, then looked back up at Bailey, whose dark eyes were laser-focused on me.

When our eyes met, the slightest smile parted her lips. That smile made my head spin and my stomach flip all at once, and I realized I probably should have taken the time to eat something. I continued to stare into those dark eyes, unable to tear myself away, somehow hypnotized by the sight in front of me.

"Sissy, I'm hungry."

The sound of Sophia's voice brought me back to reality. Bailey removed her eyes from mine and rolled them at her little sister. "I told you to eat before we left the house."

The little girl shrugged. "I wasn't hungry then. I'm hungry now."

"You know what? I was just thinking the same thing. Do you like peanut butter and jelly? You guys could come in and I can make us some sandwiches before we go skating." A heavy feeling settled in my gut as I looked to Bailey for reassurance that I hadn't overstepped my boundaries.

Her expression seemed surprised, but not in a negative way. Her smile was soft and kind. "Are you sure?" she asked softly. "We don't want to impose. It's this one's fault she decided not to eat."

"You wouldn't be imposing at all," I answered quickly. "I can whip up a mean peanut butter and jelly in no time."

"That would be great. Peanut butter and jelly is Sophia's favorite."

"After ice cream, of course," Sophia said with a sweet smile.

"Well, if you eat your peanut butter and jelly, then behave at the skating rink, maybe Emma would agree to get ice cream with us afterwards." Bailey winked at me and my mouth went dry.

It took some effort to get my next words out and I hoped Bailey didn't notice the slight crack to my voice when I said them. "Ice cream sounds wonderful. It's my favorite too."

"Let me guess…Chocolate?" Bailey winked once again, and I thought I might melt right there on my doorstep.

I shook my head. I shouldn't be having thoughts like that. Bailey was my friend. Just my friend. And that was perfect. I had Elijah. He was cute and sweet and had kissed me last night. That was good. That's how it was supposed to be.

"So, not chocolate?" Bailey asked, looking slightly confused by how I was acting.

"Oh yeah, sorry. Definitely chocolate. A chocolate ice cream sundae with hot fudge is my go-to." I cleared my throat and moved to the side to make space for them to come inside. "Sorry. Come in!"

I did a sweep of the house wondering how it looked through Bailey's eyes. The house was simple and very traditional. The walls were mostly bare, filled only with pictures of my family and bible verses.

Bailey's eyes went right over to the stairs, where they slowly passed over my school pictures which started in nursery school and went all the way up until last year, her smile growing as her eyes moved. "Aw, you were adorable."

"I was? Not anymore?" I let out an awkward chuckle as soon as the words left my lips. Why had I just said that? What did I want her to say in return?

Bailey's smile dropped as she turned back around to look at me. "Oh. You still are of course. I mean, maybe adorable isn't the word. I feel like that's what you say about little kids. But yeah. You're very pretty."

Her eyes darted to the floor, but I couldn't take mine off of her. The more I stared, the more uncomfortable I felt. It was as though someone had walked into the house and turned up the heat and now my body was burning up. I wanted to look away, but I couldn't. As uncomfortable as it was, it was also exhilarating. Simply watching Bailey sent a thrill through my body that made me feel alive, albeit being uncomfortable.

"So, where is the peanut butter and jelly?" Sophia asked, pulling me from my thoughts and breaking the trance that Bailey seemed to have over me.

I clapped my hands together and flashed her a toothy smile, hoping to look excited rather than like I had just been caught doing something I shouldn't be. "Peanut butter and jelly, of course. Right this way."

I pointed in the direction of the kitchen and took a deep breath as I began to lead them down the hallway. I avoided looking at Bailey as I got out the bread and carefully spread the peanut butter and jelly across it, being more meticulous about this sandwich than I ever was before. Once I finished the three sandwiches, I carried them over to the kitchen table and finally chanced a glance at Bailey, whose eyes were already on me.

When our eyes met, she looked away and focused on the sandwich now sitting in front of her. "These look great, Emma. Thank you."

I sat in a seat across from them and watched as Sophia took a big bite of her sandwich. "What do you say, Sophia? Does it pass the test?"

Her eyes were comically wide as she smiled a peanut butter and jelly-filled smile at me. "This is the best PB and J I've ever eaten. It's so much better than Bailey's."

"Wow, thanks, kiddo," Bailey said with a laugh as she reached a hand out and tickled her sister's side.

Sophia laughed as she squirmed away from her. "Moms always tell us to be honest. That's what I'm doing." She took another big bite and smiled contentedly.

We were all quiet as we finished our sandwiches. When everyone was done, I picked up the empty plates and carried them to the sink. I was just about to ask if they were ready to leave, when I heard the front door open and my parents' loud voices bellow through the hall and into the kitchen.

When they reached the kitchen, Bailey quickly stood up and greeted them with a warm smile. "You must be Mr. and Mrs. West. I'm Bailey Caldwell. I go to school with Emma. I'm a sprinter on the track team too." She put a hand on Sophia's head. "This is my little sister, Sophia. We're all going skating today."

My dad smiled from ear to ear as he closed the remaining space between him and Bailey and reached a hand out toward her. "It's very nice to meet you, Bailey. Emma has told us so much about you. At least, she did this morning. Normally she just mumbles answers to me when I ask her about school, but she couldn't stop talking about you at breakfast. She's lucky to have made such a good friend already."

I cringed as I felt my face burning up in embarrassment. Why did my dad have to say that? It's not like I talked about her *that* much at breakfast.

My mom slapped him on the arm playfully and shook her head. "Stop it. I think you're embarrassing her." She brought her attention to Bailey and reached out a hand to her as well. "What my husband is trying to say is that it's very nice that Emma is adjusting so well. We were worried about how it would be for her moving her senior year."

"I completely understand," Bailey answered sweetly, impressing me with how good she was at schmoozing parents. "I'm sure the move wasn't easy on any of you, but I'd just like to say that Bellman is very happy to have you."

"Well, we better go," I said, inserting myself between my parents and Bailey, before they could say anything else to potentially embarrass me.

Bailey waved to my parents as she followed me out of the kitchen. "It was very nice to meet you, Mr. and Mrs. West. I hope that I will see you both again soon."

When we arrived at the skating rink, Bailey helped her sister out of her car seat, then held her hand as she jumped out of the car. She continued to hold it as we walked through the parking lot, and as I watched the two of them skip hand in hand, a sense of longing settled in my gut. I wasn't sure what I was longing for. Maybe it was the sisterly bond that I was wishing for. I told myself that had to be it as my eyes settled on Bailey's slender fingers, a strange chill running down my spine at the sight.

I forced myself to look away when I felt the same discomfort from earlier settle throughout my body. Instead, I focused on the skating rink. The lettering spelling out *Roller Paradise* was old and rusted. Inside, it was dark and kind of smelled like a mixture of feet and concession stand nachos. Straight in front of us was the large skating area, while off to the right was the concession stand and a small arcade, and to the left was skate rentals and a row of lockers.

"Not much to look at, but we enjoy it," Bailey leaned in close to whisper, causing my body to betray me once again as the hair on the back of my neck stood up.

Instead of responding, I followed Bailey and Sophia to the rental area where we each received matching brown skates. Bailey helped Sophia with her skates, before putting on her own. I slipped mine on as well and soon the three of us were heading onto the rink. Bailey took Sophia's hand once again and held it tight as the little girl struggled to stay on her feet.

Sophia looked at me with a strained smile as her feet slowly scooted back and forth on the skating rink. "Emma, can you hold my other hand? I'm a little scared."

I skated up next to her and took her tiny hand into mine, squeezing it to reassure her that she was safe. Bailey gave me a thankful smile that reached all the way to her eyes, a slight crinkle forming right at the edges of them as she tried to focus on me through the dim lighting. Even though every part of my body was begging me not to, I had to look away. Staring into Bailey's eyes was like falling. The whole world seems to slow down around you and you wonder how much it will hurt once you hit the ground. I didn't want the fall. I knew I couldn't handle the pain.

Instead, I focused straight in front of me, careful to skate at a pace that would be good for Sophia. After a few laps, she gained more confidence and dropped both of our hands, skating just a little in front of us.

"Thanks for being so patient with her," Bailey said as she skated closer to me. "I know a day filled with peanut butter and jelly sandwiches and helping a little girl skate probably wasn't the wild senior year you had in mind."

"Lucky for you, I wasn't looking for a wild senior year, so this is perfect." I chanced a peek at Bailey and was surprised to find her dark eyes already focused intently on me. "Seriously, though. This really is perfect. I'm an only child and have never been close to any of my cousins. It's really nice to see what it would be like to have a sibling."

"Well, feel free to borrow her anytime." Bailey laughed lightly and quickly squeezed my arm. Her touch barely lasted a few seconds, but I continued to feel it long after her hand was gone.

As much as I was telling myself not to, I longed to feel that touch again. To have her fingers linger even longer. *Stop it, Emma. You're not like that. You can't be. It's not okay.*

We were both quiet for our next few laps around the rink, until Sophia turned to us with tired eyes. "My legs hurt. I think I'm all skated out." Her eyes lit up as an idea clearly popped into her head. "Emma should come over and we can all watch *Frozen* and have Moms order us pizza."

Bailey lifted an eyebrow at her sister. "You really think Mom and Mama are going to order us pizza *after* we have ice cream?"

Sophia clasped her hands together and looked up at Bailey with the cutest puppy dog eyes. "We could go home first, then get ice cream when we take Emma back to her house. Mom and Mama won't even know."

Bailey shook her head, the smallest smirk parting her lips. "If I agree to watching *Frozen* with you for the second time *this week*, we'll have to see about the ice cream. Also, we don't even know if Emma can come over. She might have to get home to her family."

Sophia now turned her puppy dog eyes on me. "Please?"

I looked to Bailey for reassurance that she also wanted me there and the hopeful look in her eyes seemed to beg me to come just as much as Sophia's puppy dog eyes. I knew there was no way I could say no to either of them. "Let me just text my parents, but it should be fine."

Both Caldwell sisters gave me a satisfied grin, but one in particular made my stomach do flips. What was I getting myself into?

# Chapter 5: Bailey

As I walked up the sidewalk to my house with Sophia and Emma by my side, my mind went back to what Wyatt said the night before. It wasn't the first time I had thought about it today. His words came to my mind every single time we shared a prolonged glance or something passed between us that felt different than the way I felt around my other friends. Each time, I pushed these thoughts away. Just because I felt different around Emma didn't mean I liked her. At least, not like that. Certainly not enough to make me question everything I thought I understood about myself.

Still, I could feel my palms sweating as I opened the door and called for my moms. Introducing them to Emma was different than introducing them to my other friends. It felt more important somehow. Like I needed them to like her just as much as I did. I had no idea why, but refused to acknowledge that it had anything to do with what Wyatt had accused me of.

My mom came down the stairs first, a big smile on her face as she focused on Emma. "You must be Emma," she said cheerfully. "You can call me Kacey or Mom. Whatever you prefer. Either of those are much easier than Mrs. Caldwell since we have two Mrs. Caldwells in the house."

"And you can call me Kari or Mama," my mama said as she walked around the corner and held out a hand to Emma.

Emma took her hand and shook it firmly. "It's very nice to meet you, Mrs… I mean Kari." She shook her head and smiled shyly. "Sorry. It's going to take me a little to get used to. My parents have it ingrained in me to not call adults by their first names."

"Oh God, don't call me an adult. It makes me feel so old," my mama said with a laugh. "I guess having a senior in high school should also make me feel old though."

She gave me a look that told me she was about to get nostalgic again, so I quickly pushed Emma away. "We need to start this movie before she starts to cry again." Once we were partially down the hall, I turned to look at my moms. "Are you guys going to watch with us?"

"Watch *Frozen* again?" my mom asked sarcastically. "I watched it enough with you when it first came out. Payback time. You got this. We'll just let you girls know when the pizza comes."

We went into the family room and Sophia threw herself onto the middle of the couch. "I want to sit in between you two!"

I shrugged at Emma who smiled sweetly as she took a seat on the right side of Sophia. "So, are we watching the first or second one?"

"The first because it's my sissy's favorite."

"The music is better in the first, and I will fight anyone who tries to tell me differently," I joked as I brought the movie up on the TV, then went to join them on the couch.

Emma put her hands in the air in surrender. "Hey, I'm not going to fight you on that."

I sat down on the couch next to Sophia when the movie started and she excitedly bounced up and down beside me, reciting every single line. We only made it about a half hour before the pizza came and we had to pause it. After forty-five minutes of my parents grilling Emma about every part of her life, we were finally able to escape back to the family room to continue watching the movie.

This time, Sophia grabbed a handful of blankets and hopped onto the recliner on the other side of the room. She yawned as she wrapped the blankets tightly around herself. "Just trying to get comfy," she said through another yawn.

"Guaranteed she'll be asleep within a half hour," I announced to Emma who had taken a seat on the same end of the couch she had been sitting before.

I hesitated as I contemplated where I should sit. When Wyatt and I watched movies, I always spread myself across the couch and fought him for space until we ended up with someone's feet across the other person's lap. That didn't seem right with Emma since we were just getting to know each other, so I sat down on the other end of the couch, careful not to take up too much space. That still didn't stop me from looking over at her multiple times while we watched the movie. I loved the way she threw her head back just the slightest bit when she laughed. I loved the fact that a kid's movie that I'm sure she had seen multiple times was making her laugh so hard. I especially loved the slight blush that hit her cheeks every time she laughed like she was embarrassed by it. The slight blush that somehow made her look even cuter. *Wait...*

I forced my eyes back to the screen, only to bring them back to her a few minutes later. I realized in the few minutes I was actually focused on the movie that she had wrapped her arms tightly around herself. "Are you cold?" Without waiting for an answer, I jumped from the couch and went to the closet where we kept the blankets, finding that Sophia had left just one. I walked back to the couch and threw it at Emma. "Last one. Lucky you!"

Emma took the blanket and draped it over herself as I sat back down on the couch. "Thanks." She looked over at me and studied me for a minute as if she wanted to say something, but was hesitant. "Are you cold? We could… share… if you want."

Her voice was low and quiet and something about the way she said those words caused goosebumps to spread across my body. There seemed to be more to them. Something behind them that I wasn't willing to think into right now. Instead, I scooted down the couch to a spot close enough to Emma for the blanket to be draped over both of us. Throughout the movie, our bodies seemed to get closer, until I felt her leg resting against mine. My first reaction was to pull away, but something was keeping me there. Almost like some sort of magnetic pull. An attraction keeping our legs resting against each other.

Even though it was the slightest connection, I could feel every little spot her leg touched mine. The skin underneath my jeans tingled in anticipation. But anticipation of what? My heartbeat picked up as my mind wandered to what it would feel like if I hadn't decided to wear jeans today. If it was my bare skin resting against hers. I didn't have to consider it for long because the slightest movement of Emma's body caused my arm to be pressed against hers as well. I didn't dare look at her as I thought about how easy it would be to reach out and take her hand in mine. *Why was I thinking about that? Why was I even considering it?*

Against every ounce of willpower, a force I had no control over pulled my eyes toward Emma's. At the same moment, her eyes were slowly burning a path toward mine as well. As soon as they met, a spark ignited and my whole body lit up. It was so strong, I couldn't possibly imagine that she didn't feel it too. I opened my mouth to speak words that I hadn't even considered yet, when the sound of Emma's phone caused me to jump and break the connection.

I looked down at the phone that was sitting on her lap to see two text messages, both from Elijah. The first said, *I hope you're having a good day* but it was the one that immediately followed that caused my heart to drop. *I hope this isn't weird, but I can't stop thinking about last night, especially the end of the night.*

My body went rigid as I felt Emma's do the same. Without thinking, I sprang to my feet, suddenly feeling the need to get far away. My eyes darted to where Sophia was sitting, now fast asleep. "I… Um… I just realized Sophia has like fifty blankets. I shouldn't be hogging the only one you have. I'll just sit with her."

I squeezed myself onto the chair with Sophia, careful not to wake her up. After a few moments, I forced myself to look at Emma. Her face was red, but not in the cute way from earlier. Instead, it was a look of extreme embarrassment. Her eyes were staring into the carpet and refused to meet mine.

I felt guilty about making her feel uncomfortable, but before I could say anything, Emma began to slowly shake her head and bring her eyes to mine. "Just so you know, all we did was kiss. It was a goodnight kiss. That was it. I swear."

I felt bad that she felt the need to explain that to me. I wanted her to know that I would never judge her for what she chose to do with a guy. It wasn't like that at all. It was… well, I don't know what it was. I couldn't explain it because I had never felt this way before. My friends talked about guys, hook ups, and sex all the time and not once did it make me feel like I wanted to jump out of my own skin. Like I wanted to think about *anything* else but that. Be anywhere else in that moment.

"You don't have to explain yourself to me. I'm not judging you. I'm sorry if I made you feel that way."

Emma shook her head. "No, it's fine. Really. I just feel like that text made it sound a lot worse than it was. I'm not even sure why he said it. It was barely a kiss." She put her head down and rubbed a hand along her temple. "I just don't want you to have the wrong idea. I'm not that kind of girl. I've never... Well... I'm a virgin. God, now I sound like such a dork. I'm sorry."

"You don't sound like a dork," I said quickly. "I've never had sex either."

"You haven't?"

"Nope. I've made out with a bunch of guys and have gotten a bit... handsy... like twice, but I've never gone all the way. I'm not against it or anything. I just want my first time to be special and with someone I really care about."

"Me too." Emma's smile started out small, then slowly spread across her face, causing my smile to return as well.

Neither of us said anything else, both turning our attention back to the movie, but I knew we were good. Something about that little conversation made me feel better. I couldn't explain it, but it felt like a weight had been lifted from my shoulders. I felt light and happy again—the way I was starting to find I almost always felt when I was around Emma.

When the movie ended, I looked at Sophia who was still fast asleep and ran a hand through her hair. "It looks like maybe the ice cream will have to wait until another time," I whispered to Emma.

With those words, Sophia's eyes popped open like a character from a cartoon. "Ice cream? I'm ready!"

After saying goodbye to my moms, we got back in the car to head for ice cream at a small ice cream parlor about halfway between my house and Emma's.

"So, have you been here yet?" I asked Emma as we got out of the car.

"I haven't actually, but I've been dying to try it."

"It's the best ice cream in town," Sophia said excitedly as she skipped ahead of us.

I shook my head as I laughed at my little sister. "She's right. It really is the best ice cream in town."

"Well, then I'm glad I get to experience it tonight… and with you." Her last words were quiet as if she was telling me a secret, and suddenly it felt like our moment in my family room never ended. We weren't touching, but I still felt connected somehow. Connected in a way I had never felt with another person.

Before I could overthink it, I reached my arm out and draped it over her shoulder, ignoring the shudder that went through my body with this one simple touch. "And I'm glad your first time is with me." I cleared my throat when I realized how that sounded. "Your first Bellman Breeze experience… I'm glad it's with me, too." I cringed. Why was I acting so awkward? It was so unlike me.

Luckily, Emma didn't seem to notice. She simply smiled and put her arm around my shoulder as well, wiggling her eyebrows at me as we continued to walk together. "Can't wait."

When we reached the front of the line, Sophia jumped up and down, trying to make herself tall enough to be seen by the worker. "I want chocolate ice cream with rainbow sprinkles please." She stopped jumping so she could turn around and smile at Emma. "I love rainbow sprinkles. I love everything rainbow."

"Spoken like a true lesbian's daughter," I joked as I placed my hand that wasn't resting on Emma's shoulder onto Sophia's. I focused on the worker who was patiently waiting for the rest of our order. "She'll have that in a kid's size cup. I'll take a medium twist in a cone and my friend here will have a chocolate ice cream sundae with hot fudge and… whipped cream?" I looked to Emma for reassurance. "Is that right?"

"It's perfect."

Once we had our ice cream, we found an empty picnic table and sat down, Sophia beside me and Emma across from us. Sophia sloppily licked the ice cream off of her spoon before plunging it back in and scooping up way more than she could handle, causing ice cream and sprinkles to go all over her face, hands, and the table. Her eyes went wide as she focused on Emma's ice cream while still taking big bites of her own. "That looks really good."

Emma held it out toward her. "It's great. Do you want to try a bite?"

Sophia bobbed her head up and down causing even more of her ice cream to spill onto the table.

Emma laughed softly as she took in the scene and started to delicately scoop at her sundae. "How about I get it for you so I make sure it's the best bite possible?"

Sophia smiled as she watched Emma run the spoon through her sundae and get a bite with a little bit of everything on it. Emma carefully reached across the table and directed the spoon to Sophia's mouth so it would end up where it was supposed to be rather than in a melted mess with the rest of her ice cream.

As she ate her bite of Emma's sundae, her eyes went comically wider. "Yum. That's even better than chocolate with sprinkles."

I tapped her shoulder and gave her a stern look. "What do you say to Emma? That was very nice of her to share her ice cream, wasn't it?"

Sophia nodded again and looked over at Emma with a big chocolatey grin. "Thank you. You're really nice and super pretty. I wish you were my big sister."

I scoffed, only feeling slightly offended since I knew how little it would take to win back my sister's affections. "Wow. Thanks, kid."

Sophia sat up taller and leaned toward me to plant a messy kiss on my cheek, before looking back at Emma. "I wish you were my *other* big sister. I wish I had two and you were one of them." She smiled between the two of us before her eyes focused on me. "Emma is as pretty as a princess, right, Bailey?"

I looked across the table at the girl already staring back at me, a shy smile on her face that I was starting to find I really enjoyed looking at. I didn't know what to say because the words coming to my mind would have been embarrassing to say out loud. She wasn't as pretty as a princess. She was even prettier. The way her eyes lit up when she looked at me, the way her blonde hair seemed to shine when even the slightest bit of light hit it, the way her lips held me completely entranced—I was pretty sure she was the most beautiful human I had ever laid eyes on. *Shit. What was I saying?* "I think you're right, Soph," I said, just barely above a whisper, the words hanging between us like clouds in the sky ready to burst just before a storm.

Emma's eyes pierced mine for a split second before she cleared her throat and tore them away from me, focusing on Sophia instead. "I'm not quite sure if I'd say I'm as pretty as a princess, but you know what? I've always wanted a little sister. Maybe you could be my honorary little sister." Her eyes slowly made their way back to me, slightly hooded as though it was hard to look at me. "That is, if it's okay with Bailey."

"Hey, like I said before, you can have her anytime."

Emma stuck her hand out for Sophia to high five, seemingly not worried about the chocolatey fingers she would have to endure. I couldn't help my wide smile and the warmth that settled over my body as I watched my little sister's face light up, somehow even happier than usual. God, this was bad. This was *so* bad.

***

"This is bad, Wy," I repeated a few hours later as I laid in bed and stared up at the ceiling.

"Wait. What's bad?" Wyatt asked from the other end of the phone, clearly confused by my unconventional *hello*.

I closed my eyes, hoping it would somehow protect me from what I was about to say. What I was about to admit. "I hung out with Emma today. We took Sophia skating, then we all watched a movie and got ice cream. She's… I think… you were right."

"Right about wha—oh. OH! Wow! Wait. Is my best friend actually finally admitting that she's bisexual?"

His giggles on the other end of the phone while I was going through a crisis made me want to reach through the phone and slap him. "It's not funny, Wy. I… Ugh… I like her."

"And that's fine, Bails." His voice took on a softer, more comforting tone. "You should understand better than anyone that people can't help who they fall for. It's nothing to be ashamed of, and it's not like you have to worry about being rejected by your family or friends."

I groaned, unsure how to put into words exactly how I was feeling. "I'm not worried about being accepted, Wy. This is all new to me. The way I feel… I've never felt this way about anyone. Guy or girl. I mean, I might as well just find a way to forget about it. It's not like it could or would ever go somewhere."

"Why not?"

I ran a hand across my forehead, frustration coursing through my body. For a guy who was normally smart, Wyatt was acting pretty stupid right now. "She's straight, Wyatt! She practically has a boyfriend. She's the daughter of a pastor and dating the son of her church's youth group leader. Nothing about her screams gay." As I thought back on our day together, that felt like a lie. The moments that made me come to my revelation felt too strong to be one-sided. I shook those thoughts from my head. I couldn't think like that. There were *so* many reasons I couldn't think like that. "Even if she was, which I really don't think is the case, I haven't even come to terms with what this all means. I don't even *know* that I'm bi. I've only ever had feelings for guys. Legitimate feelings. I know I like guys. That's not a question. But girls… that's different. Emma is the first girl to make me feel *like this*. I don't want to jump to any conclusions about what that means, especially when it doesn't really matter."

Wyatt sighed, and I could tell he was feeling my frustration. "So, what are we going to do?" Sweet, sensitive Wyatt. Always looking for the solution. Unfortunately, life wasn't always that simple.

"We're not going to do anything. I'm going to just forget about this. It's not going anywhere. Emma and I are friends, and I'm going to make the most of that."

"But, what should I do about Elijah?"

"What do you mean?"

"He's one of my boys. Before I knew how you felt, I was all about him and Emma. But you're my best friend. I don't want to encourage something that ends in you getting hurt."

"That's really sweet, but Elijah and Emma are going to happen whether you encourage it or not. If it's what they both want, that's how it should be. Supporting Elijah doesn't mean you're not supporting me."

"You're talking about everyone else, but what are *you* going to do? You know I just want you to be happy, Bails."

His words made me smile in spite of how I was feeling. I was lucky to have a best friend like him. That's really all I needed, right? "I'm going to do what I do best—completely immerse myself into school and my social life. What else do I need?" But even saying those words felt like a lie. I knew exactly what I needed. It was the one thing I was never going to get.

*** 

The following Friday after school, I stood in the gym and surveyed my surroundings. "I can't believe we only have three weeks until homecoming. I feel like we still have so much left to do."

My friend and Vice President, Ben, looked at me like I was crazy, the same way he always did when I started to get overwhelmed with class president duties. "What do you mean? We have the theme picked out, are voting on homecoming court on Monday, starting ticket sales that day too, and the gym will be completely decorated on the first day of spirit week when we have the class decorating contest."

"*That's* what I'm worried about. We *need* to win. The seniors always win spirit week, and we haven't even started on the decorations for our part of the gym yet."

Ben rolled his eyes at me as if I was being ridiculous. "The seniors always win because it's rigged. Plus, we gave ourselves the seventies, which is the most fun decade. All we need are disco balls, tie-dye, and banners that say things like *far out*."

I knew he was right. When we chose *Through the Decades* as the homecoming theme, we already had decoration ideas in mind. We then assigned the 90s to the freshman, 80s to the sophomores, and 50s to the juniors because we had to include the rock and roll era.

Ben put an arm around my shoulder and flashed me his signature grin that helped him get his way with most people, especially teenage females. "Here's what we're going to do. Tonight at my party, we'll recruit more people to help and we'll start on it this weekend. Think your moms will be cool with you having people over on Sunday? I'm going to need Saturday to recover."

"Sounds great, Ben," I answered quickly, distracted by the feeling of my phone vibrating in my pocket, somehow knowing who it was going to be from.

*Elijah asked if I wanted to get pizza with some of the soccer guys after they get done with practice today. I'm going to meet them at the school and we're going to walk to the pizza shop then walk back to the football game. Would you want to come along? I think Wyatt is going.*

She didn't have to explain it to me. The soccer guys did the same thing almost every time there was a home football game. Wyatt always invited me to go, but I turned him down most of the time because I knew that all of the girls who went with them were either girlfriends or soon-to-be-girlfriends. I worried about either feeling like a tag-along or being the new conquest for one of the single guys on the team. The few times I did agree to go were when I actually *was* hanging out with one of them, but those times were few and far between.

But suddenly, I felt interested in going again. Why though? Because I had nothing else to do or was I really just a glutton for punishment? Whatever the reasoning, I quickly typed a reply saying I would be there, then calculated how much time I had until I needed to be back at the school.

Approximately one hour. I put my phone back into my pocket and slipped away from Ben, saying a quick goodbye before hurrying to my car.

Just over an hour later, I was back in the school parking lot. I got out of my car at the same time Wyatt was walking out of the locker room. A smile split his face when he saw me. "Well, look who decided to show up. Decide you just couldn't resist my charms any longer?"

Before I could respond with an equally sarcastic comment, Elijah walked out of the locker room and began waving his arms at someone behind me. "Emma! Hey!"

Wyatt looked past me as a knowing smirk came onto his face. "Oh, I get it. You didn't come for me. It all makes sense now."

I playfully punched him on the shoulder. "Whatever. Keep your opinions to yourself."

Wyatt laughed and shook his head. "You've got it bad, girl."

"I've got nothing. I just want to spend some time with my friends. Is that so hard to believe?"

"Yes. It's actually impossible to believe." He chuckled once more, before his face became strangely serious. "There is something I should tell you though." He opened up his mouth to say something else, but stopped when both Emma and Elijah ended up beside us.

"What's up, guys?" Elijah practically shouted, clearly way too excited about this pizza outing.

"Ready to stuff my mouth with pizza. That's what's up," Wyatt responded before giving me an apologetic smile and walking a few steps to join the rest of the group.

Elijah reached his hand toward Emma, the simple gesture causing my stomach to hurt. "Coming, Em?"

Emma looked at his hand, then back at me. "You go ahead. Bailey and I need to have some girl talk, but we'll be right behind you guys."

Elijah shrugged and joined the rest of the group, allowing the two of us to fall a few steps behind as we walked to the pizza shop. "So, what's up?" I asked.

"That's actually what I wanted to ask you. You seemed extra stressed this week and I wanted to make sure you were okay. It's part of the reason I wanted you to come along. I was hoping maybe some pizza would help you smile."

Why did she have to be so sweet? It only served to make the aching in my heart even worse. "I was stressed. With homecoming coming up there's just a lot to get done." Not to mention the fact that I was putting more into it than I even had to in order to keep my mind off of other things. I moved those thoughts to the back of my mind, as I had done many times this past week, and smiled over at Emma. "But pizza will definitely help."

We made small talk the rest of the way to the pizza shop, then sat down beside Elijah and Wyatt. When we were almost done eating, I noticed some of the guys whispering around us. Specifically, they were whispering to Elijah and egging him on about something. I turned toward Wyatt for an explanation, but he simply gave me an uncomfortable smile and squeezed my knee.

Since I wasn't getting anything out of Wyatt, I looked back at Elijah who was now beet red, but staring intently at Emma. "Please don't kill me for this, but the guys told me I had to ask you this way." He stood up on his chair and pulled his shirt up revealing *HoCo?* written across his perfectly chiseled stomach. "Emma West, will you go to homecoming with me even though I look like a complete tool right now?"

Emma laughed as she nodded her head, accepting his offer. Obviously, I knew this was coming eventually, but it didn't make it any easier. I pushed the remaining bit of my pizza away, my appetite now completely gone. I started to stand to head to the bathroom so I could have a chance to breathe when a hand latched onto my wrist and stopped me. I turned to Wyatt who had a grin on his face that told me he was up to no good. He stood up on his chair just like Elijah had, but instead of facing me, he turned the other direction.

"Bailey Caldwell, I have something to ask you," he yelled, still facing away from me. He wiggled his butt slightly and acted like he was about to pull down his pants and moon the whole restaurant. Instead, he turned back toward me, already laughing hysterically at himself. He continued to laugh as he tried to catch his breath. "I'm just kidding. I don't have anything written on my ass, but I would be over the *moon* if you went to homecoming with me." He wiggled his eyebrows as he reached a hand out toward me. "What do you say? Bestie homecoming date?"

I laughed in spite of how I had been feeling just moments before, which I knew was exactly what Wyatt was going for. I took his hand and pulled him into a hug. "There is no one I'd rather go with." *Well, almost no one.*

# Chapter 6: Emma

"Where did you say you were going again?" my dad asked as I rushed around the house to finish getting ready before Elijah picked me up.

"I'm going to Bailey's house to work on decorations for homecoming."

My dad watched me closely as I picked up my phone off the kitchen counter and began fidgeting with it. "Bailey is a very nice girl. What do her parents do for work?"

"Well, her mama mainly works with kids on the autism spectrum, and…" My eyes stayed glued to my phone as I felt a rush of nerves run through my body. "And her mom works for some IT company. She does something with computers. I'm not really sure."

Silence hung between us, but I refused to look at my dad. I was scared to see his reaction to the news that Bailey had two moms.

"Your friend has two moms? As in… they are together?"

I jumped at the sound of my mom's voice having been unaware that she had joined us in the kitchen. Still not looking at either of my parents, I nodded my head. When their silence continued for much too long, I forced myself to look between them. Their eyes were locked with each other as if they were having some sort of silent conversation to decide how to respond.

"Well, that's… okay," my mom finally spoke, her lips forced into the slightest smile.

"Different strokes for different folks, right?" my dad added with a small chuckle. "They raised a very respectful young lady, and that's what really matters."

I was so happy when the doorbell rang, saving me from this conversation and my parents attempt at hiding their deeply ingrained homophobia. "That's Elijah! I better get going," I said as I darted out of the room.

"Make sure to tell him that I'm very excited for homecoming!" my mom yelled after me.

I didn't respond, instead slipping out of the door and shutting it tight before they could insist on inviting Elijah in. An offer I had no doubt he would accept so he could impress my parents.

"Whoa. Someone's in a hurry," Elijah said with a laugh when I practically ran into him.

"Just trying to avoid my parents holding us up. Should we go?"

Elijah pointed his hands toward his car, like he was directing me. "If that's what you want, that's what we're doing. After you."

I turned and quickly headed toward his car, because that was exactly what I wanted. I needed to get to Bailey's. She had been quiet during the whole football game and even ducked out of Ben's party, claiming she didn't feel well. It seemed like an excuse, but I wasn't sure what had caused the change. She was fine until we both got asked to homecoming in the pizza shop. I had spent all of Saturday contemplating the reasons that would have upset her. Maybe she didn't like the way Wyatt asked her. Maybe he wasn't the one she really wanted to go with and now she was stuck. The thought that kept creeping in no matter how much I tried to ignore it was just maybe she had felt the same pang of jealousy when Elijah asked me as I felt when I was forced to watch Wyatt ask her. I quickly chased this thought away every time it came to my head. Bailey wasn't jealous. Sure, sometimes it felt like we shared this connection I couldn't explain—a connection that felt awful and wonderful all at once. A connection I wanted to both dive into and run away from. But, that didn't mean she had feelings for me.

Plus, I wasn't jealous either. The feeling that I thought was jealousy had to be something else. I was happy to be going to homecoming with Elijah. Even though his invitation was ridiculous, it was also silly and fun—just like him. I could picture him picking me up at my house, a corsage to match my dress held proudly in front of him. My parents would insist on taking way too many pictures and he would hold me tight as they did. It was nice. It was right. Just how I had always imagined it. Exactly what I had always known.

"You're awfully quiet today."

Elijah's voice pulled me from my current internal battle and made me realize we were pulling up to Bailey's house, where there were already a bunch of cars in the driveway. "I'm sorry. Just tired I guess."

Elijah reached across and placed his hand on my leg, playfully shaking it back and forth. "Well, wake up. We have a day full of making the best homecoming display Bellman High has ever seen. Plus, depending what time we get done, I have a surprise for you."

The promise of a surprise was more daunting than it was exciting, but I forced a smile at Elijah. I didn't want to ruin his excitement with my unnecessary anxiety.

Once we were inside, Bailey's moms ushered us to the backyard where many of our classmates were already hard at work. My eyes scanned the crowd, not taking long to settle on Bailey, who was helping to paint a large banner.

As if she could feel my eyes on her, Bailey turned toward me, her already wide smile growing even bigger as she motioned for us to come over. Her hair was pulled into a high ponytail, and the sweatpants and T-shirt she was wearing were covered in paint. Her outfit was far from fancy, but that didn't stop me from losing my breath when I was standing in front of her.

"Thanks for coming! Surprised to see you're helping out your class's competition, Elijah, but I'll take any help I can get. We might actually get most or all of this done today, which is really exciting." Bailey looked around as though she was studying her surroundings before bringing her focus back to us. "You can either hop in on one of the banners or help with cutting things out."

"I don't think we're really dressed for painting, so we'll help with cutting," Elijah answered before I could.

I could have sworn I saw Bailey's smile drop as Elijah took my hand and began pulling me to where people were busy cutting, but she quickly recovered, smiling at me until I was forced to look away and causing my stomach to do somersaults that I wished it wouldn't.

The day went by quickly as we all worked hard to get as much done as we could. Right when my stomach started to grumble, Bailey's mom walked out with pizza and wings for us. By this point, most people had grown restless, so they immediately abandoned their work to eat and socialize.

"Hey, stranger," Bailey said when she sidled up beside me as we filled our plates.

Her intoxicating scent filled my nostrils even over the smell of the food and it was like I was completely surrounded by her. I had to grasp the table with the hand that wasn't holding my plate to steady myself. Bailey had the power to make me feel completely unbalanced, and I had no idea if I loved it or hated it. All I knew was I couldn't avoid it. If I was near her, the world seemed to spin around me while I stayed in place. Stuck in a place I didn't want to be, but couldn't bring myself to leave.

But why? Shouldn't this have stopped by now? I had Elijah to focus on. Elijah. The sweet church boy who gets excited about goodnight kisses and holding hands and looks at me as though I put the stars in the sky.

"Emma?" Bailey's voice interrupted my downward spiral, and I realized I still hadn't said anything to her.

"Sorry. It's been a long weekend." A lie. The only thing tiring about this weekend was the constant struggle to keep my mind from wandering to places that it shouldn't.

"Go a little too crazy at the party on Friday night?"

I shook my head. That definitely wasn't the case. I wasn't even at the party long enough to go crazy. "No. I had like a half a beer. It wasn't as fun as last time, so Elijah and I left early." What I wanted to say was it wasn't the same without *you*, but I wasn't going to go there, even if it was the truth.

"You guys have a party of your own?" Bailey's smile remained on her face, but I noticed it didn't reach her eyes like it normally did.

"Not at all. I went home and went to bed because I'm super cool like that."

There it was. That shimmer in her eyes that contrasted the darkness and made them like no eyes I'd ever seen before. Eyes I could get completely lost in…

"You're not talking about me, are you?" Elijah joked as he chuckled and put a hand on my shoulder.

Even though it seemed to take all my might, I forced my attention from Bailey to Elijah, turning completely and running my hands up and down his sides the way I figured I was supposed to. "Hey, you. I was wondering where you were."

Elijah pointed his thumb back toward where we had been working. "I was just helping to clean up so we can head out once we're done eating."

Head out? My stomach dropped at the thought. Aside from our conversation that Elijah had just interrupted, I hadn't had a chance to talk to Bailey all day. I turned to say something to her, only to realize she was gone, already fluttering around the party like the social butterfly she was.

Because that's what she did. She made everyone feel special and important. It's why she was so popular. It's what made her so likable. But it's also what could cause a person's heart to get confused, and as I felt the twisting of my own, I knew I couldn't let it happen to me. "We could just take the food with us if you want," I said when I turned back to Elijah.

Elijah's eyes went wide as if he hadn't expected that response from me, but at the same time, a smile lit up his face. "I'm down. We're not going too far, so we can eat when we get there. I guess we should say goodbye to everyone, huh?"

I slipped my hand into his and tried my best at a flirtatious grin. "Or we could just leave quietly and apologize at school tomorrow. It will get us out of here quicker."

I was ready to be anywhere but here. The striking reality that I was kidding myself about Bailey had hit me hard, even though I knew it shouldn't. It wouldn't matter if I was right about our connection. This wasn't who I was. I was a good daughter who went to church every Sunday and made her parents proud. I didn't make ripples. It was easier that way, and the easier way had to be the happier way, right? Right. So, I was determined to be the girl I knew I could.

Elijah must have been fine with my idea to sneak off because he wasted no time in pulling me around the side of the house and back to his car. I felt a little guilty about not saying anything to Bailey's parents or her sister, but made a mental note to apologize for that later.

After just a few minutes of driving, Elijah parked his car in the school parking lot, then grabbed our plates and a blanket and motioned for me to follow him. We walked until we reached the soccer field, where he laid down the blanket on one of the far edges.

"So, this is your idea of a romantic date?" I asked, eyeing him suspiciously. "Dinner on the soccer field?"

Elijah sat down and motioned for me to sit next to him. "You don't give me enough credit. I happen to know that this is one of the best spots in town to watch the sunset. And according to my research, that should start in about…" He looked down toward his phone. "Forty-five minutes."

"Ah, so you've done this before?"

"I have. Only by myself though." Elijah cringed. "Although, when I say that out loud, it sounds kind of lame."

I reached out and placed my hand on top of his, squeezing his gently. "I don't think it sounds lame at all."

Elijah turned his palm up, so he could intertwine his fingers with mine. We continued to sit like this while we ate the pizza we had taken from Bailey's house. When I finished my two slices, I laid back on the blanket and held my stomach, surprised by how full I felt. "That was good, but I'm thinking I should have stopped at one. Those were big slices."

Elijah mimicked my motions by laying down and placing a hand on his stomach as well. "Yeah. It was good though." He stared over at me and went weirdly quiet, opening his mouth a few times like he wanted to say something, but was overthinking it. "Do you want to know one of the best parts about coming here at this time?" He scooted over to me, close enough that now our arms were touching too. "No one else is ever here."

As he continued to stare, I knew exactly what he was getting at. He slowly moved closer to me as if he was asking permission for what he was about to do next. He let go of my hand so he could push up onto his arm and stare down at me, pausing once more as if he expected me to push him away. But I wasn't going to do that. It's not like he was planning on taking my clothes off in the middle of a soccer field. It was a kiss. Hopefully not a long, drawn out one where his tongue attacked mine for much longer than was comfortable, but just a kiss. Something that all seniors in high school did when they were dating a guy.

As if sensing my silent approval, Elijah closed the distance between us and placed a soft kiss on my lips. Since I knew he hadn't brought me out here for a few innocent pecks, I opened my mouth to his, allowing his tongue to slip inside. He wasn't as aggressive and sloppy as my ex-boyfriend, which was nice. He was slow and hesitant, and the kiss was pleasant. It wasn't the fireworks that a lot of girls talk about, but was that really even a thing? It seemed highly unlikely that something like kissing could really make your body feel that way.

I was happy to be able to catch my breath when Elijah pulled away a moment later. He pushed up onto his elbows as a boyish grin came onto his face. "Wow. That was awesome. You're a great kisser."

I laughed at his compliment, amused at how much pleasure he had gotten from the kiss. "You are too, Elijah. Not that my list is very long, but you're definitely number one." Which was true. Even without the fireworks, his kiss was still better than any I had gotten in the past.

"So, if it's not too much for me to ask, how long is your list?"

"Of people I've kissed? It's… umm… three. My middle school boyfriend, high school boyfriend, and you."

"What about sex?"

My face heated up at his question. Why were we even talking about this? Sex with Elijah wasn't anywhere on my radar, and I hoped he didn't think it was. Things would have to get a lot more serious before I even considered that. "Zero. I've never had sex. What about you?" Even though I asked the question, I wasn't sure if I wanted to hear the answer.

"Twice. Both with the same person." He hesitated, his face turning the slightest bit red, before he continued. "My first time was after homecoming last year."

"Oh." I swallowed hard as I thought about our impending date less than three weeks away.

Elijah swiftly grabbed back a hold of my hand. "We had been dating for over a year at that point. It's not like I expect something to happen just because it's homecoming. I promise."

I let out a breath, comforted by his reassurance. My mind slipped back to a very similar conversation I had with Bailey just a week ago, the only difference being that she was also waiting. Waiting for the right time and the right person. The sincerity on her face as she spoke about it told me she would never give up her virginity after a dance. She would probably wait for the perfect moment and make the wait completely worthwhile. Exactly how I wanted to do it. Although "the wait" wasn't really that difficult for me. The thought of sex didn't get me excited, which only served to further prove that I was right to be waiting.

"Did I completely ruin the moment?" Elijah asked, breaking me from my thoughts.

"No. You're fine. I was just thinking. What's your favorite color?" *Anything to change the subject.*

Elijah laughed. "These are the deep thoughts running through your mind right now? Mine is green. How about you?"

I told him my favorite color was blue and then we continued to go back and forth, asking each other silly questions and forgetting about the heavy conversation from just moments before. When the sun started to set, Elijah put an arm around my shoulder and pulled me closer to him. He was right. It really was beautiful. Watching the sunset with Elijah holding me tight really did feel romantic. So much so that I didn't even mind how he pulled me in for another long kiss after the sun was completely down. *Exactly how it was supposed to be...*

***

"My moms were asking about you last night. They were surprised they didn't see you before you left. I was too." Bailey's tone wasn't accusing, but there was something more behind it that I couldn't quite place.

It also wasn't lost on me that she had barely made eye contact with me since we got to weightlifting class. Now, over halfway through the period, I found myself missing those eyes. Missing the way they seemed to see right through me, past everything I was hiding and right into my soul, in the most scary yet exhilarating way possible.

"I'm sorry. I should have said goodbye. You're not mad at me, are you?" My voice sounded so weak and I wanted to slap myself for being so pathetic.

"Mad?" Bailey chuckled. "Of course I'm not mad. It was crazy. A lot of people slipped out without saying goodbye. I guess I was just surprised that you were one of them."

I shrugged. "You just seemed busy. I didn't want to bother you."

"I'm never too busy for you." And there it was—that eye contact. The already warm room seemed to get about 100 degrees hotter under the heat of that stare. Unfortunately, it was gone much too quickly when Bailey looked away to pick up a set of dumbbells. "So, you and Elijah hung out after the party?"

I avoided looking at her as I picked up a set of weights as well. "Yeah. We went to the soccer field and—"

"Made out?" Bailey interrupted with a laugh.

"Wh-What?"

"Let's just say the soccer boys aren't very creative." Bailey lifted an eyebrow in a way that told me she had also spent alone time on the soccer field. The idea made me sick. I wanted to believe it was because I was disappointed that my night with Elijah wasn't as romantic as I originally thought, but as Bailey brought her eyes back to mine and licked her lips as she got ready to say something else, causing my stomach to do somersaults, I knew that wasn't the case. "Since things seem to be getting pretty serious with you and Elijah, would you want to go to the soccer game with me on Thursday night? It's about an hour away, but Wyatt says it's an important one, so I told him I'd go."

"That sounds great!" I answered a bit too enthusiastically. "I'm sure Elijah will be really happy."

***

Thursday couldn't come soon enough and because of that, the week crawled by. Even two ice cream dates with Elijah weren't enough to make it go by faster. When Thursday finally came, Bailey and I had our plans finalized. Since the JV team played first and there was no reason for us to be at that game, we decided to get food after school, then head to the game.

"So, I thought we could go to this cafe in town. It's over by the university," Bailey said as we walked to her car. "It's called Emma's. Have you been there? Figured you should visit your namesake."

"I haven't. My dad's been saying we need to go ever since we passed it when we went to visit Bell U though."

"Should we go somewhere else? I don't want to interfere with a special family thing."

Bailey's sweetness made me laugh. "No, it's fine. He'll just be excited that I went there."

"Awesome. Emma's it is."

Less than ten minutes later, we were heading into the restaurant, which was a cute little cafe with a very hometown feel to it. We had barely sat down when a woman who had to be well over seventy came rushing over to our table, arms flailing around waving as she made her way closer.

Once she reached us, she put one hand down on the table as if to stabilize herself and took a deep breath. She grinned widely as she focused her attention on Bailey. "Why if it isn't Bailey Caldwell. It's been too long since you've been in here. Leave the rest of the crew at home tonight?" She raised an eyebrow as she looked from Bailey over to me.

"Just giving my new friend here the full Bellman experience, and what's Bellman without a trip to your restaurant?" Bailey smiled over at me, her attention causing my stomach to do flips I wish I could ignore, but couldn't no matter how hard I tried. "Emma Rogers, I'd like you to meet Emma West. Her family just moved here a few months ago."

It was that moment when the realization of who this lady was finally hit me. "Emma? So, this is your place?" I asked as I looked around.

"For the past thirty-five years," she said proudly.

"Wow, that's amazing. You've done a great job." She really had. The restaurant was still in immaculate condition and was pretty full for a random Thursday.

Even though I wouldn't have thought it would be possible, the old woman's smile grew even bigger. "Thank you. I appreciate that. It's easy to keep things going when I hear such kind words." She leaned closer to Bailey and grabbed a hold of her cheek like a crazy relative would do. "Also, the regulars sure do help too. I've been serving this one since she was just a little munchkin. Seems like just yesterday that I saw her march in here with her moms for the first time, all wide-eyed and excited."

Bailey laughed softly as she shook her head at the woman. "We're going to need some time to decide since Emma is new here, but do you think you could start us out with some of your amazing onion rings?"

"With the secret sauce?" the woman asked with an exaggerated wink.

"Always with the secret sauce," Bailey returned.

"You got it. A Coke for you," she said as she pointed toward Bailey, then she looked back at me. "And what would you like to drink, sweetheart?"

"I'll take a Coke as well, ma'am."

"Coming right up!" She gave me one more wink before floating back across the restaurant, stopping at multiple tables along the way.

"So, that's Emma," Bailey said with a laugh.

"I take it you come here a lot?" I asked, ready to learn about every facet of Bailey's life.

Bailey nodded. "Oh yeah. It's one of my family's regular spots. My moms and I came here for breakfast not long after we first moved here, so it's been special to us ever since."

Bailey's face took on an almost dreamy state as she talked about her family, getting a far away look in her eyes as if she was lost in the memories. Meanwhile, I became lost in her. Her zest for life, the love she had for her family, the way she developed the slightest crinkles at the corner of her eyes when she smiled.

"What is it?" Bailey asked, interrupting my thoughts. I realized she was now focused intently on me, probably wondering why I was practically drooling over her like an idiot.

"Sorry. I was just thinking about how cool it is that you're so close to your family. I feel like most people our age either aren't that close to their parents or won't admit it even if they are. It's refreshing."

Bailey shrugged as if it was no big deal. "I think family is the most important part of your life, whether it's your blood or your chosen family. They are the people who will be with you through every single chapter of your life. That's why it's so important to never take them for granted." She smiled and tilted her head slightly. "What about you? Are you close to your parents?"

I nodded, hoping Bailey didn't notice my hesitation as my mind went right to the issue keeping me from being as close to my parents as I used to be. *Aside from the fact that we can't talk about these feelings that I may or may not have for girls that I'm trying desperately to suppress.* "We're definitely close. My parents are great. They are two of my best friends."

"Why the hesitation?"

*Of course she would notice that.* I looked down at my hands that were resting on the table. "I just feel like the older I get, the harder it seems to be to share certain things with them. You know what I mean?" I shook my head as if answering my own question. "Probably not. Your moms are like the coolest parents ever."

When I looked back up at Bailey her eyes were studying me in that way that only she could. The way that made me believe she was seeing so much more than anyone else could. "We are all pretty open with each other, but I totally get it. I feel like sometimes it's harder to share things with the people we're closest to because we worry about how they will react since their opinion means more to us than anyone else's."

She had no idea just how true that was for me. I couldn't imagine telling my parents that the question I asked my youth pastor back in Texas wasn't just a fleeting thought. Admitting to them that those feelings might actually be real was the scariest thought in the world. What if they couldn't accept it? What if it changed the way they looked at me? I could deal with judgments from random strangers, but the thought of losing my parents because of these feelings killed me. No. I couldn't think like that. I wouldn't have to tell them about these feelings because I wasn't going to let them control me. I didn't need to. I had real feelings for Elijah. Sure, it wasn't the same as what I felt when I was with Bailey, but I could get there. I *would* get there.

"Are you okay? Did I say something wrong?"

The sound of Bailey's voice brought me back to reality and I realized she was staring at me intently, her eyebrows furrowing in concern as she waited for my answer. I shook my head and held up the menu that was sitting in front of me. "No, sorry. I just zoned out thinking about what I should order."

The concern left Bailey's face, immediately being replaced by that signature smile that had my stomach betraying me and tying up in knots once again. "No problem. We really should figure out what we're getting. We don't want you to miss any of your boy's game."

My mind wandered as I watched Bailey's lips move as she spoke. As much as I didn't want them to be, those lips were so distracting. They looked so soft and inviting. Like a forbidden fruit I wanted so badly to bite into. God, what was I thinking? What was she even saying right now? Game. My boy's game. Oh yeah. Elijah. He was the one who deserved to occupy my thoughts. He deserved my full attention, and I was going to work to get to that point for him. By homecoming, I was going to be the best date he could possibly ask for.

# Chapter 7: Bailey

"Spirit week! How pumped are you?" Wyatt asked when I picked him up for school on the Monday leading up to homecoming.

"So pumped," I said as I threw a fist in the air, trying to muster as much fake enthusiasm as possible.

Wyatt gave me a look that told me he wasn't buying it at all and sighed dramatically. "Don't lie to me. You look miserable. I hate seeing you like this. I don't think I've ever seen you fall so hard for someone."

That's because I never had fallen this hard. I did everything in my power to suppress the feelings I was having for Emma, but it seemed the harder I tried, the stronger my feelings became. I wanted to be her friend, but that was getting harder too. Every moment I spent with her made me want her that much more. Everything I learned about her made her that much more appealing to me. I thought with time I would find things *not* to like, but that didn't seem to be the case.

Remembering where I was, I reached out and put my hand on Wyatt's. "I'll be okay, Wy. I promise."

"Okay good." Wyatt opened his mouth like he was about to say something else, then shut it as if he thought better of it.

"What is it, Wyatt?"

"Nothing. We should probably get to school."

Now I *really* knew something was up. Ever since this year had started, Wyatt had tried to convince me almost every day that we should skip first period and get breakfast before school. I shut my car off and crossed my arms, staring over at him as I lifted an eyebrow. "Just tell me."

Wyatt took a deep breath and closed his eyes. When he opened them back up, it looked like he was in pain. "It's just... Elijah is planning to officially ask out Emma at homecoming."

And just like that, the sick feeling that I was becoming much too accustomed to returned. My stomach churned and I thought I might throw up. I turned the car back on and started to drive, desperate to keep myself from thinking about Emma all dressed up for homecoming, her hair styled in a way that accentuated her beautiful face, and that face lighting up as she told Elijah she would love to be his girlfriend. Ugh. When had this happened? When had I fallen *this* hard? I needed to shake this.

"Bailey? You okay?"

I nodded my head slowly. "I am. This is fine. Actually, it's great. This is just what I need to move on."

I refused to look over at him, but I could feel Wyatt studying my face. "Is that what you want though?"

"What do you mean?"

"Moving on. Do you really want that?"

I laughed out loud at his question. "Of course I want that. I don't want to have these feelings. Dating wasn't part of the plan for this year. Dating a *girl* certainly wasn't part of the plan."

"Why do you act like dating a girl would be such a terrible thing? You have two moms and a bisexual best friend."

"We've been over this. It's so cliche. The gay girl with gay parents. I don't want people to think that I was somehow influenced by them."

"Anyone who would think that is an idiot."

I shook my head as I pulled into the school parking lot. "I'm not even sure why we're having this discussion. Emma and Elijah are going to date, and I'm going to be just fine. End of story."

Wyatt huffed as he grabbed his backpack and opened the door. "Just take care of yourself, okay? Don't overdo it on your presidential duties this week just to try to keep your mind off of things."

I promised Wyatt I wouldn't even though I knew that's exactly what I was going to do, starting with the gym decorating that afternoon. Anyone on the homecoming committee or in the student council was getting out of fourth period to decorate. I almost forgot that I had convinced

Emma to join the homecoming committee until I saw her walk into the gym.

I forced myself to look away from her, which proved to be harder than it should have been. She was like a magnet and I had to fight the forces that were trying to pull my eyes to her. Unfortunately, she didn't have the same reservations, and soon I felt her presence beside me. "Where do you want me, boss?" she asked cheerfully, completely unaware of the inner demons I was currently fighting against.

I pointed toward the top of the bleachers where some of our classmates were hanging up banners, far from where I was needed. "They could use your help up there."

"Oh… okay." Emma hesitated for a moment before turning away from me to head up the bleachers.

I tried to direct my focus on anything other than Emma, but I kept finding my eyes drifting up to where she was. Between every order I gave and every prop I helped move, my eyes would search for her once again, not stopping until they landed on her. When the school day was coming to an end, my eyes found her one more time. Only this time, my eyes met hers. A small, almost shy, smile spread across her face. I tried to force my gaze away from her, but that magnetism was back, pulling me in once again.

I watched as she walked down the bleachers and closed the space separating us until she was standing right in front of me. She tilted her head as she continued to smile at me. "You're quite the busy lady."

"Yeah, you know, presidential duties." I laughed awkwardly, suddenly unable to act normal. Ugh. What was happening to me?

Emma looked down at her feet, as if she could sense the tension between us as well. "Yeah. I'm sure it's a crazy week for you." She looked back up and locked eyes with me once again. "So, are you going to the soccer game tomorrow night?"

I had told Wyatt that I was, but now that seemed like a terrible idea. I needed some time away from Emma, and of course she was going to the game. Not only was she going, but she was going to watch her soon-to-be boyfriend. I needed to shake this and I couldn't do that by sitting there and watching her swoon over Elijah. Wyatt would understand if I didn't go. He had to. "I can't make it," I lied. "Too much stuff to do to prepare for homecoming."

"Of course. That makes sense."

Emma wasn't going to make this avoidance thing easy on me though. *Missed you at the game tonight*, her text read on Tuesday night. Before I could even respond, another came through. *Still busy? Any interest in an ice cream break?*

An ice cream break with Emma sounded amazing, even though I technically didn't need a *break* from anything since all I had done all night was play games with Sophia and tried to ignore the aching feeling in my heart. I couldn't though. I didn't skip one of my best friend's final soccer games just to put my heart through the ringer anyway. *I can't tonight. I'm sorry.*

I was surprised when, instead of receiving a text back, my phone started to ring. "Hey, what's up?" I answered, trying to sound as nonchalant as possible.

"Everything okay?" Emma asked, her voice laced with concern.

"I'm good. Sorry for being weird. I'm just tired."

"That's why you need a break," Emma said sweetly.

She needed to stop being so nice. This would be so much easier if she wasn't the sweetest person in the world. "Yeah, I know. I just want everything to be perfect. I've been so focused on making homecoming a success that I haven't even gotten my homecoming court outfit for Friday."

That part wasn't a lie. Anyone on the homecoming court had to dress up for the school pep rally and the football game. Unlike the dress we would wear to the dance on Saturday, we were expected to get a suit for that. At this point, I hadn't even decided if I was going to look for a suit with pants or a skirt. Pants were more practical, but the skirt seemed cuter. At this point, I was probably at the mercy of what I could find since I had put off buying my outfit for so long.

"I'm free the rest of the week if you want help finding an outfit."

"No plans with Elijah?" I couldn't help myself. As much as I didn't want to think about their relationship, I also knew acknowledging it was the only way I could possibly move on so things could go back to normal with Emma. At least as normal as possible.

"Well, tomorrow night we have youth group and he did ask me to go out for dessert afterward. But I can probably get out of both of those things in order to help you out."

Why was Emma willing to drop anything to help me with something so trivial? Was she *this sweet* with all of her friends? I shook my head. There was no need to overthink this. It didn't matter. Even if she did treat me differently than she treated other people, what difference did that make? She was about to have a boyfriend and I was about to move on from this stupid crush that couldn't go anywhere anyway. "I wouldn't want you to change your plans for me. Seriously."

"Okay. Then how about Thursday?"

Man, this girl wouldn't give up, would she?

"Sorry if I seem overbearing right now. It's just... well, I... I don't just want to spend my time with Elijah and, so far, you're the only other person I feel close enough to to ask to hang out."

With that confession, I was overcome with guilt. Emma was just trying to make friends to share her senior year with and I was standing in the way of that because of my stupid heart and idiotic feelings. No matter how much it hurt to be around her right now, pushing her away wasn't the right thing to do either. "Thursday sounds great."

***

"Ready to go?" Emma asked as she skipped over to my car after school on Thursday.

I tried to ignore the way her blond ponytail bounced as she did and how her smile tilted up the tiniest bit more on the right side than the left and the way these little things about her somehow felt like big things to me. "Let's do this," I said with the widest grin I could muster.

"What do you think of this one?" I asked as I came out of the dressing room wearing a fitted black pantsuit.

"It's nice," Emma answered quickly, but her answer didn't convince me. I wanted more than nice.

Her reaction matched what I felt when I looked in the mirror. It was okay, but it was nothing special. I sighed as I went back into the dressing room. I had tried on five different suits so far and none of them seemed right. Since I had gotten through all of the ones we had picked out, I had to start all over.

As I slipped out of that suit and went to put my own outfit back on, there was a knock on the dressing room door. "I think I found a good one," Emma said from the other side.

She threw the suit over the top of the door. I was surprised by what I saw. It wasn't like anything I had tried on so far. It was cream colored with a long sleeve jacket and a pencil skirt. "You think this is going to look good?" I asked through the door.

"Oh yeah. I bet the light color is the perfect contrast to your hair and eyes."

I wasn't convinced, but I decided to try it on since I was desperate to find something. When I turned to look in the mirror, I was shocked. Emma was exactly right. This was definitely the suit. I ran my hands over the front of it and smiled at my reflection in the mirror. "I think you were right," I said as I opened the door to the dressing room so she could see.

Emma's eyes slowly ran up the length of the suit before reaching mine, a look in her own eyes that I couldn't read, but wanted to get lost in. "That's…" Emma swallowed hard as she continued to stare at me. "You look absolutely breathtaking."

Speaking of breathtaking, the way she was looking at me mixed with the soft sincerity of her words had me feeling like I couldn't breathe. I tried to say something, but words were escaping me. All I could do was gaze back into the eyes that were focused intently on mine. I was suddenly transported to another world. A world where what I was feeling wasn't so complicated. A world where Emma felt it too. A world that wasn't filled with expectations and soon-to-be boyfriends. "Emma, I—" I cleared my throat and shook myself from this other place, grounding myself in my current reality. "I agree. This one is perfect."

For a moment, it almost seemed like Emma was disappointed with the words that had left my mouth, her lips twitching slightly downward as I said them, but just as quickly, a wide grin spread across her face and her eyes began to sparkle again. "Told you."

***

Wyatt's reaction to my outfit when he met me outside of the gym to be my escort for the assembly didn't have nearly the same effect as Emma's. In true Wyatt fashion, he wolf-whistled when he saw me and insisted I twirl in circles for him. "Girl, if you don't come out of this weekend with a boyfriend or girlfriend, I might just sweep you up for myself."

"No, you wouldn't," I said with a laugh. I took his arm the way we were taught to and leaned in closer to him. "Also, don't say that so loud. I'm not completely convinced I'm bisexual, and I don't need rumors going around that I am before I've even figured it out."

"What would you say you are?" Wyatt whispered. He pulled away for a second, then leaned back in, an obnoxious smirk on his face. "Emma-sexual?"

I elbowed him in the side, hard enough to make him groan at the contact. "Shut up. I'm getting over that."

"Are you really? Because I was watching you in the gym before you came out to change. You looked at her five times."

I shook my head as we began to follow the rest of the court into the gym. "Creep."

"Want to know something else?"

"Not really, but I'm sure you're going to tell me anyway."

Wyatt laughed and patted my hand. "I happened to be watching her too. She looked at you *seven* times." Wyatt looked around the gym while I stared straight ahead the way we were supposed to. "Eight. She's watching you right now."

I tried not to react to the thought of Emma watching me. Wyatt had no idea what he was talking about, and putting thoughts like that in my head was only going to make things worse. "Everyone is watching me right now," I said with a scoff. "That's the point of this assembly." Aside from people who were bored with this whole thing, all eyes were on the homecoming court. It would have been more weird if Emma wasn't watching.

"Don't be so conceited. Everyone else is watching the *whole* court. She's just watching you."

I couldn't help my curiosity and looked up to the spot in the bleachers where I knew she was sitting. Sure enough, Wyatt was right. Our eyes connected as soon as they landed on her. I could feel my face heating up and I hoped it wasn't turning red. That shy smile that had the power to completely destroy me came onto Emma's face and I had to hold onto Wyatt tighter, afraid I might fall over from going weak in the knees. As if that wasn't enough, she wiggled her fingers in the most subtle wave that sent a sensation through my body that was anything *but* subtle. I smiled back to acknowledge her gesture, then let out a sigh as I turned my attention back to the walkway in front of me.

I zoned out as Ben spoke about each member of the homecoming court and reminded everyone that they would be announcing the winner during halftime of the football game. "Ready to accept your crown tonight?" Wyatt asked from beside me.

I shrugged my shoulders. Being crowned homecoming queen was never that important to me, but now it was the last thing on my mind. I would give up that crown a million times to get lost in Emma's ocean blue eyes just once.

\*\*\*

"Where is my homecoming queen?" I heard Wyatt shout from downstairs as I put the finishing touches on my make up.

I looked over at Chloe, who was doing her makeup beside me, and rolled my eyes. "He's ridiculous. I don't know why he has to make such a big deal out of this." I pointed to the crown that I was required to wear to the dance after being crowned homecoming queen the night before.

"You don't have to play it cool just because you beat me," Chloe said with a smirk. "We all knew you were going to win. We're both hot, but you're much nicer. Plus, no one wants to crown the girl who is dating the enemy as the homecoming queen."

I laughed. "You're just lucky we won last night. Otherwise, I don't know if the football guys would be as cool about Jackson coming to homecoming."

"I really don't care who won last night as long as *I* get lucky tonight."

I lifted an eyebrow at Chloe. "Planning on finding somewhere to sneak off to at Ben's party tonight?"

"Obviously. We *never* get to have sex. I need some loving." Chloe stopped applying her makeup to look over at me. "What about you? Whose date are you planning to steal tonight?"

I laughed incredulously. "Excuse me?"

"Oh, come on. I don't remember there ever being an after-dance party that you haven't found a guy to spend the night making out with. Clearly, it's not going to be Wyatt, so I figure you must be planning on stealing someone else's date at the after-party."

*Not this year,* I thought to myself. There was only one person who came to my mind when I thought about kissing and that absolutely couldn't happen. That would *never* happen. "I guess we'll just have to wait and see, won't we?" I wiggled my eyebrows at her in the hopes she wouldn't see right through my attempts at avoiding the subject.

Luckily, that seemed to work, and she focused her attention back on the mirror as she finished her makeup. Downstairs the doorbell rang, then my mama shouted up to tell us that Jackson had arrived. Within a few minutes, everyone else who was going out to dinner with us before we headed to the dance had arrived as well.

Emma was going to the dance with a group of soccer players from Elijah's grade and their dates which was both a blessing and a curse. It felt weird to not have her there. All feelings aside, she had already become one of my best friends and I enjoyed having her around. On the other hand, it was nice that I didn't have to watch her and Elijah together. Dinner was much more enjoyable when I wasn't stuck on every touch and every whisper between them.

As soon as we walked into the dance, that all too familiar bubbling returned to my stomach and I found myself searching for Emma once again. For a little bit, I had almost been able to get her off my mind, but being in a space that I knew we would both be occupying tonight brought it all back.

A few minutes after arriving, when I heard another big group enter the gym, I knew she was part of it. It wasn't because I heard any voices I recognized, but instead, I felt her presence. It was like all of the air had been sucked from the room, the walls were closing in, and I couldn't breathe. Yet, I welcomed the feeling. It was that comfortable discomfort that I was learning to love and hate all at once. I slowly turned around and wasn't surprised to see Emma across the gym. She was wearing a dark blue dress that fell just above her knees. Her blonde hair was partially pulled back with a few curls framing her face. She closed her eyes and threw her head back while she laughed at something someone said, as one of her hands rested on Elijah's arm. Any breath I had left was completely sucked from my lungs as her eyes opened back up and settled on mine.

The eye contact was short-lived because Emma quickly looked away, putting her focus on Elijah as she leaned in close to whisper something in his ear. I tried to ignore how my heart dropped and disappointment coursed through my body. I forced myself to look away, staring down at my heeled feet to keep myself from being tempted to sneak another peek that would only hurt me.

"Shouldn't you be having more fun? You *are* the Homecoming Queen."

I looked up and all of those terrible feelings washed away. "Emma." Her name came out in a breathless whisper that I hoped she didn't notice.

She tilted her head in a way that I tried, and failed, not to find so endearing. "Were you expecting someone else?"

"No. I just thought you'd want to be with your—" I stopped myself when I remembered Elijah probably hadn't asked her out yet. "Your date."

Emma waved a dismissive hand in the air. "I just spent all of dinner with him and his friends. I wanted some time with my best friend."

"I'm… I'm your best friend?" God, why did I sound so pathetic right now?

Even in the dark gym, I could still see Emma's face turning red, causing me to feel guilty for making her feel uncomfortable. "Oh God, I'm sorry. I guess that might sound a bit pathetic since we haven't known each other that long. You've been here forever. You have so many close friends. It's just that I'm new and you've been so cool and welcoming and—"

I put up a hand to signal for Emma to stop her nervous rambling. "Don't apologize. You're my best friend too."

Emma looked like she was about to say something, but closed her mouth instead and started to laugh. "Don't let Wyatt hear you say that."

"That's different. Wyatt's like my brother. You're…" *The girl I can't stop thinking about kissing. My unrequited, unrealistic crush.* "It's not different with you."

Something flashed in Emma's eyes as she looked deeply into mine and somehow I knew whatever she was about to say was important. I watched as she opened her mouth, waiting with bated breath to see what she had to say.

"Sorry to interrupt, but can I have this dance?"

I tried my best not to glare at Elijah as he stole Emma's attention away, but I wasn't sure if I was successful. I was pretty positive I really wanted to hear whatever it was she wanted to say. Did I really, though? What did I expect? It's not like she was going to confess her love for me, and I wouldn't have wanted her to anyway. It didn't even matter.

The moment I thought we were having was officially over as Emma allowed Elijah to whisk her onto the dance floor.

I needed to get away. Maybe get a drink of water or perhaps some fresh air. Anything was better than watching Emma with Elijah. I turned to walk away, but walked right into a person instead.

"Where's the fire?" Wyatt asked with a laugh. "I was just coming over here to dance with you. No running away now."

I sighed as I rested my arms on his shoulders. Wyatt was stubborn. There was no use fighting him since I knew he would win in the end. "You don't have to dance with me you know."

"Well, unfortunately I don't seem to have any other options."

I scoffed at his honesty. "Wow, thanks. You really know how to make a girl feel special."

"You *are* special, hence why I'm dancing with you right now. I saw your face when Emma went to dance with Elijah. I'm not going to let you be miserable at your last homecoming dance ever. So, I'm making it my duty to make sure you have fun, even if I'm not actually the person you want to be here with."

I pulled Wyatt closer to me and lay my head on his shoulder, enjoying the comfort of being close to the person I trusted more than anyone else. "There is no one I'd rather be here with than you, Wy."

Wyatt threw his head back in laughter as if I had just told a joke, rather than spoken the truth. "You keep telling yourself that."

"I mean it."

"Then I take it you wouldn't be interested in knowing that your girl has looked at you more throughout this song than her date that she's dancing with?"

I sighed in frustration. I knew Wyatt was just trying to cheer me up, but this wasn't the way to do it. "First of all, I don't believe that. Second of all, it doesn't matter anyway."

"Are you sure about that?" Wyatt pulled back so he could look at me, and I was surprised by the serious expression on his face. "I would never tell you this if I didn't think it was true because I wouldn't want to get your hopes up just to have you be disappointed. But I don't think this crush of yours is one-sided."

I hated the way hearing him say that made my heart beat faster. I had to keep these feelings under control, and that wasn't going to happen if my heart was convinced it had a chance. "Drop it, Wyatt. I told you that's not even what I want. I honestly just want to move on, and that will be a heck of a lot easier once Emma and Elijah become official. Which they will. Because you're wrong. There is no way Emma West likes me as anything more than a friend."

# Chapter 8: Emma

"Sorry I stole you away from Bailey."

"What?" I focused my attention back on Elijah as we danced together.

He nodded over to where Bailey was dancing with Wyatt, a scene I couldn't seem to keep my eyes off of even though I knew there wasn't actually anything going on between them. "I know since you spent dinner with my friends, you probably want to hang out with your friends now, so I'm sorry about pulling you away to dance. I just thought you would want to."

"Of course I want to. You're my date. I want to dance every slow song with you." Even as I said the words, I wasn't sure if I was trying to convince Elijah or myself.

A wide smile worked its way across Elijah's face. "I'm really happy to hear that."

I liked how something as simple as that could make him so happy. It was charming and refreshing. For that reason, I moved my hands to the back of his neck and pulled him closer to me to kiss him. Much to my surprise, he deepened the kiss, making out with me right there in the middle of the dance floor.

When I pulled away, his smile was even bigger. "Wow. That was… wow."

*You'll get there, Emma,* I reminded myself. Just because Elijah was clearly feeling more than I was now, didn't mean that I wouldn't feel it soon enough. It was still early. Every kiss seemed to get a little better than the last so that had to mean something. Plus, guys were just predisposed to like physical affection more, so of course Elijah was more into things like kissing.

I felt better when the song switched to a fast one and we went back and forth seeing who could do the craziest dance moves. This was what I liked about Elijah. I enjoyed how goofy we could be together. It was fun and comfortable, and I couldn't see myself ever growing tired of spending time with him. That was a lot more than I could say for my ex.

Yet, near the end of the dance when we were both exhausted and Elijah went to grab us water, Wyatt shared news with me that had me reacting differently than I would have expected. I was watching Bailey dance with some of our classmates and contemplating going over to join them when I felt an arm come to rest on my shoulder.

"We need to talk," Wyatt said, his tone much more serious than usual. "I shouldn't be telling you this, but Elijah is planning to ask you to make things official tonight."

"Oh." His words took me by surprise. It seemed so soon. Right? Wasn't this fast? Wasn't it too early to make things official?

"You don't seem happy about that."

I shook my head. "It's not that. I'm just surprised I guess. I wasn't expecting it."

"Good surprised or bad surprised?

"Good obviously," I said with a nervous laugh.

Wyatt continued to stare at me without saying a word as if he was waiting for me to say something else. It was almost as if he expected me to change my mind. After a few seconds that felt much longer under that intense stare, he finally spoke again. "Okay, cool. I'm only saying this because I care about Elijah, and you, of course, but if you're not sure about this, you don't have to say yes. You shouldn't say yes."

Why was he talking to me like this? I didn't like it. Not one bit. I hated having my feelings questioned. "I'm sure," I answered stiffly.

"Good. Then I'm really happy for you guys." Wyatt brought his hands up in a praying motion. "But do me a favor and forget I even mentioned this. Elijah would kill me if he knew I ruined the surprise."

"I promise."

Forgetting about it proved to be impossible though. It was all I could think about for the rest of the dance. By the time we got to Ben's for the after-party though, Elijah still hadn't asked. I was starting to think that maybe Wyatt was wrong about the whole thing or maybe Elijah realized it was too soon. I waited for one of the bathrooms to open up and switched out my dress for a pair of sweatpants and a long sleeve shirt.

As soon as I was out of the bathroom, Elijah was back by my side, now wearing a Bellman Soccer outfit. "Want to get a drink?"

I nodded my head and as we walked through the party I watched for any sign of Bailey. Elijah monopolized almost all of my time at the dance so, much to my disappointment, we had barely spent any time together. I was hoping we could have some girl time while the guys played beer pong or flip cup. Unfortunately, she didn't seem to have arrived yet.

When we got to the kitchen, Ben offered to make us mixed drinks. My eyes went wide when I saw just how much alcohol he was putting in it. I took a sip and coughed at the potency. Ben laughed as if he was proud of himself for the effect it was having on me. "You need to just chug it down. It's easier to take that way." He lifted an eyebrow as if he was challenging me, and since I was never one to back down from a challenge, I took a deep breath then quickly finished off the contents of my cup. I cringed as I sat the cup back down on the table, before mustering up a cocky smile.

Ben looked from me to Elijah, looking both shocked and impressed. "Quite the lady you got there, little E."

Elijah slipped an arm around my waist and pulled me into him. "She's pretty awesome, isn't she?" He leaned closer to me as if he was waiting for a kiss, but a voice pulled my attention away.

I looked out toward the hallway where the voice was coming from, and there she was. Even though I had just seen her at the dance, seeing her again now still made the whole room seem to disappear. All I could focus on was her. Her green floor-length dress that hugged every curve. Her dark hair that was styled perfectly for the crown, almost as if it was made for her. Those dark eyes that had now come to focus on me, suddenly making it hard for me to breathe. I forced my eyes away, quickly looking toward the ground. *Stop that. It's not… You're not… She's not…* Ugh, I couldn't even think straight anymore.

99

Luckily, my internal battle was cut off by the sound of Elijah's voice. "Could we go somewhere private to talk?"

I nodded my head and followed him out the back door and to the edge of the lawn, where I took a seat beside him. "So, what's up?"

Elijah looked out into the distance, then at me, then back out into the distance. "I wanted to ask you a question."

Wyatt was right. This was it. Elijah was going to ask me to officially be his girlfriend. I became nervous at the thought, but nerves were normal, right? This was a big step. It was good though. It's exactly what I needed. I squeezed his hand, to encourage him to look at me. "Of course."

"Well, um, I guess I just wanted to know... did you actually want to go to homecoming with me?"

Okay. Not the question I was expecting. I furrowed my eyebrows as I stared at Elijah's unsure face. "Of course I did. You're awesome, and I thought we had a lot of fun together, didn't you?"

"I did." Elijah turned so he was fully facing me and took both of my hands in his. "Listen, Em, I really like you. I think you're really cool. You're like no other girl in this school, and the fact that you've been hanging out with me this past month and a half has blown my mind. But tonight... even with how much fun we were having... I couldn't help but think that you'd rather be there with someone else. Rather be dancing with someone else. Kissing someone else. Just be honest with me, Em, you like Bailey, don't you?"

He spoke softly, looking me in the eyes and squeezing my hands for reassurance. His voice wasn't accusatory or angry. It was gentle and comforting, but that didn't stop my body from tensing up at the accusation. I felt like I was back in Texas again sitting with my parents as they waited for my explanation, disappointment written all over their faces. Suddenly, my heart beat picked up, and I felt like I couldn't breathe.

I jumped to my feet, desperate to get away. Away from the guilt. Away from the questions. Away from the person I didn't want to be.

Elijah scrambled to his feet and tried to reach his hand out toward me, but I pulled mine away before he could take it and started to walk away from him.

"Em, listen, it's..."

I spun around, a fire burning deep inside of me, but I wasn't sure if I was more angry at him or myself. "No, Elijah, you listen. You have no right to say something like that. I'm not... That's not." I shook my head in frustration. "Just leave me alone okay?"

He tried once again to reach his hand out toward me, but I turned my back to him, crossing my arms over my chest to try to protect myself from the outside world. Protect myself from being seen for who I truly was. The person I wouldn't allow myself to be. "Please, Elijah," I said with a quiver to my voice. "Please leave me alone."

I heard him take a deep breath like he was getting ready to say something else, but instead he huffed and walked away.

When I was sure he was gone, I sat back down, bringing my knees up to my chest as I stared out into the darkness. How had this happened? I was supposed to be running away from these feelings, not toward them. This part of me should have stayed in Texas, where it could be forgotten and buried. Instead, I was right back where I found myself before. Trying to convince someone that I wasn't this person. Trying to convince *myself* that I wasn't. I couldn't be. It wasn't part of the plan. It wasn't my parents' plan for my life. It wasn't my plan for my life. This was messy, and I didn't do messy. I avoided messy at all costs. I wanted *easy*. I wanted *normal*. I wanted to kiss Elijah and feel that special spark. I wanted to feel proud as I introduced him to people as my boyfriend. I wanted all of the things that I might not ever be able to have.

With these thoughts swirling around in my head, I wrapped my arms around my legs to pull them even closer to my body as if I was trying to protect myself from the outside world, and I started to cry. I cried for everything I was and everything I might not ever be. I wasn't sure how long I was sitting there, but it seemed like forever before I heard a voice behind me.

"There you are! I've been looking all over for you," Bailey said, sounding breathless, but relieved. I quickly tried to wipe at my eyes, but it was too late. Bailey took a seat beside me and pulled me tightly into her arms. "Hey, what's wrong? Did you and Elijah have a fight?"

I shrugged my shoulders, unsure how to answer that.

"I don't understand. Did he say something that made you cry?"

My bottom lip quivered, making my voice come out in a shaky whisper. "Just the truth."

"I don't understand."

I wiped my eyes once again and looked over toward Bailey, who looked like she might start to cry. "I didn't tell you the whole story about why my dad was relocated to a different church or why my break up with my boyfriend was so hard." I took a deep breath, barely able to believe that I was actually about to admit this to her. "When my boyfriend had sex with my best friend, I was really upset, but not for the reason you might think. I was heartbroken, but not over my boyfriend. When that happened, I realized that my feelings for my best friend might go… beyond friendship. Coming to this realization scared me, so I talked to my youth pastor because I trusted her." I shook my head as I started to cry again, and Bailey pulled me even closer to her. "It turns out I shouldn't have. She told my parents. She told everyone on the church staff and a bunch of people in the congregation. Soon, it seemed like most of the town knew. The Methodist Church claimed my dad was being moved because they needed him here, but I know that's not true. They just didn't want him there, because… because of me."

"And what about your parents? How did they react?"

"With denial. I told them I was asking for a friend and they believed me, because people will believe anything if they want to badly enough."

"And what about you and Elijah?"

I looked away from Bailey and up at the stars sprinkling the sky. "I want Elijah. Well, I want to want him. Even he could see what I've been trying to deny. I don't want to have these feelings. I don't want to be… God, I can't even say it." I laughed sarcastically through my tears. "And the crazy thing is, maybe I'm not even… you know. I've never even kissed a girl. How am I even supposed to know if I am?"

"You could… kiss me."

"W-what?" There was no way. I had to have heard that wrong.

Only, the way Bailey's face immediately turned red told me I hadn't. She vigorously shook her head back and forth. "I'm so sorry. I have no idea why I said that. Can we please just forget I did?"

There was no forgetting. Now that she put it out there, it was all I could think about. My eyes dropped to her lips which looked so soft and oh so inviting. All control was lost as I continued to stare, Bailey's words hanging between us like a carrot on a string, pulling me forward. Literally. Before I could even fathom what my body was doing, I was leaning closer to Bailey, our lips just inches apart as I stopped to take one last deep breath. I looked from her lips to her eyes to see if she was going to try to stop me, but there was no trepidation there, only what appeared to be desire.

I sighed as I gave up. I gave up on trying to be perfect. I gave up on trying to control this. I just gave up, and I gave in. I closed the remaining few inches between us and connected our lips. As soon as they touched, I felt it. Fireworks. Freedom. That bubbling in the pit of my stomach that so many girls talked about. It was a sensation I wanted to hold on to forever. I never wanted it to go away. I wanted to embrace it, wear it, wrap myself in it. I moved a hand to Bailey's cheek and ran my finger along it as I dared to open my mouth to hers, moaning softly as our tongues met for the first time.

God, this was good. Oh my God, it was *so* good. Oh no. I quickly pulled back, suddenly very aware of what was happening. "Shit," I whispered as I pulled my eyes away from Bailey. I couldn't even look at her. I couldn't believe I had just done that. I didn't want to believe how good it felt. How much sense it made. How my lips fit perfectly with hers. I couldn't think about any of that. "I need to go," I mumbled as I quickly stood to my feet.

I made my way through the party, avoiding all eye contact, and found an empty room with a couch. I threw myself on to it and curled into a ball, squeezing my eyes shut tightly and wishing I could be anywhere but here. Exhausted from all of the emotions I was experiencing, I let myself drift off to sleep as one thought continued to run through my mind: what the hell had I just done?

*** 

"Hey, Emma? Em?"

I opened my eyes to find Elijah staring down at me. "Can I give you a ride home?" he asked softly.

I looked around and noticed there was now sunlight streaming through the window meaning I had slept through the night. "Is that really the best idea?"

Elijah shrugged. "Do you have any other choice?"

He had a point. It's not like I could get a ride home with Bailey. I didn't even know what happened to her after I kissed her and ran away the night before. "Alright. Let's go."

I stumbled through the house until I found the bag I had packed and then I followed Elijah out to his car. We were silent for most of the drive, and even though I had no interest in talking, it was still killing me.

Elijah finally spoke when we were just five minutes from my house. "Listen, Em, I really think we should talk."

I shook my head. "I can't." The disappointment on Elijah's face made me feel awful. He really didn't deserve any of this. "We're almost at my house and I need to get inside and get ready for church. Maybe we could go somewhere after the second service."

"Sounds good to me," Elijah said with a sweet smile. He reached out and grabbed my hand, squeezing it gently. Only this time, instead of keeping a hold of it, he let it drop.

While at church, I could barely focus on my dad's sermon. Since I always attended both services, I had two chances to hear it and still had no clue what it was about. All I could think about was that kiss and what it meant. Well, I knew what it meant. It confirmed everything I was trying my hardest to deny. That's what made it so scary. What made it even scarier was what it could mean for my friendship with Bailey. I meant what I said when I told her she had become my best friend these past few months. Was that over now? How would it be possible to get back to that?

It's not like we could ever be anything more than friends. That's not what I wanted. At least, it's not what I should want. It would make my life way too complicated. I didn't want complicated. I was sure Bailey didn't either. Neither of us could deny that the kiss wasn't just one-sided, but that didn't mean Bailey actually wanted me. I had no reason to believe she even liked girls. If she did, wouldn't she have just said something? It's not like it had the potential to ruin the relationship with her parents like it could with me.

When the second service was over, Elijah met me outside of the church. He was wearing khakis and a blue button up and looked incredibly handsome. Why couldn't he just give me butterflies the way he was supposed to? Instead, looking at him only made me feel guilty.

"Do you just want to go for a drive?" Elijah asked, clearly aware this wasn't the type of conversation I wanted to have anywhere there was even the slightest chance of someone else hearing.

"That sounds like a good idea," I said as I followed him toward his car.

Once inside, I was overcome with anxiety once again. What was I even supposed to say to him?

"Listen, Em," Elijah began to say, but I shook my head and put up a hand to stop him.

"I need to say something first." I closed my eyes and took a deep breath. There was no way I could look at him for this, but I knew it needed to be said. "Elijah, I'm... I'm gay."

Much to my surprise, Elijah let out a small chuckle. "I think we established last night that I already figured that out."

I couldn't help but smile a little. I didn't know how he was being so cool about this given our relationship. "That's just the first time I've ever said it out loud. I've never been able to admit that before, even to myself. I knew I had certain feelings, but I was too scared to label them before. I'm still scared."

Elijah reached across the car and grabbed my hand, flashing me a smile before looking back at the road. "This is great, Em."

Really? Because it sure didn't feel that way, and I was shocked he would think it was. "It is?"

"Okay, so it's not so great for me since I'm clearly not your type, but I'm really happy for you. This is a big step in the right direction. You can be yourself."

Did he think...? Oh no, that wasn't happening. "I can't, Elijah."

The smile dropped from his face as he looked over to study mine. "You can't what?"

"I can't be gay. I mean, I won't be." I shook my head in frustration. "I don't know. I just know this isn't what I want."

"It might not be what you want, but it's who you are. You can't change something that's part of you."

"Then I just won't act on it. I can't. My dad's a pastor, Elijah. The church would never accept it. *He* would never accept it."

Elijah sighed and pulled his hand away from mine to rub it over his forehead. "When you say that, you know what I hear? I hear that you're willing to give up your own happiness just to make other people happy, and that's not fair. If they can't be happy for you, they don't deserve to be happy."

I took his hand back in mine and squeezed it. I needed a way to show him how much I appreciated his support. "Why are you being so cool about this? This is so unfair to you. I shouldn't have led you on when I was questioning all of this."

Elijah shrugged. "I imagine it can't be easy. If I was going through something like this, I would hope people would be understanding of that, and give me the benefit of the doubt. I'm just trying to do that for you."

I couldn't help but laugh a little. "You're making this really hard, you know."

Elijah furrowed his eyebrows. "How so?"

"Do you know how much I wish I could like you? You're such an amazing guy, and when you're this sweet, it makes it that much harder that I can't just like you the way I want to. I wish I could just be like 'screw it' and date you anyway, but that wouldn't be fair to you."

"It wouldn't be fair to either of us."

I nodded my head slowly, wondering where I went from here. Did this mean I was destined to spend my life alone? Were my only two choices really to either give in to my feelings and risk losing my family, friends, and church, or give up the chance to ever fall in love? This was a lot to process, and I felt exhausted. "Could you take me home? I really need to rest and think about everything."

Without saying anything, Elijah turned the car around and drove me home. We were both silent the rest of the way, since Elijah must have been able to sense that's what I needed. When we pulled into my driveway, I said a quick goodbye and hopped out of the car.

"Emma, wait," Elijah said before I could shut the door. "Remember what I said. You deserve to be happy. If I'm right about you liking Bailey, which I'm pretty sure I am, you should tell her. I'm not sure what her feelings are, but Bailey is cool. I don't think it would ruin your friendship if she didn't feel the same way. I think it's worth putting yourself out there."

I nodded and closed the door, slowly heading into the house. I wanted him to be right. I hoped what happened last night wouldn't ruin my friendship with Bailey. I had no idea how she felt about that kiss since we hadn't talked since, but I didn't think I wanted to know. I wanted to move on and just pretend it didn't happen, which was probably going to be hard since I could still taste her on my lips.

# Chapter 9: Bailey

I held my breath as I waited for Emma to come into homeroom on Monday morning. I had no idea what to say to her after what happened after homecoming. The kiss was unexpected, to say the least. All night at homecoming, I was waiting to hear that Emma and Elijah were officially dating. When I went to find her at the party, the last thing I expected was to find her crying and I definitely didn't expect the story she told me about struggling with her sexuality.

But that kiss... what could even be said about that kiss? It was perfect. It was so much better than any kiss I ever had with a guy and even blew my first kiss with Tina Blake out of the water. But it couldn't happen again. Even if I wanted it to, which I did and didn't all at once, Emma clearly regretted it. Our lips had barely parted before she was running away.

I couldn't stop thinking about what it all meant. She said she liked girls. Did that kiss mean she liked me? I really didn't know. All I knew was this didn't feel like a crush anymore. It went so far beyond that. It was bad. So very bad. Why did I have to open my dumb mouth and tell her to kiss me? It's not like I was drunk. I was mildly buzzed at most, but the words slipped out before I could stop them. And then her lips were on mine and it felt like I was floating. It was such an out-of-body experience, almost like I was watching the scene play out in front of me.

I was so lost in my own thoughts, I almost missed the final homeroom bell ringing. I looked to Emma's seat and realized it was empty. Skipping school? She was really committed to avoiding me. The urge to text her that I had been having ever since Saturday night grew even stronger, but what was I supposed to say? *I'm sorry I suggested we should kiss? Kissing you might be the greatest thing in the entire world but I don't think it should happen again?*

I decided to wait until we could talk in person, but I didn't get that chance until Wednesday since Emma was out on Tuesday as well. She avoided eye contact with me throughout homeroom so I decided to wait until weightlifting class to say something. There was no way for her to avoid me there since we were partners.

By the time third period came, I was so nervous I could barely think straight. I had no idea what we had talked about in my first two classes, my mouth was dry, and the rest of my body was drenched with sweat. Pretty much, I was a hot freaking mess, which was so unusual for me. I could normally keep it together even when I was falling apart. It was different with Emma though. She had an effect on me no one and nothing else did.

I didn't see her as I got changed in the locker room, but as soon as I walked into the weight room, my eyes found her immediately. I took a deep breath before walking over to where she was standing at the bench press. Unsure what to say, I began changing the weights on one side as she did the same on the other, both of us completely silent.

I sighed loudly. This was ridiculous. We couldn't spend the whole period not talking. I had to say something. *Anything*. "You weren't here the past two days." Okay, so it wasn't earth-shattering, but it was something at least.

Emma looked up at me and blinked a few times as though she was surprised to hear me speak. "Yeah. I was… sick."

"Sick?" When Emma didn't say anything in response, I decided I should probably address the elephant in the room. "Listen, we should really talk about what happened at Ben's party."

"We should. But we can't do it here. Please, Bailey." It was at that moment that I realized just how scared Emma looked.

It was heartbreaking, and all I wanted to do was reach out and touch her and tell her everything would be okay. But would it? The fact that I couldn't even comfort my friend because everything was such a mess told me it might not be.

"Okay. How about tonight after school?"

Emma shook her head as she looked down at the weights. "I can't. I have youth group."

"Tomorrow?" I asked, not caring how desperate I sounded.

"Tomorrow won't work either. I'm sorry. I have plans with Elijah."

Oh God. That was still a thing? I figured after Elijah had accused her of liking girls it was over. I looked around for the nearest trash can, convinced I was going to throw up. "Oh. Elijah. I didn't know."

"Oh no. It's not like that." Emma shook her head and reached her hand out toward me, then moved it to her side as though she thought better of it. "He's just helping me work through some stuff." I wasn't sure how to respond to that, but luckily I didn't have to, because Emma spoke again instead. "My parents have some church conference this weekend so they're going to be away. You could come over Saturday to talk if you want."

"Saturday is perfect."

***

On Friday night, I told everyone I was staying home from the football game because I was tired from all of the homecoming festivities the week prior. The truth was I was freaking out over my upcoming conversation with Emma and the last thing I wanted to do was spend the night surrounded by my classmates pretending to be okay.

Around the time the football game was supposed to be starting, there was a knock on my bedroom door. When I yelled for the person to come in, I was surprised that it was Wyatt instead of one of my moms.

I sat up in my bed. "Wyatt? What are you doing here?"

Wyatt motioned for me to move over and sat down beside me. "I came to find out what happened at Ben's party. You've barely talked to me since you made me drive you home early. I thought it was weird, but I decided not to make you talk since you were clearly upset. It's been almost a week though. I'm your best friend. If you can't talk to me, who can you talk to?"

"It's not that I don't want to talk to you, Wy. It's just that this isn't just my story to tell."

"Ah, so this has to do with Emma, huh? I kind of figured since Elijah told me he didn't end up asking her out. What happened? Did she confess her feelings for you?"

"Not exactly." I wasn't sure if I should share this with Wyatt, but I knew he would get it out of me eventually. He had a way of doing that. "She… kissed me."

Wyatt's eyes went wide as he let out a low whistle. "Wow. I wasn't expecting that. So, how was it?"

I groaned as I covered my face. "It was indescribable, like nothing I've ever experienced in my entire life."

"Isn't that a good thing?" Wyatt asked with a light chuckle.

"No. It's terrible. We've barely talked since it happened."

Wyatt elbowed me in the side while giving me a goofy grin. "Here's an idea, doofus, how about you talk to her?"

"We're getting together tomorrow to talk, but I honestly have no idea what's going to come of it."

"Hopefully some more mind-blowing lady kisses."

I gave him a look to try to convey that I wasn't happy about how nonchalant he was acting about all of this. "It's not that simple. I don't think this is what either of us want."

"You know what I think?"

"No, but I'm sure you're going to tell me."

Wyatt laughed even harder this time. "I think this is exactly what both of you want, but you're too scared to admit that because then you'd have to define what that meant, and I think that terrifies you."

"I don't know, Wy. If it's okay, I really don't want to talk about it. It's all I've thought about all week and I can't take it anymore."

"So, snacks and trashy TV for the rest of the night?"

I threw a hand over my chest. "You sure do know the way to my heart."

***

111

I was happy I was able to have a relaxing night with Wyatt because driving to Emma's house I felt anything but relaxed. I had no idea what was going to happen with this talk, but I hoped we could get back to some semblance of normal. I really missed my best friend.

I sat in Emma's driveway for a minute before finally shutting off my car, then slowly made my way up to her front door. I took a deep breath before I knocked, then held it while I waited for her to answer.

It wasn't long before the door was opened and I was staring into those gorgeous blue eyes. I stood there frozen, fine with getting lost in them for the moment. Emma apparently felt the same way because she didn't move either.

Much too soon, Emma cleared her throat and moved to the side. "Sorry. Come in." Her eyes moved around her house as though she was trying to look anywhere but at me. "Do you want a drink?"

"Water would be good."

Emma nodded her head and I followed her to the kitchen where she silently poured me a glass of water. I took a long sip before sitting it back down on the counter. "So…"

"So…" Emma repeated.

We both started to laugh at the same time and I shook my head at my own awkwardness. "We're making this really weird, aren't we?"

"We are. I'm sorry. I just don't know what to say."

"Well, why don't you start by telling me how you feel about everything?"

"This can't happen…"

Not exactly an answer, but it was a start. "Okay."

Emma shook her head like she was frustrated. "It's just… this *can't* be who I am. My parents have certain expectations. Being gay doesn't fit those expectations."

"That's fine, Emma, I completely understand. I just want things to go back to normal between us. You don't have to—"

"But that kiss!" Emma interrupted. She threw her hands in the air and began pacing around the room, quickly burning a path back and forth across the kitchen. "I wanted it to be bad. I *really* wanted it to be bad. It wasn't though. It was… ugh." Emma stopped pacing, coming to a stop just a few inches in front of me. She was close enough to touch and I had to remind myself *not* to do that. She looked into my eyes and just stared at me while tears came to hers. "I don't want to be gay."

This time I did reach out and push a piece of hair behind her ear. "Listen, Emma, I get it."

Emma shook her head. "No. No you don't. The thing is, I don't want to be gay, but I need to do this."

She put a hand on each of my cheeks and crashed her lips into mine, shocking my body to life.

All of the feelings I tried to suppress all week came back, now stronger than ever. Emma didn't waste any time slipping her tongue into my mouth, and that was more than okay with me. Our tongues connecting caused synapses to fire through my whole body, making it so I didn't just feel the kiss on my lips, but everywhere. My body tingled as the kiss continued, and I never wanted it to end. I wanted all of this to last forever. Nothing had ever felt like this before, not even our first kiss.

Without even realizing it, I began to run my hands up and down Emma's sides. I moaned when I realized what I was doing and just how much I enjoyed it. I loved the way she felt beneath my fingers. I loved the way her body flexed in response to my touch.

Then Emma moved her hands from my cheeks onto my hips, squeezing gently as she pulled our bodies closer together. That's when I experienced something I never had from a kiss before—the throbbing in my center; the need for more. More kissing. More contact. More of Emma. Everywhere.

I forced myself to pull back because I had no idea what I might do if we continued down this road, and we *really* needed to talk. Emma groaned as I pulled my lips away from hers and it was so endearing I almost said *screw it* and just went in for another kiss.

Instead, I pulled back enough to look into her eyes and was shocked by what I felt just from that. I never knew someone could touch you without their hands until I became lost in Emma's eyes and felt her throughout my entire body. "I'm pretty sure I've liked you from the first time I saw you," I said in a breathy whisper before rubbing a finger down her cheek.

Emma sighed and leaned into my hand, closing her eyes as a content smile parted her lips. "My plan was to lay low this year. I wanted to focus on school and track and possibly make a friend or two. Then I met you and everything changed. You were all I could ever think about and I loved and hated it at the same time. Ever since I realized I was attracted to girls, I just wanted to forget about it. I wanted to pack that part of me so deep in the closet that no one ever found it. But kissing you made me realize everything I would be giving up if I did that. Now that I know what it feels like to actually want someone, I don't think I could accept anything less than that." Emma pulled her face away from my hand and shook her head as her smile dropped. "But I'm not ready to let this define me. I'm not proud of this part of me, and I'm not sure what to do. Being close to you feels so right, but accepting that this is who I am feels wrong, because I just never saw myself this way. Sorry. I probably sound like such a jerk right now. Please don't think that I have any issue with people being gay. It's not like that. I guess I just never thought it would be me."

"Hey, I get that," I reassured her. "I have two moms and I absolutely love it. I've never seen a better example of love than what they share. Still, I never even considered that there was a chance that I liked both guys and girls, and even that is a lot to wrap my head around."

"So, what do we do now?" Emma asked, a shakiness to her voice that made me want to wrap her up in my arms and never let go. Protect her against the outside world and everyone that could hurt her.

What were we supposed to do? Now that I had more of Emma there was no way I could go back to just being her friend, but it didn't seem like either of us were ready for more. "What if we try not to think into it too much? We could take things as they come and just do what feels right."

Emma nodded her head slowly as if she was still contemplating it as she was agreeing. "I think I like that idea. There is one thing that definitely feels right to me."

"And what's that?"

Emma looked down at her feet, suddenly appearing so much more shy as a red blush took over her cheeks and she spoke so softly I almost couldn't hear the words. "Kissing you."

There was no missing that though. Warmth spread throughout my body at the same time a smile spread across my face and even though there was still so much that was up in the air, I felt content with where we were at. "I was hoping you'd say that."

\*\*\*

*Doing what felt right* with Emma involved a lot of kissing, hand holding, and constant texts and phone calls. A month had passed and we hadn't defined exactly what this was between us, but that was more than fine with me. I was happy with where we were at and I didn't need any labels to ruin that.

It was now a week before Thanksgiving and Emma and I were watching a movie in my room. We had pillows propped up on my bed and were sitting against them. A few minutes into the movie, Emma leaned her head on my shoulder and I grabbed ahold of her hand.

She giggled when my fingers intertwined with hers which made me laugh too. "What is it?"

Emma sighed and leaned even closer to me. "Nothing. I just really really like how it feels when you hold my hand. I kind of feel it through my whole body. I hope that's not weird to say."

I squeezed her hand, making the feelings already coursing through my own body even more intense. "Definitely not weird. I feel the exact same way. I wish I could hold your hand forever."

And I really did. I never knew I could enjoy holding hands so much until I held Emma's. Her hands were soft and her touch was light and she always ran her thumb along the back of my hand as if it was the most natural thing in the world. And it really did feel that way with her—perfectly natural, like our hands were somehow made to fit each other's perfectly.

"So, I was thinking," Emma said hesitantly. "I'm sure you have plans with your family, but on Thanksgiving, how would you feel about coming over to my house later for dessert?"

"Wait, really?"

I was both shocked and flattered by her question. Most of our time together the past month had either been spent at my house or anywhere else that wasn't hers. Come to think of it, the only time I went there since this whole thing started was the one time I picked her up and her parents insisted that I come in. I knew she was worried about the two of us being around them, because she was convinced they would somehow catch on to the fact that we were more than just friends.

"Really. I miss you when we're apart. Plus, Thanksgiving is going to be lame this year because it's just going to be me and my parents. We're having lunch and then the rest of the day is free. I figured seeing you would make it better. Unless, of course, you think it's a stupid idea. It probably is. You can forget I even mentioned it. I just—"

I placed a quick kiss on her lips to stop her from rambling, which was hard since I found her rambling absolutely adorable. I kept a hand on her face and ran a finger along her cheek. "I would *love* to spend Thanksgiving with you. In fact, I can't think of anything better. The only problem is that we always decorate for Christmas on Thanksgiving. It's a tradition."

"Oh yeah, I get it. No big deal," Emma said as she stared down at the bed and pulled at a loose thread on the comforter.

"We're doing a Thanksgiving lunch as well. What if I came over to your house for dessert and then we came back to mine to decorate?"

"You want me to help your family decorate for Christmas?"

The genuine surprise in Emma's voice was so cute that I couldn't resist leaning in and placing another kiss on her lips. "Of course. It will be great. I'll have all my favorite people together in one place."

"I'm one of your favorite people?"

I had to laugh at the fact that even this seemed to surprise her. "Is that really so hard to believe?"

Emma shrugged. "This all just feels like a dream to me. Being here with you is almost too good to be true."

"If you think things have been good already, just wait until you spend a holiday with me."

Emma tilted her head and placed a few kisses on my neck that had my body begging for more. "I can't wait."

\*\*\*

I wiped my sweaty palms on my pants before knocking on Emma's front door. Even though I had met her parents before, it felt different now. I had to keep reminding myself that it wasn't any different for them. I was still just their daughter's friend in their eyes, not the girl who spent many nights over the past month making out with her and secretly wishing for more, even if that thought scared me to death.

I was relieved when it was Emma who came to the door, buying me a little more time before I had to impress her parents. Emma looked good, no great actually, and I wondered how I was going to stop myself from spending the whole day just staring at her. She was wearing tight blue jeans and a plaid button up shirt and her hair was pulled up into a loose bun.

Before I could say anything, she pulled me into the house. She quickly shut the front door, and in a move completely out of character for her, pushed me up against it and pressed a hard kiss upon my lips. When she pulled away, I quickly looked around to make sure there was no one around to catch that liplock.

"Sorry about that," Emma said while running her thumb along her bottom lip. "My parents are at the neighbor's house dropping off a pie. They'll be back any minute, but I couldn't resist. I missed you so much."

"You just saw me two days ago." I laughed, but I completely understood where Emma was coming from. I had gotten so used to seeing her every day at school that I could definitely feel the loss with having the past two days off.

"Okay. So, I might be a bit pathetic, but I can't help it. I can't get enough of this cute face and amazing body." She had just started to wrap her arms around me when the sound of voices traveled in from outside. Emma quickly jumped away from me, her demeanor suddenly completely different. The cool, confident girl from just a moment ago was gone and she was replaced by someone who was scared and unsure.

I hated to see her like this. The urge to grab her hand was so strong, but I knew that would only make things worse. It wasn't something we could do, no matter how much I wanted to.

A minute later, Emma's parents walked through the front door, looking surprised to see us standing right there. "Oh, Bailey," her mom said, putting a hand over her chest as if we had frightened her. "It's so nice to see you again. We were very happy when Emma told us you would be coming over today. She talks about you so much that we've been excited to get to know you better."

Her dad nodded his head. "Yes. We were worried about what it would be like for her moving right before her senior year, but she's been very lucky to make friends like you."

I could feel my face turning red from his compliments. If he only knew just how close we had become this year, would he still be happy about this friendship? "I'm the lucky one, sir. Emma is…" I hesitated, reminding myself I needed to be careful with the words I chose. "She's an amazing friend. I feel very blessed to have her in my life."

"Isn't that just the sweetest thing?" her mom said as she squeezed my hand gently before dropping it. I was starting to feel less anxious about spending time with her parents, but that didn't last very long. Mrs. West leaned close to me like she was going to whisper something in my ear, but spoke loud enough for everyone in the room to hear. "Maybe you can tell me the truth about why she isn't dating Elijah anymore. He is such a nice boy. It's a shame."

I swallowed hard as Emma's eyes went wide. "I told you, Mom. We both just decided that we're better as friends."

Her mom threw both hands in the air. "I know what you told me. I just thought maybe your friend here could talk some sense into you."

She looked at me as if she was waiting for me to agree with her, but what was I supposed to say? Agreeing with her would make Emma's life harder, but disagreeing could put me on her mom's bad side. Luckily, I didn't have to worry about it because Emma spoke up instead.

"We should eat. We don't have a ton of time before we need to go back to Bailey's house."

"I agree. Don't want to keep her parents waiting." Her dad began to walk down the hall and motioned for us to follow. "I hope everyone saved room."

The kitchen counter was filled with way too much dessert for three people. There was pumpkin pie, apple pie, and at least five different types of cookies. Her dad must have seen the surprise on my face because he started to chuckle when he looked at me. "We always make extra so we can take leftovers to members of the congregation."

Her mom now looked at me too and somehow I could already tell that whatever she was about to say was going to make me feel uncomfortable. "What church do you go to, Bailey?"

Great. Another question that could come back to bite me whether I told the truth or lied. In the end, telling the truth seemed like the better option though. "Oh. My family doesn't actually go to church. My moms have raised me to believe in God, but they didn't want to become members of a church that wasn't fully accepting of our family."

"Well, just for the record, we accept everyone at Bellman Methodist." I wanted to believe her dad, but I wasn't convinced. How far did that acceptance spread? Did it still count when it was your own daughter? Because, if so, wouldn't Emma's parents have stood up for her at their old church rather than running away and pretending it never happened?

I forced a smile as I went to sit down at the kitchen table, hoping her parents didn't notice just how uncomfortable I felt with this conversation. "I'll keep that in mind," I said as sincerely as possible.

"So, what do you want to eat?" Emma asked as she subtly squeezed my leg underneath the table, which I took as a silent apology.

I looked around the table, considering what I wanted to eat and wishing we were alone so Emma didn't have to move her hand from my leg. "I'll take a slice of that delicious looking pumpkin pie and a chocolate chip cookie please."

Emma prepared a plate for me and then herself while her parents did the same. With the topics of boyfriends and church out of the way, the rest of the time with Emma's parents was really nice.

Of course that didn't stop Emma from turning red with embarrassment once we were in my car to go back to my house. "I'm so sorry about my parents," she said as she put a hand over her face.

I grabbed that hand and intertwined our fingers together over the middle console. "There's nothing to be sorry about. I had a really nice time."

"But my mom. She—"

I squeezed her hand to try to reassure her. "Like I said, I had a really nice time. Seriously."

Emma sighed and closed her eyes. "Fine. If you say so. I'm just happy to be out of there and headed to your house with your cool parents."

"Cool parents? You might change your mind about that after you see some of our Christmas decorating traditions. You might find me a lot less cool too."

"I highly doubt that's possible."

*Oh, you have no idea.*

# Chapter 10: Emma

"Maybe you shouldn't go through that one," Bailey said as she tried to grab the box I was holding out of my hands.

I pulled it out of her reach. "Now I'm *definitely* opening it. You have me intrigued."

I sat it down on the floor and opened it to find what looked to be a bunch of framed pictures. As I pulled out one at a time, I thought my heart might explode. Each one was a Santa picture. The first ten were just Bailey and her mom, Kacey, then there were a few with both of her moms, and the remaining had the whole family.

I held up the very first picture where Bailey was only about six months old with one hand and placed my other hand over my heart. "This is too cute."

Bailey tried to steal it away from me, but I blocked her from it and stared down at it. Bailey's mouth was wide open and her face was beet red. Her mom looked proud, but also exhausted, as she held her in her arms. "This is a really cool tradition. I can't believe you guys never missed a year."

Bailey sat down beside me and studied the pictures sitting in front of us. "It actually started because my mom couldn't afford professional pictures of me when I was first born, so she got a picture of us with Santa so she would have a nice picture of the two of us together. Then it just kind of became a thing from there." She picked one up that had her and both of her moms and ran her finger along the frame. "This is my favorite one. It was our second Christmas in Bellman and just a few months after my moms got engaged. I was so excited to have Mama in the picture with us."

I looked down at the picture at Bailey's big toothy grin and laughed. "I can tell." I let my eyes drift from the picture over to Bailey and became lost in those dark eyes staring back at me. I cleared my throat and looked away once I remembered we weren't alone, forcing my eyes over to where her moms were putting lights on their Christmas tree. "So, how did you two get engaged?" I asked, hoping they didn't notice the way my voice cracked as I spoke.

"I'll take this one if that's okay." Bailey's eyes looked nostalgic as she stared into space. When there was no argument from her moms, she continued. "Mama proposed at my grandma and grandpa's house. My aunt had been in a bad car accident a few months earlier and we were having a party to celebrate her recovery. First she got down on one knee and asked me if I wanted to officially become family, and then she proposed to mom."

*My heart.* Just when I thought Bailey and her family couldn't get any more perfect, she tells a story like that. It was all just way too sweet. "That's amazing," I said to Bailey's mama, Kari.

"What can I say? I had a long time to think about it." She hitched her thumb at Bailey's mom. "This one kept me waiting."

Bailey's mom wrapped her arms tightly around her wife and stared at her lovingly. "But I was totally worth the wait. Right, sweetie?"

Her mama leaned down and placed a quick kiss on her mom's lips. "Totally."

I couldn't help but watch their interaction intently. Their love for each other was absolutely beautiful. My parents were extremely happy together and had the type of relationship people strive for. But it was different with Bailey's moms. They had the type of love that could only come from really fighting for each other. It was a love that other people would never understand because they didn't have to go through such hardship to get their happy ending. Just like Bailey, her moms seemed to appreciate what they had so much more because of what they had been through.

"Ew," a little voice said, interrupting my thoughts.

I looked toward the voice to find Sophia squeezing herself between her two moms. "Kissing is gross," she said as she scrunched up her nose.

"Is that so?" Bailey asked as she jumped to her feet. She walked across the room to where the rest of her family was and bent down to be on her sister's level, then peppered kisses all over her face while she tickled her sides.

Sophia giggled as she tried to pull away. "Stop. Stop," she said between laughter.

"Say kisses aren't gross," Bailey demanded as she continued to tickle her.

"Fine," Sophia laughed. "Kisses aren't gross."

"Thank you," Bailey said as she pulled away. Then she turned and winked at me, and I was happy I was sitting or else I would have fallen to the ground because it literally made me weak in the knees.

Not trying to fight the feelings I had for Bailey had shown me just *how much* another person could affect you. I always thought the cliches of what it was like to fall for someone were exaggerated, but I was learning that they actually didn't do those feelings justice. There was no way to put into words exactly what it felt like to be around the person that your heart chose. I found it both exhilarating and terrifying all at once. Bailey made me so happy, but I also knew she had the power to break me as well.

Bailey must have noticed that I was getting lost in my own thoughts because she furrowed her eyebrows when she looked at me. "Em, could you come to the basement with me? I think there is one more box of ornaments down there."

I stood up and followed her downstairs and was happy when Bailey turned around and wrapped me in her arms as soon as we were alone. She kept one hand on my hip and used the other to push a piece of hair behind my ear.

Even this simple motion had my body buzzing. That one touch had me craving so much more. Luckily, Bailey must have felt the same way because soon her lips were on mine, stealing a kiss that was so much better than the one at my house. It was soft and slow and made me wonder how I ever let myself believe that I was actually satisfied kissing anyone else. When Bailey ran her tongue along my bottom lip, I opened my mouth to hers and had to work not to whimper when our tongues made contact. Yes, this was so much better than I ever expected it could be. The longer whatever this was went on with Bailey, the more I craved for things to go further. When I was around her, I barely had control of my own body. It felt like I was at her mercy, and strangely enough, I absolutely loved it. I had worked so hard to gain control of my life, but losing control was *so, much, better.*

Not even considering how close her family was, I ran my hand up and down her arm, then brought it to rest on her hip, letting it slip below her sweatshirt so I could feel her skin underneath my fingers. Bailey let out a quiet moan which encouraged me to squeeze her side, loving everything about the warmth of her skin on mine.

Bailey pulled back from the kiss, but kept her forehead resting against mine, and stared deeply and longingly into my eyes. "Emma, I…" She sighed as her dark eyes pierced mine, giving the sensation that she was touching me without actually doing anything. "I can't even put into words the way you make me feel."

I closed the short distance between our lips to place another kiss on hers. "Trust me, you don't have to. I feel it too." I grabbed her hand and moved it to my chest, over my rapidly beating heart. "See?"

The sweetest smile made its way onto Bailey's face. "Wow, I…" She giggled lightly as she shook her head. "Just wow."

"I know."

"Hey, Bails, did you find that box?"

The sound of her mom's voice broke up the moment we were having and caused me to jump away from Bailey, suddenly feeling miles apart rather than just inches. I moved my eyes all around the room as if I was searching for the box. "There's really more ornaments? And here I thought you were just trying to get me alone," I joked.

"Oh, trust me, I was definitely trying to get you alone. The ornaments just happened to be the perfect excuse." Bailey closed the distance between us to place one last kiss on my lips before walking across the basement to grab the box of ornaments. "Got it, Mom," she yelled upstairs.

As we headed back upstairs, I was saddened by the fact that we had to snap back into *friend mode*. There was nothing I wanted more than to hold Bailey's hand while we decorated and to steal kisses between putting ornaments on the tree. But that couldn't happen and probably never would. What was happening with Bailey was like another world, completely separate from our real life; the two universes never to collide. What made that so exciting also made it tragic, and I hated to think about it.

So, I forced myself not to. Instead, I focused on the task at hand. I gushed over the ornaments Bailey had made as we hung them on the tree, I laughed along to funny stories about past Christmases, and when we fulfilled their final tradition of watching *Elf* together, I restrained myself from cuddling up to Bailey the way I desperately wanted to.

When the night came to an end, I was happy Bailey had driven us to her house so she had to drive me back to mine, giving us some alone time.

As we came to my house, I pointed to the church just beyond it. "Park in the church parking lot. I want to say goodbye to you properly." I was glad it was dark out so Bailey couldn't see how red I was sure my face was from being much more forward than usual.

Bailey pulled into a parking spot far from my house and smirked as she lifted an eyebrow. "Bringing me to the church parking lot to make out with me?"

"Maybe," I answered flirtatiously. I loved that Bailey brought out this side of me. It was so different and exciting.

Bailey laughed the most delicious laugh as she leaned across the middle console. "You heathen. What would the pastor say?"

My stomach turned at the mention of my dad. When I was alone with Bailey, I could normally turn off all thoughts of my parents and the rest of the world. I didn't want to think about them and how they would feel about all of this, but now I couldn't think of anything else.

"Shoot. I ruined the moment, didn't I?"

"Yeah. My parents are kind of the *last* thing I want to think about when I'm about to make out with someone." *Especially when that someone is a girl.*

"Give me a chance to redeem myself?" Bailey asked as she leaned in even closer to me, stopping when her face was just inches from mine. "Even though I know for a fact that you've watched *Elf* multiple times—because let's be honest, who hasn't—you still laughed hysterically through the whole movie. Even my sister didn't laugh as much as you."

"I'm confused. *This* is how you redeem yourself?"

"You didn't let me finish." Bailey pushed a piece of hair behind my ear. "I could barely pay attention to the movie because I just kept watching you laugh. I couldn't stop, almost like I was studying your laughter; memorizing everything about it. The way just your right eye squints a little when you're laughing. How you snort the tiniest bit when you laugh hard enough. The sparkle in your eyes that shows just how happy you are. Watching you do something so simple made me fall even harder for you."

I didn't even know what to say. I could barely breathe. Everything she said was so perfect. I couldn't believe she noticed all of that about *me*. Not only that, but somehow it made her like me more. I had no idea how I got so lucky.

"So, what do you think? Did I redeem myself?"

I still couldn't find the words, so instead I closed the remaining few inches between us and kissed her long and hard.

Somehow every single kiss with Bailey was better than the last and this one wasn't any exception. It was like I found something new to like about every kiss. This time, it was the way I could tell Bailey's lips were curved into a smile as they connected with mine. It was like she was passing that happiness from her lips to mine and warming my heart in the process.

As hard as it was, I forced myself to pull away after a few minutes, unable to contain the smile she had put on my face. "As hard as it is for me to say this, I should probably get home. I don't want your moms wondering why you've been out so long."

Bailey groaned. "I guess. If I must." She smiled as she placed a few more quick kisses on my lips. "It's just so tough. These lips are so inviting." She continued to kiss me chastely, both of us giggling from her very welcomed attack.

After another minute passed, I put my hand on her chest and pushed her away. "Enough," I said with a laugh. "You're a very bad influence."

"What can I say? You bring out the worst in me." Bailey winked at me, then got back in position to drive and pulled out of the parking spot. "Thanks for such a good day, Em," she said once we were in my driveway.

"Thank *you*."

We both sat in our seats, just staring at each other as if we had so much more to say that we were keeping inside. I put my hand on the door handle and started to open my door, but never took my eyes off of Bailey. "I really do need to go. Please text me when you get home, okay?"

"Of course."

The staring continued for another minute since I was unable to tear my eyes away from hers. It was like I was under a spell, her dark eyes hypnotizing me. When I finally mustered up the strength to look away, we both started to laugh again. I unbuckled my seat belt and pushed out of my seat stopping to look at Bailey one more time once I was outside of the car. "Bye, Bails."

As I walked up the sidewalk to my house, I felt like I was floating. I had to imagine this is what it would feel like to walk on a cloud. I took a deep breath as I came to my front door. I wasn't ready for this magical feeling to be replaced by the inevitable feeling of guilt and fear that I always got around my parents after hanging out with Bailey.

"Honey, is that you?" my mom yelled as soon as I came in the door.

She responded the same way almost every time I came home and depending what mood I was in, I either found it amusing or annoying. Who else would it be?

"Yes, Mom," I answered, trying not to sound annoyed.

I had no reason to be annoyed at her. It had been a really good day and spending time with Bailey put me in a great mood. But now that I was home, reality set back in. Being with Bailey was like a dream, but it wasn't the real world. In everyone else's eyes, we were just friends. To my parents, that's all we could ever be. I was pretty sure that's all they would ever accept and that thought had me on the verge of tears.

I had to bite them back when my mom walked into the hallway, her eyebrows furrowed in confusion. "What are you doing, sweetie? Everything okay?"

I forced a smile onto my face. "Everything's great, Mom."

She waved her hand to signal for me to come over. "Your father and I were just about to start a movie. Come join us."

"I don't know. I'm really tired," I lied.

My mom's lips turned down in a slight frown, making me feel guilty about being so distant. "Are you sure? Won't you join us for just a few minutes to talk?"

"Talk? What do you want to talk about?"

I could feel my face becoming red as I turned over in my mind what it was she could possibly want to talk about. Did she notice something pass between me and Bailey? Was it possible they somehow saw our kiss when she first got to the house? No, there was no way. What if she saw Bailey's car pull into the church parking lot and she wants to know what we were doing over there? What was I supposed to tell her?

"I just wanted to hear about the rest of your day." My mom turned her head, a confused smile coming to her face. "Are you sure you're okay?"

God, what was wrong with me? I was acting crazy. Of course my parents didn't suspect anything. I tried my best to smile once again, but I had gotten myself so overwhelmed that it was proving to be especially difficult. "Sorry. Like I said, I'm just tired. It was a long day."

"That's why we want to talk to you. We'd love to hear about the rest of your day. Can you give us a few minutes? It feels like you never share anything with us since we moved." I went to argue, but my mom put up a hand to stop me. "Don't even think about trying to fight me on that, young lady. We had to hear about you and Elijah breaking up from the youth choir director."

I tried not to cringe thinking about that. Why did church women feel the need to spread rumors? Elijah's mom had apparently mentioned something to her best friend, who happened to be the choir director, who in turn decided to tell my parents. "Elijah and I didn't technically break up. We were never officially a couple."

My mom sighed. "Well, either way, I wish you would have told me."

"Sorry, Mom."

"It's okay. I'm probably just being overly sensitive because you're going away to school next year." My mom lifted an eyebrow and I knew exactly what was coming. "Speaking of which, how are those college applications coming?"

"They're coming. I was going to work on them more this weekend." I walked past my mom and started toward the living room so we could join my dad.

"Have you come up with a top choice yet?" my mom asked as we walked into the room.

"If we're talking about colleges, I sure hope it's Bell U," my dad said, inserting himself right into our conversation.

"Bellman is definitely near the top."

If I was being completely honest, out of all the schools I was applying to, Bellman checked the most boxes for me. I liked the size of the school and was really interested in their track program. Not to mention, I liked the idea of staying in Bellman. I didn't feel like moving to a whole other town all over again so soon. The only issue was that Bellman was Bailey's first choice, and even though I loved the idea of being at the same college as her, I didn't want it to look like I was choosing it just for her. Admittedly, I had to make sure I wasn't doing that. I worried whether I had convinced myself Bellman was a good choice because of Bailey. I certainly didn't think so, but I seemed to be overthinking everything these days.

My mom sat down on the couch and patted the spot beside her. "Your father and I are definitely rooting for Bellman, but we'll be happy with whatever school you choose. But anyway, how was the rest of your day?"

I sat down in the spot next to my mom. "It was great. Bailey's family has a bunch of traditions that are really sweet."

"That's nice." My mom crossed her hands over her lap the same way she always did when she had more to say. "Bailey is a very sweet girl."

"She is…" I let my words hang between us because I had a feeling there was a *but* coming.

"You should bring her to church sometime." *There it was.*

I shook my head. "I don't really think church is her thing."

"I just think it's a shame. Having two moms is no reason to shut out God."

Really? That's where she was going to go with this conversation? My blood started to boil, making my whole body feel warm, and I tried my best to remind myself to stay calm. "She's not shutting out God. She believes in Him. The problem isn't her shutting God out, it's the church shutting *her* out."

My mom nonchalantly waved a hand in the air. "Has she ever tried? I highly doubt a church would shut her out. The church obviously has certain beliefs, but that doesn't mean they don't love and accept everyone."

"Really, Mom?"

There was no way I was going to bring up what happened at our last church, but that's exactly where my mind went. The way my mom's forehead wrinkled as her lips curved downward told me that's where her mind went too.

"Yes, honey. The church makes certain decisions out of love, even if it doesn't always feel that way."

"Your mother is right," my dad added firmly in his *end of story* type voice. "The church will always do what is best for everyone, especially those they are trying to help."

I crossed my arms in front of my chest. This was not the argument I should be partaking in given the secrets I was trying to hide far away, but it felt like my parents were attacking Bailey's family, and I couldn't let that slide. "Bailey's family doesn't need any help. They are all wonderful people."

My dad sat up straighter in his chair and cleared his throat. "I never said they needed help. In fact, the Methodist Church is very accepting of same-sex couples. You should know that. It's been a fight within the Church for a few years now about whether or not someone who chooses to be with a person of the same gender should be allowed to become a minister. They are even discussing Methodist pastors doing same-sex wedding ceremonies. We are very progressive, sweetheart." He studied my face, then smiled at me the way a parent would smile at a young child. "And your mom and I have no problem with Bailey's two moms. I'm sure they are very nice women. They raised an extremely respectful daughter. We just obviously believe church is important."

My mom nodded her head at everything my dad said, then placed a hand on my knee. "And if I'm being honest, I'm a bit concerned Bailey had something to do with things not working out between you and Elijah. You used to spend a lot of time with him and now you spend most of your time with her."

Just like that, my anxiety got the best of me again, causing the worst thoughts to run through my mind. What was she getting at? Did that mean she suspected there was something more between me and Bailey? Were my parents going to try to keep us apart? That thought made my stomach hurt. I couldn't imagine being forced to keep my distance from the one person I wanted to spend all of my time with.

"That's not true. I've always spent a lot of time with both of them. I still do. Elijah and I are just better as friends." My voice was almost shaking as I spoke because my mom had me so overwhelmed.

"No need to get upset," my mom said with a chuckle. "I just wanted to make sure. Some girls who don't have boyfriends get jealous when their friends do. I wanted to make sure that didn't influence your decision."

It took everything in me not to roll my eyes at my mom. This whole conversation was ridiculous. "No, Mom. I really am tired though. I'm going up to bed."

"Okay, honey. I'm sorry if I upset you. I'm just a mom, and I worry."

But what kind of mom worries about her daughter being influenced into not dating someone? Shouldn't she be happy if she believes her high school daughter is focused on school and friends rather than boys? I didn't even want to consider her reasons for wanting me to date Elijah, so I wiped those thoughts from my mind and stood to leave the room.

"Em, wait," my dad said when I was almost out of the room. When I turned around, he looked concerned. "I hope you don't think that your mom and I dislike Bailey. We both think she is great and we're very happy that you have her as a friend. I don't want you to get the wrong idea. We would love to have her here anytime."

I could tell by the tone of his voice that his words were sincere. I mean, my parents weren't monsters. They might be small-minded in some ways, but they could never dislike someone like Bailey. Heck, I don't think they could dislike anyone. I also knew he felt the need to point that out because he was smart enough to realize I would never be home if I didn't feel comfortable having my friends over, and that's the last thing he wanted.

"Thanks, Dad. I appreciate it. Bailey is one of the greatest people I've ever met. I know the more time you spend with her, you'll like her even more."

"I don't doubt it," my dad said, giving me a sweet smile before I turned to leave the room and head upstairs.

I waited until I was halfway up the stairs to call Bailey. It only took two rings before she answered. "Hey, you. How's it going?" she asked, her voice immediately easing the anxiety I felt over my conversation with my parents.

"I'm good. Much better now that I'm talking to you."

"What's wrong? You sound strange." The concern in Bailey's voice was strangely comforting. It made me happy to see how much she cared.

"I'm fine. It's nothing." I didn't want to lie to her, but I also didn't want to tell her that my parents had reservations about her. I knew how upset she would be to hear that and she didn't deserve it.

"If you say so." Bailey sighed, then yawned. "Do you want to watch a movie while we fall asleep?"

Watching a movie while we were on the phone had become a regular thing for us these past few weeks. It happened at least a few nights a week, especially on the weekends. Normally, we only made it about a half hour before one or both of us fell asleep, but I lived for those nights. I loved when Bailey fell asleep first and I could hear her breathing get heavier on the other end. She would always wake up as I quietly said goodbye and would groggily say goodnight back to me. She had the most adorable sleepy voice I ever heard and just hearing it caused butterflies to flutter in my stomach.

Tonight, I wasn't in the mood for that though. My parents had really thrown me off and all I wanted was to go to bed. I hated that their words were causing me to push Bailey away for now, but I knew after a good night's sleep, I could get back on track. "I'm actually really tired. I think I'm just going to pass out."

"Are you sure you're okay?" Bailey's voice became quieter and more unsure, sounding less confident than I've ever heard her before. "Are *we* okay?"

"We're more than okay, Bailey. We're great. I promise."

"Okay good, because I... I'm really happy."

I smiled in spite of the uncomfortable conversation with my parents. I couldn't help myself. Bailey was happy. I made her happy in the same way that she made me happy, and right now, that was more than enough for me.

"I'm really happy too. You know what else? I'm suddenly not so tired. Let's watch that movie."

# Chapter 11: Bailey

"So, I was thinking," I said as I ran a finger along Emma's arm and watched the December snow fall outside my bedroom window. "How would you feel about maybe getting dinner in town tomorrow, then going to see that Christmas movie you keep talking about?"

I held my breath while I waited to hear Emma's answer, unsure why I was so nervous. We hung out all the time. Why should this be any different? Except, I knew exactly why it felt different. I didn't want it to just be a normal hang out. I wanted it to be like a date. I wasn't sure if I could call it that since Emma and I hadn't officially stated exactly what it was we were doing. It sure felt like dating. We were certainly more than just make-out buddies. I had friends with benefits in the past and what I felt for Emma went well beyond that. Still, neither of us were ready to define it in fear of making it *too real*. But I wanted to take this step. I wanted to get dressed up and tell Emma she looked beautiful, then hold her hand in the car before treating her to dinner and a movie, just like I would if she was my… I could feel my heart rate pick up as that word threatened its way into my thoughts. No, I wasn't ready for that yet. Definitely too real. I had to admit I was getting closer though. I hated the secrets. I hated the sneaking around. I wanted more.

"I would love that," Emma finally answered after what felt like much too long. "Did you want to meet somewhere or…?"

Emma's voice trailed off and I could read between the lines of what she was asking.

"I'll pick you up." I opened up my phone and found that there was a showing of the movie at 8:30. "How does 6:00 sound? That way, even if we get held up at dinner, we'll have plenty of time to get to the 8:30 movie."

Emma leaned into me and kissed me softly on the lips, making my head spin with just that simple contact. "Six sounds perfect. I can't wait."

Neither could I, which of course made the twenty-four hours leading up to it seem to last forever. After changing my outfit about ten times, I settled on green corduroys and a white sweater with a pair of knee high boots.

When I came out of my room, I was so distracted by my thoughts that I almost ran right into my mom. She grabbed onto my shoulders, forcing me to stop right in front of her. "You look nice," she said as she raised an eyebrow and looked at me with those dark eyes that made me feel like I was staring into a mirror. "Do you have a date tonight?"

"A date?" I asked, hoping the stuttering of my voice didn't completely give me away. "N-No. Not a date. Just hanging out with Emma. We're going to grab some food, then go see a movie. That's it."

"Well, that sounds like a nice night." My mom smiled at me in a way that had me wondering if she knew more than she was letting on. "Emma is great. I'm glad you've made such a good *friend*."

"Um, yeah." I pointed to the stairs behind my mom. "I better go." I cringed as I walked away. Could I have made that interaction any more awkward? Probably not.

I took a few deep breaths as I drove to Emma's house. I had to get control of myself before I saw her parents. Acting that way in front of my mom was one thing. If my parents caught on to what was going on between us, it really wasn't a big deal. Emma's knowing, on the other hand, was a huge deal. They were always extremely nice and welcoming to me, and I could tell they loved their daughter more than anything, but it was also pretty obvious that they wouldn't accept whatever this was between us.

When I pulled into her driveway, I stared at myself in the rearview mirror. "You've got this, Bailey. No big deal." I checked my reflection one more time and was about to shut off my car when there was a knock on the passenger door.

I looked over to see Emma standing there, shivering as she waited for me to unlock the door. She was absolutely breathtaking. Instead of being pulled up like it usually was, her hair was curled and resting just below her shoulders. She was also wearing a sweater, but hers was blue which brought out the color of her eyes. She had a tan peacoat over it that fell halfway down her tight jeans. Her purple lips only served to make her look even more cute. Oh, shoot. Purple lips. I still had her standing out in the cold.

I scolded myself as I quickly unlocked the door. I was messing this up already. "I'm sorry. I was just about to come to the door to get you."

"Don't worry about it. I figured it was easier this way." Emma stared down at her hands giving me the impression that she was just as nervous as I was.

I grabbed her hand and was happy to find that was enough to bring a relaxed smile to her face. "I'm really excited for tonight," I said, unable to contain my own grin. "I made us reservations at Bulldog Bistro. Have you been there yet?"

Emma shook her head. "I haven't. I heard it's really good though. Let me guess—this place has some special memory for you too."

By the way she said it, I could tell she was just joking around, but that still didn't stop me from blushing. I could feel Emma's eyes on me and I could tell she noticed.

"Oh gosh, Bailey, I hope you don't think I was making fun of you. I think it's awesome how you have so many good memories in Bellman. It also makes me feel really special that you want to take me to all the spots that are important to you." Emma continued to study my face, tilting her head slightly while she did. "So, what's the significance of Bulldog Bistro?"

I hesitated to answer. I actually wasn't planning on telling Emma the real reason I chose Bulldog Bistro. But now that she asked, I didn't have any other choice. "After my mom and I moved back here, this is where she brought my mama on their first official date. Sorry. I know that's probably strange. That doesn't mean that I consider this... Well, I mean, we don't need to call this—"

Emma squeezed my hand to stop me from rambling. "I know we haven't *defined* anything, and even though I'm still having a hard time coming to terms with my feelings and what all of this means for the future, I want to call this what it is. I want it to be a date." She blew out a breath and smiled a sweet smile that made her look completely content. "Ever since I realized I might be gay, it's been so scary for me, but being with you is the opposite of that. When I'm with you, I feel free. I finally feel like myself. So yeah, I want this to be a date."

Her words caused tingles to run down my spine. I never thought I would have that reaction to being on a date. It was amazing, and if I was being honest, a little bit scary, but in the best way. "In that case, I hope I can make this the best date of your life."

"I don't think that's going to be a problem."

If dinner was any indication, it certainly wasn't going to be a problem. We spent the meal telling each other funny stories from growing up. Emma told me about how she ruined her Christmas dress when she was eight years old because a boy from her church told her he could beat her in a race and she insisted on proving him wrong right after their Christmas Eve service, but unfortunately she slipped on a patch of ice and ripped the dress. I told her about the phase I went through where I tried to learn as many big words as possible and insisted on working them into all of my conversations.

When the meal was over, Emma playfully tried to fight me over paying, but I insisted the whole night was my treat. I was happy when we got to the movies and she actually didn't fight me as I paid for our tickets and popcorn.

As we sat in the dark theater, it took everything in me not to reach out and hold her hand. I figured no one would notice, but I knew Emma would be too scared that they would. Yet, halfway through the movie, I noticed her staring at my hand, almost longingly, like she was actually considering it. I sat it on the arm rest between us, leaving the decision up to her. Emma fidgeted in her seat and pulled her coat out from under her. I wasn't sure what she was doing until she draped it over the armrest, then moved her hand under it joining it with mine. She gave me a nervous smile that made me wish I could kiss her, but the hand holding was going to have to be enough. And it really was. Emma's hand in mine made me feel like I could float right out of my seat.

I was disappointed when the movie ended and Emma disconnected our hands before pulling her coat away. Luckily, as soon as we were back in my car, her hand was back in mine. "You did it," she said as she ran her thumb over the back of my hand.

"Did what?"

"You made this the best date of my life." She laughed and shook her head. "Not that you had much competition. This is the first date I've been on with someone I actually liked."

"Well, I've been on dates with people I actually did have feelings for, and this was still by far the best. No one has ever compared to you." It was scary to be so honest with her, but I couldn't hold it in.

"I wanted to ask you something, but I've been afraid to."

Emma's voice quivered, so I squeezed her hand reassuringly. "You can ask me anything."

"Well, my parents are going to a conference next weekend, and they will be gone from Thursday until Saturday night. I was just wondering if maybe you wanted to stay at my house on Friday night."

Her question surprised me, and nerves shot through me as I thought of all the possible implications that came along with that invitation. A night alone with Emma, at her house, in her bed... I swallowed hard as my body temperature seemed to rise exponentially.

"I just really want to spend time together where we don't have to worry about anyone else. I don't think I'm ready to go any further than we already have, but I'd love to spend a whole night making out with you without getting anxious that my parents could walk in the room."

I let out the breath that I didn't realize I was holding. Apparently, I wasn't ready for more either, no matter how much I might want it. "A night of making out sounds great. I just have one condition." When Emma looked at me with worried eyes, I squeezed her hand once again. "I want you to snuggle with me as we fall asleep."

"That I can *definitely* do."

***

"I can't believe you're having an adult sleepover with your girlfriend tonight," Wyatt said with a laugh as I drove him to school that Friday. "My little Bailey is growing up. I can't wait to hear all about your first time."

I shook my head at his ridiculousness. "First of all, Emma isn't my girlfriend. Second of all, we already talked about it and we're *not* having sex tonight. And lastly, even if we were, I wouldn't tell you all about it."

Wyatt pushed his bottom lip out into a pout. "That's so unfair. I gave you a detailed description of my first time with a girl and my first time with a guy."

I tried not to gag as I thought back on just how detailed Wyatt had gotten. "Yeah, trust me, I never asked you to do that."

Wyatt crossed his arms in front of his chest, continuing to pout. "Whatever. When are you going to make things official?"

"Official?"

"Yeah. This has been going on for a while now. When are you going to make Emma your girlfriend?"

"That's not really what either of us wants." Although the more time that passed, the less true that was becoming. I wasn't so sure how to feel about our plan to do what felt right anymore, because being able to call her my girlfriend *did* feel right. I was starting to think maybe that was what I wanted.

"Are you sure about that?"

*No.* "Of course." I tried to make myself sound as convincing as possible, but I could tell by the look Wyatt was giving me that he wasn't buying it. I laughed and rolled my eyes, trying to keep the conversation light. "I told you, Wy, I'm not trying to be that cliche girl with two moms who has a girlfriend. The bigots and haters would have a heyday with that."

"You know what I think?"

"No, but I'm sure you're going to tell me."

"I don't actually think you're scared of being a cliche. I think you're scared of what you feel. Scared that if you define it, it gets that much more real. You're not scared of being with her, Bails. You're scared of losing her."

His words hit me hard. I didn't want to believe him. The last thing I wanted was to admit that I didn't have complete control of the situation. I lived my life meticulously, making sure every piece fell into place exactly as I wanted it to. But this was different. I had no control over what happened between me and Emma. Part of whatever this was and wherever it would go was being led by Emma, the other part was being led by my heart. I was in trouble. Deep trouble.

*** 

Wyatt's words continued to run through my head when I got to Emma's house that night. I tried to forget about them. The last thing I wanted was to ruin our alone time with such a stupid worry. Emma greeted me at the door already wearing her pajamas and looking much cuter than someone should in flannel pants and a green long sleeve shirt.

"Sorry," she apologized as she looked down at her outfit that she clearly caught me staring at. "It was a long week and I really wanted to make myself comfy."

I inadvertently licked my lips as I ran my eyes over her body once more. "You have absolutely *nothing* to apologize for. I think you look amazing. I have to say though—I am pretty jealous. Now I wish I was in my PJs."

Emma pointed down the hall toward the bathroom. "I'm not stopping you."

I nodded my head and carried my bag to the bathroom where I changed into my pajamas as well. I blew out a breath and then I spoke to my reflection in the bathroom mirror. "Stop overthinking this, Bailey. You've been so happy. It would be stupid to ruin that now."

I was surprised when I walked out to find Emma standing close to the door. She lifted an inquisitive eyebrow at me. "Were you on the phone? I thought I heard you talking to someone."

*Busted.* "Not exactly. Embarrassingly enough, I was actually giving myself a little pep talk."

Emma giggled as she wrapped her arms around my waist, then gave me a kiss on the cheek. "You're way too cute."

I felt my whole body relax at her touch. Wyatt was wrong. This was perfect. This was exactly how it was meant to be. I had nothing to worry about. That feeling continued throughout our night together.

We started out by making grilled cheese and ramen noodles, stealing kisses throughout the process that had my heart soaring. When the food was done, Emma set up tray tables in her living room and turned on trashy reality TV, which we ended up not paying much attention to, spending our time just talking instead.

I patted my stomach as I finished my food. "One of the best meals I've ever had."

Emma smiled as she elbowed me in the side. "I have trouble believing that."

"Okay. You're probably right. I think it's just the company."

Emma pushed her tray table out of the way, then focused on me, her eyes serious and her mouth a straight line across. "Bailey, I..."

I held my breath as I waited to hear what she had to say. I wasn't naive, or dumb, enough to think she was about to confess her undying love to me, but I had a feeling whatever she had to say was important. I was desperate to know what it was, so I placed my hand on her knee and squeezed it. "What is it, Em?"

She moved her eyes from mine and stared down at her hands instead. "It's just..." Our eyes met again and there was something in hers that I couldn't quite read. It almost seemed to be a mixture of desire and fear. "I... ugh." Instead of saying anything else, she lunged across the couch, her body landing on top of mine as our lips came together.

We had kissed more times than I could count at this point, but this felt different. Maybe it was knowing there was no possibility of getting interrupted. Maybe it was the way Emma's body pushed into mine, making my body beg for so much more than just a kiss. As our tongues met, our bodies pushed even closer together. My hips instinctively pushed up into hers as she moved on top of me. I had never felt anything like this before. Never before had making out with someone made me feel like I was losing all control of my body. My head was spinning as my body heated up, and all I wanted was to give myself completely to Emma.

I moved a hand down her side, then ran it up inside her pajama shirt, reveling in the way her skin felt underneath my fingers. It was too much and not enough all at once. I wanted to run away, but also wanted to drink this moment in completely and never, ever let go. My body must have decided on the latter because my hand continued to move higher without another thought into what I was doing. My breath hitched when I realized my hand had made its way just beneath the sports bra that Emma was wearing. I paused for a moment so she could stop me if she wanted to, but prayed she wouldn't.

Emma moved her hand to meet mine, but instead of pulling it away, she pushed it higher, encouraging me to move underneath her bra and whimpering at the contact. I moaned as my fingers explored this previously uncharted territory.

Emma's hands were now on the move too, and before I could contemplate what was happening, one hand had dropped down between us and was running over the front of my pajama pants causing a desire I had never felt before. Then that same hand moved to the top of my pajama pants before starting to journey not just inside my pants, but also my underwear. My breathing picked up as my mind moved at a million miles a minute. Were we about to...? Is that what I wanted? My body and heart were telling me one thing, but my mind refused to let them take control.

We were on the couch in Emma's living room while her parents who knew absolutely nothing about our relationship were away. Relationship... We weren't even *in* a relationship. This was... well, officially, it was nothing. It obviously was much more than that, but in reality, we hadn't actually defined what was happening between us or what it meant for our future. I wished my strong feelings for Emma were enough to convince me this was a good idea, because I *really* wanted this to continue, but there was a voice inside my head telling me we needed to stop. It wasn't the right time or place for this.

I grabbed Emma's hand, but instead of encouraging it on as she had done with me, I brought it to a halt. "I'm sorry," I apologized as she looked down at me, frustration and confusion showing in her furrowed brows and pouty lips. "I'm just not ready for this. I'm really sorry."

Emma sat up quickly and shook her head, her face turning bright red. "You don't need to apologize. I'm the one who's sorry. We agreed this wasn't going to happen. Neither of us are ready. I just got carried away."

I grabbed her cheek to force her to look at me. "Hey, we both got carried away. Trust me, I wanted that just as much as you did. It just didn't feel right yet."

"I agree." Emma nodded slowly. "So, this is going to be a strange request given what just happened, but do you want to go up to bed now? I just feel like that would be much more comfortable than the couch. I'm not trying to seduce you into doing something you're not ready for. I promise."

I felt my body start to relax. "I think we can do that." I pointed a finger at Emma as if I was lecturing her. "I just need you to keep your hands to yourself, young lady."

Emma laughed, finally appearing much less tense. "I could say the same thing to you."

"Touche." I lifted both eyebrows in the air as an idea popped into my head to bring back the carefree atmosphere from earlier. "Race me upstairs?"

I pushed myself off the couch and began to run toward the stairs only to realize that I had never actually been to Emma's room so I didn't know where it was. I hopped up the stairs two at a time, hoping I could get far enough ahead to figure it out before she caught up. Unfortunately, it turned out her track skills were no joke and she caught up to me as soon as I opened the first door at the top of the stairs which happened to be a closet. I chased her down the hall, my new goal being to follow her lead and win it at the end. I could tell she was headed for the last door at the end of the hall and ran her into the wall before we reached it. As I started to turn the doorknob, a hand grabbed my pajama top, pulling me back. Emma opened the door and the two of us stumbled into the room at the exact same time, both of us laughing hysterically.

"Calling it a tie?" I asked as I held my stomach that hurt from laughing so hard.

"Guess we'll have to settle this on the track."

Oh yeah. I was so focused on the here and now with Emma that I had almost forgotten track season would be starting in a few months. "Speaking of track—want to be my bus buddy for away meets? We can sit in the back of the bus and hold hands under a blanket."

Emma's smile dropped away and I contemplated which part upset her. Was track season too far in the future? Was she worried about someone seeing if we tried to secretly hold hands? Either way, it was disappointing that she would feel that way.

"I tend to get sick on buses. I always had to sit in the front at my old school. Normally I was sitting by myself because no one wants to sit up front close to the coaches."

I took her hand as relief washed over me. "We can sit in the front of the bus and hold hands under a blanket."

"Now that sounds perfect," Emma said with a sweet smile. Emma hitched her thumb over toward her bed. "Ready to snuggle?"

"Born ready," I answered with a wink.

When we lay down, I took a good look around Emma's room for the first time. There wasn't much to it which I figured had to do with the fact that she had just moved in a few months ago. Her white walls were mostly bare aside from a few awards from school and track. There was a desk on the opposite side of the room from the bed that was covered with school supplies. Aside from that, the only other piece of furniture in the room was a large bookshelf that was packed full of textbooks and novels. Sitting on top of the bookshelf was a placard that read, "I can do all things through Christ who strengthens me" and a trophy with a runner on the top.

"Your room is—"

"Boring?" Emma interrupted.

"I was going to say nice, but if I'm being honest it is a bit bland. Very not you."

"So, you're saying you don't find me bland?" Emma asked with a giggle.

I placed a quick kiss on her cheek, then smiled down at her. "Not in the slightest."

Emma sighed as she looked around her room. "I guess I didn't see the point in doing much with it when I would be leaving after a year."

"Speaking of which, I wanted to wait until we were alone to tell you this, but I verbally committed to Bellman."

Emma's smile lit up her whole face at my announcement. "That's amazing, Bailey! I'm so happy for you."

I was hoping she would give some insight into her college decision and whether or not she had narrowed down her choices at all, but I didn't want to ask. I secretly, and selfishly, hoped Bellman was still on her list, but Emma had to do what was best for her.

Our conversation was cut short by the sound of a text coming through on my phone. I looked down to find a text from Ben saying he would be doing his New Year's Eve party this year. "Sweet. Party at Ben's house for New Years. Want to go?"

Emma groaned. "Do I want to? Yes. Can I? No. Apparently at this church, the youth group does a lock-in every year on New Year's Eve. My dad told me I have to go since he's the pastor. It sucks. Even Elijah's mom isn't making *him* go and she's the youth group director."

I tried not to show how disappointing this was because I knew it wasn't Emma's fault. Still, I couldn't stop myself from feeling sad over it. Even though we hadn't talked about it, I kind of figured we would be spending the night together in some way or another.

Emma cleared her throat a few times and I could tell she wanted to say something, but wasn't for some reason, so I snuggled closer to her to try to encourage her. "You could… I mean, you probably don't want to… but I would love to have you. But it's no pressure at all because I totally understand if it's the last thing you want to do."

Even with all of her rambling, I could still put the pieces together to decipher what she was saying, or wasn't saying, but wanted to. "Are you trying to ask me if I want to go to the lock-in with you?"

Emma looked at me with so much uncertainty in her eyes that I wanted to pull her tighter against me, although I didn't know if that was even possible. "Yeah, but like I said, you really don't have to. Ben's will be so much better."

I shook my head. "No, it won't. It won't be better because you won't be there. I'd love to go to the lock-in with you."

It was far from what I was planning to do on New Year's Eve my senior year of high school, but when I saw the way Emma's face lit up when I accepted her invitation, I knew there was truly nowhere I would rather be.

# Chapter 12: Emma

"I still can't believe you guys are all skipping Ben's party to come to this with me," I said when Bailey, Elijah, Wyatt, Chloe, and Chloe's boyfriend, Jackson, met me outside of the church on New Year's Eve.

"This is much better than spending the night with a bunch of guys from Bellman's football team. Trust me." Jackson looked around at the group, a nervous smile on his face. "No offense."

Wyatt slapped a hand down on Jackson's shoulder. "You're not going to offend us. I think we all agree that the soccer guys are much cooler than the football guys at our school."

Wyatt gave Bailey a pointed look and she threw her hands in the air playfully. "Hey, you're not going to get any arguments from me."

"Well, seriously, it means a lot to me to have you all here," I said as we entered through the large double doors of the church. "I know you probably didn't expect to spend your New Year's Eve playing stupid games rather than getting drunk."

Elijah, who was leading the group, turned around and walked backwards to talk to us. "I certainly didn't expect to spend my New Year's Eve with my mom, but I'm just happy to spend time with some of my best friends no matter what we're doing."

Elijah was such a nice guy that it still made me feel guilty that I had essentially used him to try to hide my sexuality, even though he had reassured me multiple times that he understood. He even told me that he believes we're better as friends anyway. I'm not sure if he meant it, but I was certainly happy to have him as a friend. Ever since things officially ended between us and I came out to him, he had become my best friend. He was the one person I could talk to about Bailey and that felt really nice.

"I'm going to pretend I didn't hear that," Elijah's mom said as she walked around the corner to greet us.

Wyatt playfully pushed Elijah as he flashed his mom a wide smile. "Ignore your son, Mrs. G. I, for one, am very excited to spend the night hanging out with you."

"I second that," Bailey said, her voice extra sweet, the same way it always was when she spoke to adults.

Chloe and Jackson muttered an agreement, but I just smiled at her. Even though I had been around her plenty of times since things ended between me and Elijah, and she had always been super kind, I still worried how she felt about me. Elijah had also reassured me that there were no hard feelings there either, especially since his mom thought the choice to be friends was mutual, but that didn't stop me from feeling awkward around her.

When we got into the recreational area of the church, there were already about twenty other kids there, most of which were much younger than us. They were all participating in the different activities that were made more so for kids their age than for us, making me feel somewhat embarrassed once again to have my friends there.

An arm slipped around my waist and I could tell by the way my body reacted that it was Bailey. "So, what are we doing first? Singing Karaoke or playing a game of basketball?"

"Oh, no you don't. You can sing karaoke with anyone you want, but only if I get the first song. That's the rule," Wyatt said, as he pulled Bailey away from me.

Bailey gave me an apologetic look as she was dragged over to where the karaoke machine was set up. She continued to sneak glances over at me while she and Wyatt looked through a book that listed all of the karaoke songs available. Every time our eyes met, a spark seemed to ignite within me, and I couldn't help but smile.

"So, I take it things are still going well between you two?"

I quickly moved my eyes to where Elijah was standing beside me then searched the room for Chloe and Jackson, relieved to find they were over at the basketball hoop rather than within earshot.

148

"I'm not an idiot, you know. I wouldn't say anything in front of anyone other than Bailey or Wyatt." Elijah stared at me as he rocked back and forth on the balls of his feet and shoved his hands deep into the pockets of his sweatpants. "Speaking of it being a secret though, how long are you planning to keep it that way? It's been over two months since you guys first kissed and from the looks of it, things are getting more serious. Don't you ever wish that you didn't have to keep it a secret that Bailey is your girlfriend?"

Hearing Bailey referred to as my girlfriend made my skin tingle and my heartbeat pick up as nervous energy shot through my body. I shook my head dramatically. "Bailey isn't my girlfriend. That's too serious and way too real. We're not ready for that. *I'm* not ready for that."

"When will you be?"

*Never* was the first thought that came to mind, but I knew Elijah wouldn't accept that. As a straight male who never had to worry about disappointing his parents, he couldn't possibly understand what it felt like. He would never know what it was like to fear losing your family over the person you were falling for. *Had already fallen for.* I shook my head, more so at myself than at Elijah. It scared me when I thought about just how deep I was in this with Bailey.

"I don't want to talk about this right now. You're right. Things are going well between us. Really well. Figuring out where to go from here would only ruin that."

Elijah shrugged as he blew out a breath, giving me the impression that he was frustrated with me. "Fine. I'll stop. But just remember—we're about to start a new year. It's a fresh start. A chance to be who you truly are."

*I wish.*

Elijah nodded his head toward Wyatt and Bailey. "Anyway, it looks like your not-girlfriend is getting ready to sing."

I watched as Bailey and Wyatt sang a terrible rendition of *Baby, It's Cold Outside*, stumbling as they tried to change the lyrics to be more politically correct. At the end, Bailey looked right at me and winked, her smile beaming the same way my heart seemed to be.

"Hey," Chloe's voice shouted from across the rec hall, grabbing my attention from Bailey. "How would you guys feel about a boys versus girls game of basketball? I'm sick of beating Jackson at one-on-one."

"Heck yeah!" Bailey said as she walked back over toward us. "Let's show these guys who the real athletes are."

We played for thirty intense minutes before we were all too tired to go anymore and decided to end it in a tie. Now that we were done playing, I could focus on Bailey who was drenched in sweat, and God, did she look good like that. I watched as beads of sweat ran down her face and my mouth went dry as I thought about all of the things I would like to do to her at that very moment. Things that most definitely weren't appropriate to be doing at church. I honestly felt like I should say a prayer and apologize for even having those thoughts while in a church building.

Bailey lifted an eyebrow when she saw me staring which only served to make me feel even more turned on. "Em, is there a water fountain in here?"

"Wa-water fountain?" I just barely squeaked out. "Um, yeah. Yeah, there is."

One side of her lips quirked into a smirk. "Wanna take me to one? I could really use a drink."

I nodded my head, still barely able to speak, then motioned for Bailey to follow me.

When we got there, she took a quick drink, then leaned against the water fountain and stared at me, that same smirk still on her face. "I honestly just wanted to get a minute alone with you."

I looked down the hall to where I could still see everyone, which meant they could also see us. "We're not really alone."

"We're far enough away so they can't hear us." Bailey bit at her bottom lip, but didn't lose her smile. "I just had to tell you that you look really good right now. Like *really* good. If this is how you always look after competing, I don't know how I'm going to make it through track season with you. You might just be the death of me."

I looked down toward my feet, giggling like a small child. How did she have the ability to turn me to absolute

150

mush with just a few words? "I was actually thinking the exact same thing," I said as I brought my eyes back to hers and became completely lost in them.

I wasn't sure how long we stood there, just staring like this, but eventually Bailey cleared her throat, breaking up the moment. "I probably shouldn't even suggest this, but is there anywhere we could sneak off to to truly be alone around midnight? I'd hate to miss out on a New Year's kiss."

I was so entranced with her that I wasn't even thinking clearly. If I had been, I would have realized what a stupid idea that was. Instead I nodded my head hungrily. "Yeah. My dad's office. It's the door right across the hall there. A few minutes after midnight, say that you're going to the bathroom, then I'll wait a minute or two before coming up with an excuse of my own."

And that's exactly what we did. A few minutes after counting down to midnight and celebrating with noisemakers and high fives, Bailey announced that she was going to run to the restroom. I counted to ninety inside my head before I told a lie about how I had to grab something out of the sanctuary for my dad so I wouldn't forget about it.

I snuck into my dad's office and the door had just barely closed behind me when Bailey's lips were on mine. "I've… wanted.. .to… do… this… all… night," she confessed between kisses.

Instead of responding with words, I wrapped my arms around her neck, pulling her even closer to me and showing her with my mouth just how much I agreed.

And just like that, I became completely lost in her once again. I was so lost in her that I didn't even register the sound of a phone ringing or the footsteps coming down the hall. I didn't even notice when the door to the office started to creak open, until I heard an older female's voice accompanying it.

"There's my phone. How did it get in he—— Oh. Oh my."

I jumped back from Bailey as soon as it hit me that we weren't alone. I looked over toward Elijah's mom, then quickly diverted my eyes to Bailey who looked just as terrified as I felt. No. No. No. This couldn't be happening.

"Sorry, girls. I didn't know you were in here." Mrs. Green cleared her throat. "I think maybe we should have a seat and talk."

*No. Absolutely not.* I could feel my heart beating rapidly in my chest as I looked all around, trying to find a way to escape. But there was no escaping this. Instead, it felt like the walls were closing in around me. I could barely breathe.

"Of course, ma'am," Bailey answered, completely surprising me. What was even more surprising was when she attempted to grab onto my hand.

I quickly tore it away from her. What was she thinking? We couldn't do that. Sure, holding hands was nothing compared to what Mrs. Green had just seen, but maybe there was a way to convince her she didn't see it.

"We should sit down, Em," Bailey said in a soothing whisper.

"No."

"No?"

I shook my head back and forth. "You need to go. You shouldn't be here. You... You should go."

Bailey tried to catch my eye, but I refused to look at her. I couldn't face her right now. I couldn't face anyone right now. I didn't even want to face myself. All I wanted was to disappear.

"I'll be right outside waiting for you." Bailey opened the door and as soon as she walked out, I regretted telling her to leave.

Mrs. Green took a seat behind my dad's desk and motioned for me to do the same. I threw myself down and ran my hand over my temple. I couldn't believe this was happening. It was like history was repeating itself, but this time it was a thousand times worse. How could I talk my way out of this one? How could I pretend it was all a lie when this inevitably spread throughout the congregation?

"How long have you known, Emma?"

"How long have I known what?"

"That you are attracted to the same gender."

Just hearing it spoken out loud by someone else was enough to make me sick. Physically sick. I had to get to a bathroom. Fast. "I'm really sorry."

I ran out of the office and past someone standing right outside the door who I assumed must be Bailey, but everything was a blur so I couldn't be sure. As soon as I was inside the bathroom, I let out all of the contents of my dinner into the toilet.

I heard the bathroom door open and soon someone was kneeling down beside me and rubbing my back. "Shh, it's okay. Everything is going to be okay, sweetheart."

Bailey's normally soothing voice didn't feel soothing to me at that moment. In fact, it was having the opposite effect. I twisted my head around as an irrational anger built up inside of me. "*Okay*? What part of this is okay?"

"I'm sorry. You're right. It's obviously not okay, but we can get through this together. I know it's scary, but you're not alone. We'll figure it out."

I shook my head. She was wrong about all of that. So wrong. "No. It's ruined. Everything is ruined. Everyone is going to find out just like before."

Bailey wrapped her arms around me and pulled me into her, placing a light kiss on my temple. "You don't know that. We can talk to Elijah's mom. Heck, we can have him talk to her. It's not her secret to tell, so she probably won't." Bailey sighed, and I could tell she had more to say. "And maybe people knowing wouldn't be the worst thing. Maybe it's time."

How could she say that? What didn't she understand? I pushed away from her and began wiping at the tears streaming down my face. "I'm not ready."

"Okay. Then we'll wait, and when the time feels right, we'll do it together. Like I said, Em, you're not going through this alone."

I knew it was irrational to get mad at her. She was only trying to help. She was trying to understand. But that was just it. She couldn't possibly understand. She had no idea what I was feeling right now. "You're wrong. I am alone. You're not going through the same thing I am."

Bailey furrowed her eyebrows as if she was confused, only serving to make my blood boil with anger. What. Wasn't. She. Getting? "I am, Em. She didn't just catch you in there. It was both of us."

153

"You don't get it! You couldn't possibly get it." I jumped to my feet and stormed out of the bathroom, hoping Bailey wouldn't follow me.

Of course she did though. "Em, stop!" she yelled once we were back out in the hallway.

I whipped around once again and pointed a finger at her. "No. You stop! Don't act like what we're going through is the same. You don't have to worry about what will happen with your parents if they find out about us. You don't have to worry about them disowning you or never looking at you the same. This isn't both of us."

Bailey slowly shook her head and tried to reach her hand out toward me, but I pulled mine away. I couldn't stand to feel her touch right now. Mostly because I knew that I *needed* it, and that scared me to death. I couldn't be so dependent on something that I could already feel slipping away. "I'm sorry about your parents, Em. I really am. But let's try to figure this out together, okay?"

I let myself look at Bailey for the first time since being caught. Like really, truly focus on her. I saw the worry lines along her forehead. I saw tears that were coming to her eyes as well that I could tell she was trying so hard to hold in. I saw the way she held her shoulders up, like she was putting a lot of effort into trying to stay strong, because she clearly wanted to be strong for both of us. My anger melted away as I allowed myself to truly see her. This wasn't her fault. None of this was her fault, which only made what I was about to do that much harder.

I opened my mouth to speak, but I couldn't form the words. Instead, my knees became weak and I fell to the ground. Before I could hit, Bailey caught me and this time I melted into her touch.

I let my head fall onto her shoulder as I cried even harder. I had no idea what Mrs. Green was going to do, but the fear was enough to zap me back into reality. It was a reality that I had successfully avoided these past two months but couldn't anymore. My family was too important to me. My faith was too important. Bailey was too important too. Hurting her now would keep her from inevitably getting hurt even worse in the future. "I'm sorry. I'm so sorry."

"Hey, you have nothing to be sorry about. *I'm* sorry. It was my idea to sneak off. I should have never suggested it."

Why did she have to be so sweet? It only made what I was about to do that much harder. "I... I can't do this, Bailey."

"Can't do what?"

I swallowed hard. I didn't want to say these words, but it was for the best. Well, the best for everyone else. All it did for me was leave me completely heartbroken. "Us. I can't do us."

"Wait. Wh-what?"

The crack in her voice made it hurt one thousand times worse. When she pulled away to look at me, I couldn't meet her eyes. I couldn't stand to see what I was doing to her.

"Please, Em. Nothing has to change. I'm sorry if I made you think it did. I'll talk to Mrs. Green. I'll make sure she doesn't tell anyone. Things can stay the same."

"No. I've been kidding myself. I can't do this. I'm not... I just... can't be with a girl."

"So, what? We just forget this ever happened?"

I wanted to tell her that I could never forget. I would always remember the taste of her lips and the way her eyes got lost in mine when there was no one else around. Instead, I slowly nodded my head. "It's for the best."

"For who?" Bailey asked, sounding completely exasperated.

"For my parents. For *you*."

"*Me?*"

"Yeah. I mean, come on, Bailey, you weren't looking for this either. You're not like me. You don't *just* like girls. You could be with a guy."

"And what about you?"

What I wanted and needed was honestly the last thing on my mind right now. I figured if I made others happy, my happiness would eventually follow. "I'll just focus on other stuff."

Bailey shook her head as if she was in utter disbelief. "And this is what you want?"

*No. Not one bit.* "Yes."

Bailey stood up fully and backed away from me with her hands in the air. "Fine then."

When I chanced a look at her, I realized all of our friends had joined us out in the hall. I had no idea how long they had been there or what they had heard. When Bailey backed right into Chloe, she lifted an eyebrow at me. "Everything okay?"

"Everything is just great," Bailey said with a smile so fake I knew there was no way she was fooling anyone. She focused on me and her smile dropped, leaving nothing but an empty expression. "Bye, Em."

She shoved past me and walked right out of the church. I looked back at our group of friends, who all seemed to be dumbfounded. Chloe grabbed Jackson's hand and motioned toward the door Bailey had just left through. "We should go after her." She put her focus on me for a split second before turning her attention to Elijah and Wyatt. "You two stay here."

Elijah and Wyatt stared at me as if they were waiting for an explanation. Before I could answer, Mrs. Green walked out of the office, her eyebrows furrowed in concern as she looked between the three of us. "Emma, could I please talk to you?"

I nodded, then reluctantly followed her back into my dad's office. I really didn't want to be doing this right now, but honestly, how could things get any worse than they currently were? I slumped back into the chair I had just been sitting in a few minutes earlier. "Please don't tell my parents," I pleaded as I stared down at my hands in my lap.

"I'm not going to tell your parents, sweetheart." A sense of relief washed over me, that only lasted for a few seconds until Mrs. Green said her next words. "I really think you should though."

"Why? So they can get me help?" I felt sick once again.

When Mrs. Green sat quietly for a few seconds, I chanced a look at her. Her eyes were kind. There was none of that judgment I had seen from my last youth pastor. "Do you want help?"

I shook my head. I was too tired to lie. "No, I don't."

"Good because I don't want that for you either."

"You… You don't?"

A small smile parted Mrs. Green's lips. "Of course not, sweetie. I know the Methodist Church is pretty split on how they feel about people being attracted to the same gender, but personally, I don't get it. I couldn't help but fall in love with my husband. Why should I have reason to believe that anyone else can help who they have feelings for?"

"I wish my parents felt that way," I said softly.

"What makes you think they don't?"

With that question, I opened up to Mrs. Green about everything, starting with my feelings for my best friend in Texas and how I opened up to my youth pastor there only to have it backfire on me. I went into detail about my parents' reaction to the rumors, the disappointment on their faces when they sat me down to talk, the relief when I lied and told them I was asking for a friend. I told her all about how this led to us ending up in Bellman, because I was sure she didn't know that. My parents had done a good job of making sure that information didn't make its way to our new church.

Mrs. Green listened intently, only responding by nodding her head, until I was done. I pushed out a breath once I had finished. She was only the third person I had told that story to, and it was exhausting to recount all of it. The fact that she was not only my parents' age, but also the mom of the guy that I had dated when I was "trying to be straight" only made it that much more intimidating.

Much to my surprise, Mrs. Green moved from the seat behind the desk to the one right beside mine and took my hand in hers. "I can't even begin to express how sorry I am that you went through all of that."

"I should be apologizing to you. I shouldn't have agreed to going on dates with Elijah when I was questioning all of this. I was just hoping that being with a nice guy like him would be enough to change me, but I shouldn't have used him like that. You should hate me."

"We all make mistakes. What kind of Christian would I be if I didn't forgive you for yours, especially when I know it wasn't your intention to hurt anyone. Elijah speaks very highly of you. He's happy to have you as his friend." She gently squeezed my hand. "I know you and Bailey have good friends to turn to during this time, but if the two of you ever want to talk to someone with a bit more life experience, I'd be happy to meet with you."

My stomach went into knots at just the mention of Bailey's name. This was all such a mess. "I ended things with Bailey. When you walked in on us, I realized I'm not ready for this. I'm not sure if I'll ever be."

"I imagine it must be extremely scary for you, but don't forget that you deserve to be happy. You shouldn't have to sacrifice your own happiness for *anyone* else. Also, I truly think if you give your parents a chance, they'll come around. I'd even be willing to talk to them with you if you'd like."

I quickly shook my head. "I'm just not ready."

Mrs. Green removed her hand from mine and patted my knee. "And that's fine. It has to be done on your time. Until then, if you ever want to talk, I'm here."

A random question burned into my mind. "Could I ask you one thing?"

"Of course."

"Aren't you worried about my parents being mad if they find out that you knew about this? You seem to love being the youth group director. What if they took that away from you?"

"My job as the youth group director is to be there for the youth of this church. And if that means keeping a secret that you aren't ready to tell yet, I'm more than willing to do that. I would hope that your parents and others in the church would respect that. I truly believe they would."

I nodded my head slowly. I wanted to believe her. I really did. But after everything that had happened at my last church, it was hard.

"Your parents are really good, caring people, Emma. You should give them the chance to prove that to you. When you're ready of course." Mrs. Green stood up and glanced down at me with a sweet smile. "I need to go make sure the rest of these kids are behaving, but think about everything we talked about."

Before she was out the door, she turned around again. "One more thing—many Christians have very strong opinions on this subject, and, unfortunately, a majority of those are different from mine. I'm not going to claim that my belief is definitely the right one, but I have trouble believing that a loving God like ours wouldn't want you to find love— no matter who it's with."

A few seconds after she walked out of the room, Wyatt and Elijah walked in. "Ready to tell us what's going on?" Elijah asked softly.

I let out a breath as I got ready to dive into the story. "Well, Bailey and I decided to sneak off so we could kiss, and as luck would have it, we chose the room that your mom left her phone in. She caught us, and I freaked out. She was actually really cool about it. She promised not to tell my parents and even told me that she doesn't have a problem with people being... you know. But I broke up with Bailey. We were kidding ourselves and living in some crazy dream world. I don't even really know what I want." Even as the words left my mouth, I knew they were a lie. I knew exactly what I wanted. I wanted the one person I was too afraid to be with and would probably never get back, even if I could let go of that fear.

# Chapter 13: Bailey

I couldn't believe that a month had passed since things ended with Emma and I was still completely heartbroken. Luckily, we didn't have any classes together this semester, a fact that would have sucked before but was definitely for the best now. Even just passing her in the hall was hard. I could feel my heart clench in my chest and it took everything in me not to say something to her.

That clearly wasn't what she wanted though seeing as how she hadn't said a word to me since that night. That awful night. I couldn't count the amount of times I had chastised myself for suggesting we sneak off to kiss. If I could have just controlled my hormones for one night, things would still be perfect between us.

But had it really been that perfect if Emma had no problem just cutting me out of her life? Both Elijah and Wyatt insisted that she was just as sad as me, but I had trouble believing that. She had been the one to break it off. She had to know that if she just talked to me, I'd be willing to work things out.

I hated to admit it, but Wyatt was right. All of that talk about not wanting to be official because I didn't want to become a cliche was a front. It was a way to try to keep myself from getting hurt. Unfortunately, it hadn't worked. Not being official hadn't made the ending hurt any less. It honestly might have hurt more since I had almost no one to talk to. Chloe had easily figured out what happened so I now had her in addition to Wyatt and Elijah. But what I really wanted was to talk to my moms about it.

Obviously, they wouldn't care that I was bisexual, but I worried it might hurt their feelings to know I kept it from them. We were always so open with each other, so the fact that I could sneak around with Emma for two months and deal with another month of heartbreak without saying a word might be hard for them to accept.

As if sensing that I was thinking about her, my mama knocked on my open door before walking into my room. "You sure you don't mind watching your sister tonight? It's the weekend before Valentine's Day. Your mom and I can stay in if there is somewhere else you would rather be or someone you would rather be with. We don't have to do anything for Valentine's Day. We *are* old."

I shook my head. "Absolutely nowhere I'd rather be, Mama."

My mama sat down beside me on my bed and stared over at me as if she was trying to figure something out. "Is there something you want to talk to me about?"

Here it was. I was actually surprised that this conversation hadn't come up sooner. My first instinct was to lie. Since things were over with Emma, my moms had no way of finding out that there was ever something going on between us. I knew the guilt of keeping it from them would kill me though, and I would end up telling them eventually. They would be less hurt hearing it now than hearing about it a few months from now.

"I'm bisexual." I spoke the words in a breathy whisper, as if I was almost trying to mask them.

"That's cool." My mama let out a brief chuckle. "Is that it? I assume that you would have to know that your *other mom* and I have no issue with that."

I couldn't help but laugh. When she put it that way, it seemed ridiculous that I hadn't said anything to them to begin with. "No, that's not it. I didn't tell you this, but I was actually seeing someone. It was never official, but Emma and I were together."

"I take it you're not anymore?"

When I went to speak, instead of words coming out, tears came to my eyes. The emotions that I had been hiding from my moms over the past month spilled out of me and I cried on my mama's shoulder as if I was a little kid again.

"Oh, honey," my mama said as she ran a hand through my hair. "I'm so sorry."

I didn't know what to say, so I just continued to cry. After a few minutes, I realized the nice sweater that my mama was wearing for her date with my mom was completely drenched. I moved away from her and wiped at my eyes, trying, and failing, to stop the tears from coming out. "I'm sorry about your sweater."

My mama tilted her head and gave me an incredulous look. "Do you really think I care about my stupid sweater? I care about *you*. All I want is for you to be happy. It's the only thing I've ever wanted since that time I saw you sitting on the back of that U-Haul."

I laughed through my tears as I wiped at my eyes once again. "You need to stop talking about that or else you're going to start crying too."

"Sorry," my mama apologized as she dabbed at her eyes, causing me to realize that they had actually started to water.

"I'm sorry I didn't tell you about Emma."

My mama put an arm around my shoulder and pulled me closer to her. "That's okay. But why didn't you? You're normally so open with your mom and I."

I shrugged. "I'm honestly not sure. I convinced myself that I didn't want to be bisexual, but the truth is, I think I was just afraid that if I told you it would become real and the more real it became, the more chance there was that I would get hurt."

My mama bumped her shoulder against mine, giving me a teasing, but sweet smile. "And how did that work out for you?"

"Not well. I feel like my heart was ripped out of my chest and stomped on about a million times."

"Oh, honey, I know that feeling all too well. Want to tell me what happened?"

I told my mom about Emma's experience in Texas and how it made her believe she needed to stay in the closet, then I took her through our relationship from the amazing beginning to the bitter end.

"It sounds like Emma is really scared. I remember that feeling. I was so worried about coming out to your grandma and grandpa when I was in high school, and unlike Emma, I had no reason to believe they wouldn't support me. The fear that you could actually lose your family because of your sexuality must be terrifying. I knew your grandma and grandpa would never disown me, but just the thought of them seeing me differently was enough to keep me from coming out for years."

Thinking about how scared Emma must be made my heart hurt even more than losing her did. I didn't think that was possible, but when my mind flashed back to the look of fear that I saw in her eyes after we got caught, my heart felt like it was breaking all over again. I hadn't let myself look back on that moment because it was easier to be mad at her if I didn't think about that and feeling angry was a lot better than feeling sad. "She won't talk to me, Mama."

"Well, have you tried talking to her?" I could tell by the way my mama lifted her eyebrow at me that she knew exactly what my answer was going to be.

"Well, no, but it was her choice to end things. If she wanted to talk, she would reach out to me."

"Whether she *wants* to talk to you isn't up for debate. I saw the way she acted around you. It was obvious how much she cared about you. You can't pretend this isn't killing her just as much as it's killing you. The question is whether she has the courage to talk to you. Maybe you need to be the strong one for both of you."

"I don't know, Mama. She has a lot to figure out. I think I need to let her do that."

"You've always been so wise, just like your mom." My mama leaned over and placed a kiss on my cheek. "Don't worry. Things will work out exactly how they are supposed to. I happen to know quite a bit about fate. If something is meant to happen, it will."

"Could I ask you something?"

"You can ask me anything. You know that."

"Did you and Mom break up in college because of me?"

My mama's mouth fell open in surprise. Clearly, that wasn't the question she was expecting. She opened and closed it a few times before finally starting to speak. "Your mom did what she had to do for her family, and even though it was really hard at the time, I wouldn't change anything about it."

We both sat in silence as the heaviness of our conversation filled the air. After a few minutes, my mama squeezed my shoulder before standing from the bed. "I'm going to go tell your mom we're changing our plans. How does a slumber party in the family room for old times' sake sound? Too lame for a high school senior?"

I smiled in spite of how much my heart still hurt. "Not lame at all." My mama turned to leave, but I grabbed her hand. "Just in case I don't tell you enough, I'm really happy fate brought you and Mom back together. I don't know what I would do without you."

My mama pointed a finger at me as she blinked back tears. "You stop that, young lady. We don't need anymore tears tonight. Tonight is all about fun and family time. Deal?"

For the first time since New Year's Eve, the smile that came to my face was sincere, and I actually felt happy. "Deal."

\*\*\*

"Yay! Movie night!" Sophia yelled as she walked into the family room with a big bowl of popcorn, leaving a path of popcorn along the way. She shoved a handful of popcorn into her mouth and turned toward me. "You should tell Emma to come."

My mama looked at me with apologetic eyes, but I forced a smile onto my face as I focused on my sister. "I don't think she can make it tonight. But how about I ask Wyatt instead?"

Sophia scrunched up her nose and squinted her eyes. "Boys have cooties, but I *guess* Wyatt is cool."

Luckily, Wyatt had put himself on Bailey duty ever since things ended with Emma, so within seconds of texting him, he responded that he would be right over. Not even fifteen minutes later, he walked through the front door.

"Not to worry. Everyone's favorite man is here," he announced as he joined us in the family room. "You are all very lucky that the students of Bellman High have terrible taste leaving me without a Valentine once again. Although, I have to say, I have the four most beautiful Valentine dates in the whole world now. I guess that makes *me* the lucky one."

I stood and gave him a hug. "Thanks for coming, Wy."

"You can always count on me, bestie." Wyatt gave me an extra squeeze before letting go. "So, what movie are we watching tonight? Let me guess… *Frozen*?"

A lump formed in my throat as I thought about the last time I watched *Frozen*. I now knew that the moment I thought I was imagining with Emma actually happened. It used to make me happy when I thought about that day, but now it just hurt.

Sophia put her hands on her hips as she glared up at Wyatt. "I want to watch *Toy Story*. Girls don't only have to be princesses. They can be cowgirls or astronauts too."

I took a relieved breath. I would have sat through *Frozen* for Sophia, but it was the last thing I wanted. I was so lucky she was going through a boy-hating phase and had probably rejected *Frozen* only because Wyatt was the one to mention it. "Which one are we watching?"

Sophia batted her eyelashes first at me and then at our moms as she smiled her sweetest smile. "I thought we could watch all four."

"We can watch *two*," Mama said with a laugh.

"*Maybe,*" my mom added.

Sophia skipped over to where the TV remote was sitting and handed it to my mom. "Number three and four please. The other ones are so *old*."

My mom lifted the controller in the air and lifted an eyebrow. "Are you calling me and Mama old?"

Before Sophia could respond, there was a knock at the door. "I'll get it!" she shouted as she ran out of the room.

I wondered who it would be and couldn't hear from the family room. A minute later, Sophia walked back into the room and tilted her head as if she was confused. "There's someone here for you mommy. She wouldn't say who she was, but she looks like you."

What the hell? Who could she possibly be talking about? It couldn't be…? No. There was no way.

The look on my mom's face told me that she had the same thought I did. She stood from the couch and put her hand up toward me. "Bailey, I think you should stay here. I'll be right back."

Mama stood from the couch as well. "I'm coming with you."

I watched them walk out of the room, then looked over at Wyatt. His eyes were wide and he looked just as shell-shocked as I felt. I tried to swallow the lump in my throat so I could say something, but it was no use.

"Why is everyone acting so weird?" Sophia asked as she threw a piece of popcorn into the air and caught it in her mouth, completely unphased by what was happening.

"Can you keep Sophia in here?" I whispered to Wyatt. "I-I'm going to go out there."

"Are you sure that's a good idea?"

No. I wasn't sure at all. Honestly, it was probably an absolutely terrible idea, but I couldn't take the not knowing. Lately, it felt like I had absolutely no control over my own life, so I was going to take control of this. "I need to know."

Wyatt didn't say anything, but nodded his head in understanding. As I walked through the kitchen and down the hallway, I prepared myself for whatever was waiting for me at the door. I stopped just far enough away so I could see the three of them, but they hopefully wouldn't see me. Sophia was right. The woman standing with my moms was a spitting image of both me and my mom. That could only mean one thing. It really was her.

The sight made me feel lightheaded, so I reached my hand out to brace myself against the wall. Unfortunately, since I wasn't paying attention, my hand hit a picture causing it to rattle against the wall and make enough noise to gather the attention of the three adults standing by the door.

Eyes that resembled my eyes even more than my mom's latched onto mine. The owner's mouth dropped open in shock as she continued to stare at me, and I had to assume my mouth probably looked the exact same as hers.

"Bailey," she said in such a low whisper that I wasn't sure if she was talking to me or talking to herself. "I'm your m—" She cleared her throat and shook her head as if she thought better of what she was about to say. "I'm your mom's sister, Ariana."

Ariana shook her head once again as we all just stared at each other in silence. "You know what? I'm going to go for now. I shouldn't have just stopped by unannounced like this." Ariana focused her attention on Kacey. "I really am sorry. I was going to call or text, but then I figured you had either blocked me or changed your number, which I completely understand. Truly." She fumbled through the purse she was holding and pulled out a pen and paper, turning around to use the door as a hard surface to write something, then handed the paper to Kacey. "That's my number in case you don't have it anymore. I know I don't deserve it, but if you could give me a call after you guys all have a chance to talk, I would really appreciate it. I'm going to go now."

Before I could even fully comprehend what was happening, she walked right back out the door without as much as a second look. I leaned my back against the wall and moved my eyes back and forth between my moms. "I'm sorry. I know you told me to wait in the family room, but I just... I don't know. I needed to see for myself."

Instead of saying anything, my mom closed the distance between us and hugged me tightly. After a few seconds, she pulled back, bringing her hands up to hold onto my arms. "Are you okay?"

"I am. Or... I will be, at least."

"What do you want to do about all of this?"

I rubbed my hand over my temple. What I wanted to do was go back to the end of last year when life was so much simpler. Back when Emma was still talking to me and the woman who gave birth to me wasn't just showing up out of the blue after years of no contact with anyone in my family. "Tonight we need to do exactly what we originally planned to do so Sophia doesn't know there's anything weird going on. Tomorrow I'd like to sit down and talk to you guys about all of this. Is that okay?"

My mom squeezed my arms before letting her hands drop. "I think that sounds like a perfect idea."

We were able to have a good night despite the giant elephant in the room. It helped that Sophia had no clue anything weird had happened and kept us all entertained. Wyatt spent the night and offered to take Sophia on a brunch date so my moms and I could talk. Sophia put up a little bit of an argument about how boys had cooties only to give in when Wyatt agreed to take her to whatever restaurant she chose. Of course she chose Emma's so she could get a *humongous* stack of chocolate chip pancakes with whipped cream.

Once they were out of the house, my mom made us our own batch of pancakes and some coffee, then we all sat down at the kitchen table to eat and talk.

"So, last night was obviously unexpected." My mom picked up her mug of coffee and took a long sip before sitting it back down. "We never shared a ton about Ariana with you, mostly because I never thought she would come back, but also because you were young and I wanted to spare you the details."

I had never seen my mom so stressed, which was saying a lot of the woman who raised me practically alone for half of my life, her grandma just barely present until she passed away right before we moved to Bellman. She took another long sip of her coffee, closing her eyes and rubbing a hand over her forehead after she sat it back down again.

"You're almost an adult so you deserve the full story and also should be able to make your own decisions. Ariana became pregnant when she was a teenager, so she never planned on being a mom. The plan was actually to put you up for adoption, but that all changed when you were born." My mom reached across the table and cupped my hands in hers. "From the moment I saw you, I knew I was meant to be your mom. When I held you, there was no question that you were *my* daughter. Ariana and I were never close. Aside from looks, we were about as opposite as two people could be. She wanted no part in being a mom." She quickly shook her head as if she thought better of the words she was saying. "That had nothing to do with you. She was just young. She wasn't ready. You were too young to remember, but she came in and out of our lives a few times before I told her it was unacceptable. I didn't want you to grow attached to someone you couldn't count on.

When we first moved to Bellman, she ended up finding us. She showed up and said she was ready to have a relationship with you, but I wouldn't let her meet you until she proved she was ready. Unfortunately, she proved the opposite."

I wasn't sure how much I actually wanted to hear this story, but my curiosity got the best of me. "What did she do?"

"She showed up drunk one night insisting to see you, then said some really terrible things to your mama. I told her to spend the night so she could sober up, but I wanted her out of our lives after that."

"So, the next day was the last time you saw her?"

My mom shook her head, looking solemn. "No. That night was the last time. She ended up leaving that night without a word." She laughed a quick sarcastic laugh. "Left without a word, but took my wallet with her."

Wow. I knew Ariana was bad, but I didn't know she was *this* bad. "Did you end up catching her to at least get your stuff back? Did she get in trouble?"

My mom removed one of her hands from mine to take Mama's hand. "No. I just cancelled the cards. That was the least of our worries that night. Do you remember your Aunt's accident?"

Oh God, no, it couldn't be. This just kept getting worse. When I was nine my Aunt Kylie was in a terrible car accident that took her months to recover from. I later learned it had been a drunk driver who hit her. My moms reminded me of that more than I could count to emphasize just how important it was to never drive after drinking, even if it's just been one drink and I felt fine. But the story they told was that a Bellman football player had done it. Now I was wondering if they made that up, not only to scare me into worrying about ruining my track career, but also to protect Ariana. "That wasn't…?"

"Oh, no. No it wasn't," my mama quickly corrected. "It really was that Bellman football player like we told you. We honestly thought it was her. It was actually a relief to find out it wasn't."

"Wow, that's—"

"A lot, I know," my mom said, finishing my sentence. "I'm really sorry to put that all on you. We just thought you needed to know the full story."

I wasn't sure what to do with all of this information. Throughout my life, I really had no feelings at all about Ariana. She was a stranger who happened to give birth to me. Now, the only feelings I had were anger and resentment. Not for how she had acted so blasé toward having any sort of relationship with me. That was fine. My family was perfect. I would have been worse off if Ariana had interfered with that. No, I was angry and resentful about how she had treated my moms. My moms were my heroes and the thought of anyone treating them badly frankly just pissed me off. Why would I want to give someone like that any of my time? Yet, I couldn't get those dark eyes off of my mind. I couldn't forget just how much they looked like mine. I wanted to. Man, did I want to. But I just couldn't for some reason.

Another set of dark eyes met mine as my mom studied my face. "You know Ariana is in the area and clearly wants us to reach out to her. What you do with that information is up to you. Personally, I want to talk to her. I know she doesn't deserve my time, but she's my sister. If I don't find out why she's here, I'm always going to wonder. With that being said, if you happen to be interested in meeting her, I'd like to talk to her first if that's okay with you. I need to know what her intentions are in showing up here. I don't want to set you up for disappointment."

My mama joined her hand that wasn't holding my mom's with me and my mom's hands that were resting on the table. "We want you to know that we completely support whatever you decide. We love you and we'll be here for you."

This was all just way too much. Dealing with losing Emma was already hard enough. Now I also had to deal with the woman who gave birth to me walking back into my life? No way. I just couldn't do it. I needed time. I needed to breathe, which I currently wasn't doing.

# Chapter 14: Emma

"Honey, are you almost ready?"

My dad's voice caught my attention and I looked up from the homework I was working on. "Ready?"

My dad furrowed his eyebrows in concern, a look I was becoming way too familiar with recently. "You didn't forget, did you? Today is your visit to Bell U. We have to leave in…" He looked down at his watch. "Fifteen minutes."

*Shoot.* I *had* forgotten about that. Mostly I had pushed it from my mind because I knew there was no way I could go to Bellman. Out of all the schools I applied to, Bellman looked the best to me, but I couldn't possibly go there. How could I go to the same school as the girl whose heart I had broken?

For the hundredth time, my mind flashed back to the way Bailey's face looked the night I ended things between us. I honestly wasn't sure what hurt more—the thought of breaking her heart or the feeling of my own breaking. Because it was. It was completely broken. I was trying to keep it together because only a handful of people actually knew what I had to be upset about, but it was getting harder everyday. It was almost two months since things ended and I still felt the loss every single day. Every *minute* of every day. It was like a piece of me had been taken from my own body. I had no idea it would hurt *this much.*

"Are you feeling okay? Should we reschedule? This is a very important day. We need you on your A-game."

I shook my head in response to my dad's question. I had to suck it up. Coach Hopkins had made time in her schedule to speak with me. I'm sure she had better things to be doing on a Sunday.

"I'll be ready soon." I tried to smile, but even I knew it wasn't convincing.

My dad stood by the door to my bedroom for another moment as if he was contemplating whether to say something else. He studied my face, concern still written all over his, then nodded slightly and walked away.

***

Just twenty-five minutes later, we pulled in front of a small building right on the edge of Bellman's campus. The sign out front indicated that this was where all of Bellman's coaches had their offices. I ran my finger over the sign until it landed on *Joey Hopkins - Head Track and Field Coach*. I took a deep breath, then said goodbye to my parents and headed toward the second floor, room five as the sign had directed.

The door to the office was open and a woman who looked to be around the age of Bailey's parents was sitting behind a laptop, deeply focused on whatever was on the screen. My heart clenched just at the thought of Bailey. Why did my mind *always* have to go back to her?

"Coach Hopkins?" I asked softly.

The woman looked up from her laptop and as soon as our eyes met, a large smile spread across her face. She stood from her chair and walked toward me, hand stretched out in front of her. "You must be Emma. I'm so excited to finally meet you." After offering me a firm handshake, she pointed toward the chair in front of her desk. "Please, have a seat."

She sat back down in the seat she had just stood from. Her face became serious once again as she stared across at me. "Listen, Emma, I'm a no bullshit sort of woman, so forgive me for starting out this way, but I've found it makes it the easiest for both of us if I start with this question. Do you truly want to be part of the Bellman track team? Because if not, there's no need to waste either of our time. I only ask because I know how parents can be. They pressure their kids into following their dreams instead of their own, and this decision needs to be all about *you*."

"Oh. Um…" I looked down at my hands which were beginning to sweat just like the rest of my body, then looked around the office. Trophies were scattered around, not-so-subtly bragging about all of the team's accomplishments.

As my eyes made their way across Coach Hopkins' desk, they paused on what looked like a family picture. Coach Hopkins was holding a little girl in one of her arms and had her hand resting on a little boy's shoulder. There was a woman standing next to her with a hand wrapped around her waist and her other hand on another little girl's shoulder. Did that mean...? Was Coach Hopkins...?

I tore my eyes from the picture, embarrassed that I still had yet to say anything. When I looked across the desk, Coach Hopkins raised an eyebrow at me, looking from me to the picture I had just been staring at. "That's my wife and kids."

*Wife.* Why didn't Bailey ever mention the Bellman track coach was in a same-sex relationship? I shook my head at myself. Why would she? It wasn't important.

Except it was. It was to me. Suddenly, I didn't feel so alone. I knew it was stupid, but it felt nice to be sitting with someone who understood, even if she actually had no idea.

"Are you okay?" Coach Hopkins asked, her voice now sounding a lot less firm. "I'm sorry if my words upset you. I know it can sound a bit harsh. I like to act like a hardass, but the truth is I'm actually a big softie."

I shook my head as I felt my eyes start to burn, tears threatening to fall. "Bellman is a great school and the track team is better here than any other schools I've looked at. I would love to go to school here. I just... I can't."

Now, a few tears *did* fall from my eyes. What was wrong with me? This was so embarrassing. I couldn't stop them though. I had been holding them in for months, lying whenever someone asked me the question Coach Hopkins had just asked. I couldn't lie anymore. Not to myself and not to her.

"I'm often hesitant to recruit athletes from Bellman High School, because a lot of kids want to get away after high school, and it's their parents trying to get them to go to school close by. Something tells me this isn't about distance for you though. Am I right?"

I nodded my head and wiped my wet cheeks with the sleeve of my sweatshirt. "Yes ma'am. I'm—" *Was I really about to admit this out loud to a complete stranger?* Before I could stop myself, the words slipped out. "I'm gay."

Coach Hopkins chuckled. "If that's what's holding you back, I'd like to ask you to please reconsider. That's not gonna be a problem on this team."

"My parents don't know," I said softly, chancing a look at Coach Hopkins.

The slight smile that had been on her face dipped into a frown. "Are you worried about how they'll react?"

"My dad's a pastor," I said quietly.

"God should never be an excuse for people to judge you. Quite the opposite, actually." Coach Hopkins ran a hand over her forehead. "Unfortunately, I know all too well that people love to blame their hatred on their religion. I really hope that's not the case with your parents."

"Was your family okay with it?" I swallowed hard as I waited for the answer that I unfortunately had a feeling I already knew.

Coach Hopkins stared past me, then smiled when she looked back at me. "The family that matters is the people who love you and accept you for who you are—*that's* your family." She looked around the room as if she was taking in everything surrounding us. "Listen, I'm not just saying this because you're a hell of a runner and we could really use you on our team. Even if it doesn't feel like it now, someday you *will* come out to your parents. And no matter what happens, if you do end up coming to Bellman, you'll have a family here. I promise."

Now, even more tears came to my eyes, and this time, I didn't try to stop them. "Thank you. Seriously. I know this isn't how our meeting was supposed to go, and I really appreciate you being so understanding."

"Trust me, kid, if someone understands how hard this is, it's me. I went through it all when I came out." Coach Hopkins' eyes moved back to the picture of her family sitting on her desk and her face lit up. "I can also tell you it's worth it though. No matter what happens, it's so worth it. I'm not going to keep you here going over all of our stats and what type of scholarship we're willing to offer you, but I do have one piece of unsolicited advice. People can't love you for who you are unless you let them."

Her words hit me hard and I had to take a deep breath because it felt like the wind had been knocked out of me. There was so much there to consider; so much to unpack. There was one thing I was sure of though. As I stood, I reached my hand out to Coach Hopkins. "Consider this my verbal commitment. I want to be a Bellman Bulldog."

Coach Hopkins took my hand, absolutely beaming in response to my words. "Welcome to the family."

***

"So, what's the deal?" my dad asked as he pulled into our driveway and turned off the car. He turned to face where I was sitting in the backseat and crossed his arms in front of his chest. "You haven't said a word since we left your meeting."

I hadn't said a word because I had too many thoughts going through my head. Everything Coach said was buzzing in my ears, like an annoying bug I couldn't swat away. There was so much I wanted to say to my parents, but I couldn't. Even with Coach's words of wisdom, how could I possibly say those words that I spent years being too afraid to speak out loud?

"I decided I want to go to Bell U. I gave Coach a verbal commitment." No matter how much I tried, I couldn't make my voice sound chipper. I wanted this to be a happy moment, but instead, it carried so much weight.

"That's amazing, honey," my mom said, her voice exuding the cheer that mine was missing. Her smile dropped when she turned toward me and saw the panicked look that I was sure was written all over my face. "Why aren't you excited? This is wonderful news."

I stared out the window, unable to handle my parents' worried eyes that were watching me intently, waiting for some sort of explanation. "I just… I'm…" I started to cry just like I had in Coach's office. "I'm so sick of playing this part."

"What part?" my dad asked, sounding completely bewildered.

I moved my focus from our house to the church building; a building that made me feel physically sick because of the memory of New Year's Eve. "The part of the pastor's perfect daughter. The one who would do anything to make you guys proud even if it's killing me inside."

"Honey, if you don't want to go to Bellman—"

"This isn't about Bellman," I shouted, interrupting my dad. "It's about the fact that I can't be who I truly am because I'm terrified."

"I don't understand," my mom said softly. "Terrified of what?"

"Terrified of losing you guys," I answered, my voice still raised. I threw my hands in the air. Why didn't they get it? How had they not put the pieces together at this point? "I wasn't asking for a friend, *okay*? Back in Texas when I asked about… I lied to you guys. I was asking for *me* because of feelings that *I* have. And if you're completely honest with yourselves, I think you've always known that. I just… I can't do this anymore."

It suddenly felt like the car was closing in around me and I was losing air. I had to get out of there before I couldn't breathe at all. I grabbed the door handle and forcefully pushed my way out of the car, not even sticking around to hear my parents' response. I thought maybe one of them shouted my name, but I wasn't listening. I was only focused on putting one foot in front of the other and getting into the house and up to my room as quickly as possible.

Luckily, that didn't take me long, and as soon as I was in my room, I threw myself onto my bed and started to cry. I cried for the girl I would never be. I cried for the girl I was desperate to become. I cried for what I could lose and what I had already lost. Why did this have to be so complicated? Why did it matter who I loved? My gut twisted as that word came to my mind. *Love.* Was that really what I felt for Bailey? If it wasn't already, it was certainly heading in that direction. At least, it had been before I tore it all apart.

My sobs were so loud that I didn't hear anyone walk into my room, and it wasn't until I felt a hand rubbing my back that I realized I wasn't alone. I could tell it was my mom by her soft touch, but I didn't turn around to look at her. I couldn't possibly face her right now.

"Could we please talk?" my mom asked. Her voice was gentle, but didn't sound as soothing as it always did when she comforted me in the past. "Listen, honey, we all question things about ourselves at times. It's nothing to be ashamed of. God made us to be inquisitive beings."

I quickly sat up and rubbed my eyes. She had it all wrong. So very wrong. I shook my head. "That's the thing, Mom. I'm not questioning this anymore. I know this is who I am."

I was surprised when my mom laughed as if I had just told a joke. "Oh, sweetie, how could you possibly know that. It's not like—" She paused suddenly and her smile quickly dropped from her face. "Oh dear. You didn't, did you? You weren't... *with another girl*?" She whispered the last part as if it were shameful.

I began to sob all over again. It was partially due to my mom's reaction, but mostly because her question made me think of Bailey once again and just how much I had messed things up between us. "If by *with* you mean was I falling really hard for someone and completely ruined it because I knew you would react exactly how you are right now, then the answer is yes."

My mom sighed as she patted me on the knee. "So, this *is* about Bailey Caldwell. I really like her. I think she is an upstanding young lady. I need to be honest though. I was worried this might happen if you spent time around people who were living an *alternative lifestyle*."

"I thought you said it was okay that Bailey had two moms."

My mom scoffed. "It's okay if they don't try to push that lifestyle on *my* daughter."

My stomach started to hurt as I listened to her voice her small-minded opinions. This was my worst nightmare coming true. Even with all of my worry over my parents finding out I was gay, I still held out hope that *just maybe* they would be accepting. Obviously, that wasn't the case.

"No one pushed anything on me, Mom. I told you. I've had these feelings since we lived in Texas. If I'm being completely honest with myself, I had them way before we even moved *there*. This has always been part of me. I just refused to see it. Then when I saw it, I refused to acknowledge it."

"I'm not faulting you for having feelings, sweetheart," my mom said softly, restoring some faith that maybe this could still be okay.

"You're not?"

"Of course not. The devil isn't ugly. Temptation is strong. It's up to us to work through it."

I groaned and ran a hand over my forehead, my body heating up from the anger that was boiling just below the surface. "Let me get this straight. It's okay for me to feel this way, but it's not okay for me to act on my feelings? Pretty much, I'm just not allowed to be happy."

My mom's mouth dipped into a frown and she furrowed her eyebrows. "Well, when you put it that way, you make me sound terrible." My mom squeezed my knee and moved a little closer to me. "Listen, honey, I'm not telling you that you aren't allowed to be happy. I'm just saying that you shouldn't label yourself based off of a few relationships. You could still meet a boy that you really like. You're not even eighteen yet."

"I'll be eighteen in like a month, and I'm pretty sure eighteen years is more than enough time to figure out who you are. You always told me it took you just two months to know dad was the one and you guys met right when you started college."

"Well, that's different."

"How is it different?" I asked hotly, not able to hide the anger in my voice. "Because your relationship is more acceptable to society?"

My mom shook her head as if she was frustrated. "I feel like I can't say anything right. I'm trying. I really am. But you argue with everything I say. What do you want from me?"

"What I *want* is for you to say that you accept me; that you accept *this part* of me." The floodgates had opened and tears were now streaming down my face.

"Honey, it's not—" My mom shook her head once again. "The Bible says—"

"I don't care what the Bible says, Mom," I interrupted, my words now being shouted through my tears. "I want to know what *you* say. I want *your* acceptance."

When my mom stared at me dumbfounded, I stood from the bed, no longer able to take it. "I can't be here right now. I can't do this. I just... I can't. Where is dad even at?"

"He went for a drive."

I scoffed once again. "Of course he did." Whenever my dad was upset or angry about something he would go for a drive. He always said it was so he had a chance to cool down before saying something he would regret. But what did he want to say this time? That he was ashamed of his own daughter?

I knew one thing. I wasn't waiting around to hear what he had to say when he got home. "You know what? A drive sounds like a great idea. I'll be back later."

I needed to talk to someone and I knew I *should* go to Elijah since he was definitely my closest friend since things ended with Bailey, but I found myself driving in the opposite direction of his house. I was driving toward the house of someone who probably didn't feel like comforting me right now. Someone who probably thought I had this coming after what I had done.

I paused and took a deep breath before knocking. When the door opened, Wyatt looked confused to see me standing there, which I had expected. The two of us had never hung out without Elijah or Bailey, and even though he had been supportive since things ended, I was sure he wasn't happy about what I had done to his best friend.

He took a step toward me. "Are you okay, Em?" he asked, his voice laced with concern.

I shook my head as I stared down at the ground. "I came out to my parents and... and..." I couldn't finish my sentence because I was too upset to speak, and frankly, I also didn't really understand what had happened. There hadn't been yelling, at least from my parents' end, but there also hadn't been any sort of acceptance. Even a reassuring

'*We'll always love you no matter what,*' would have been something.

Wyatt closed the little gap remaining between us and wrapped me in his arms. "I'm so sorry, Em." He let go just enough to pull me into the house, closing the door behind us. "What do you say I text Elijah and see if he can come over? The three of us could watch a movie or just talk if that's what you want. It's up to you. Whatever you want to do."

I mustered up a slight smile to show my appreciation. "A movie sounds great."

***

After spending a few hours with Wyatt and Elijah, I headed home, the anxiety from earlier returning as soon as I pulled in my driveway. When I walked into the house, my parents were sitting in the living room waiting for me, and the scene looked eerily similar to what I walked into after being outed by my youth pastor.

"Emma, sit down please. We need to talk," my dad said, his voice stern but also soft.

I sat down and looked between my parents. My mom was staring down at her hands that were resting on her lap and my dad was rubbing at his temples. I swallowed hard when my dad looked back at me searching my face as if I was a stranger.

After a few more seconds of silence, he finally spoke. "I hope you know your mother and I just want what's best for you. We want you to be happy."

"But I am happy."

My dad studied my face once again and this time I could tell he was searching for proof that what i just said was true. "Really? Because I would argue that these past few months you've been more upset than I've seen you in your whole life."

"That's because I lost…" I hesitated unsure how to refer to Bailey. She wasn't officially my girlfriend, but she also wasn't just my friend either. "Someone very important to me."

My dad closed his eyes and nodded his head as if he was taking my words into consideration. "Yes. Your mother told me you had *something* with Bailey Caldwell."

I had to swallow back the bile that was rising in my throat. What I had with Bailey was so much more than something. For a fleeting, perfect moment, it felt like *everything*.

"I'm going to be honest with you, Em," my dad's voice cut through the silence. "We're not sure what to do about this. You're almost an adult. You can make your own choices. We have to let you make your own mistakes, whether we agree with them or not."

*Seriously?* I tried to keep my composure; tried not to show how much his words were eating me up inside. "This isn't a choice or a mistake. This is just who I am."

"And I guess that's something we're all just going to have to figure out."

I couldn't even fathom what my dad's words meant. What were we *figuring out?* It certainly didn't sound like they were going to *figure out* how to accept this part of me. "I guess so." The room remained awkwardly silent for what felt like hours, so I stood from my chair. "If you don't have anything else to say, I guess I'll go to bed."

For the first time since getting home, my mom brought her eyes to mine and spoke. "Yes, you should get a good night's sleep for school tomorrow." And just like that, she looked back down at her hands. It was almost as if looking at me was painful for her.

She didn't know pain though. She couldn't even begin to fathom the pain I felt as I lay down in my bed. First I lost Bailey and now it felt like I was losing my parents as well. What the hell was I going to do?

***

"The pizza is here," Mrs. Green announced to everyone in attendance at youth group.

I slowly made my way over to the table she placed it on and put just one slice onto my plate. It was hard to have much of an appetite when I already felt sick with worry. It had been a week and a half since I came out to my parents and although things were cordial between the three of us they were far from normal. My parents refused to acknowledge my coming out and hadn't mentioned it since our talk that night. I decided not to push it. I had done my part. I told the truth. Now it was their turn to decide what to do with it. As if all that wasn't enough, track practice was starting the following week, and I could no longer avoid Bailey. Being in such close proximity to her again was going to completely tear me apart.

As if reading my mind, Elijah leaned in close to me to whisper in my ear. "I really think you should talk to my mom about what's going on with your parents."

I shook my head. "I can't do that to her. I already put her in a bad position. I don't want to make it even worse."

"Well, then what about Bailey?" Elijah asked as we sat down.

Just hearing her name spoken out loud made my heart rate pick up. "What about Bailey?"

Elijah shrugged as he took a bite of his pizza. "I think you should talk to her. You've barely said anything to me and Wyatt. You refuse to talk to my mom. I think it could be good for you."

I shook my head once again, this time more firmly. "I can't do that to her. It's not her place to have to comfort me. That wouldn't be fair. I don't even want her to know about it." I shot my head up to look at him. "Wait. You didn't tell her, did you? Because I told both you and Wyatt—"

Elijah stuck both hands in the air. "Whoa, calm down. Of course I didn't tell her." He put his hands down and started to play with his food as if he was suddenly nervous. "But you really *should* talk to her, Em. I think you could both use each other right now."

"What do you mean?"

Elijah groaned and dropped the pizza he was holding. "Listen, I'm not supposed to tell you this, and I'm pretty sure both Wyatt and Bailey would kill me if they found out I did, but it's for the best that you know. Bailey's biological mom came back, Em. She wants to be part of Bailey's life. Wyatt was there the night she just showed up out of nowhere and he said Bailey was really shaken up by the whole thing."

The sick feeling in my stomach seemed to move throughout my whole body now. I couldn't believe that Bailey was going through such a big life-changing event and I had no idea. I couldn't imagine how she felt right now. I knew I wouldn't have to imagine for long though. Elijah was right. I needed to talk to her. My problems now seemed so minuscule, and all I cared about was being there for Bailey. I had to let her know that I still cared about her. I needed her to know that even though we weren't whatever we used to be, she could still count on me. Now I just had to work up the courage to do it.

# Chapter 15: Bailey

"Earth to Bailey."

I could hear Wyatt's voice from across the lunch table but I was too caught up in looking at the text I had just received from Ariana to process that he was talking to me.

After Ariana showed back up, my mom met up with her to find out what her intentions were. She explained to my mom that she had spent the last few years getting her life together and felt awful about how she had treated us. Whether we were willing to have any sort of relationship with her or not, she still wanted the chance to apologize for everything she had done throughout the years.

She rented an apartment in a town about a half hour away from us and was working as a waitress. My mom had met up with her a few times since their first meeting and was cautiously optimistic that Ariana might truly mean what she said this time. Everyone was leaving it up to me how, or if, I pursued a relationship with Ariana. I had decided to start out by texting her. Yes, I knew it was strange to exchange random texts about my day with the woman who had birthed me and then wanted nothing to do with me for most of my life, but I wasn't sure of any other way to handle this. I didn't want to write Ariana off completely, but I also wasn't sure if I actually wanted to let her into my life. Texting was easy. I could pretend she was just a pen pal, rather than my biological mother, which allowed me to keep her at arm's length.

But the text I had just received asking if I would be willing to get dinner with her sometime had the power to change everything. I had no idea how to feel about that request. Was I ready for that? Was it something I *ever* wanted to do?

My thoughts were cut off by the sound of someone whistling. I looked across the table to find Wyatt staring at me. "What, dude?" I asked, sounding more irritated than I intended.

"Don't dude me. I was just trying to ask if you were going to finish your fries."

I threw one at him which he tried, and failed, to dodge. It bounced off the side of his face, then landed on his lap. He picked it up and proudly put it into his mouth. I rolled my eyes at him. "I have more important things than your stomach to worry about right now. Ariana wants to get dinner with me."

Wyatt's eyebrows lifted high as his face became more serious. "Wow. That's a big step. How do you feel about that?"

I shook my head as I stared down at my tray and pushed it toward him. "I don't think I'm ready."

Wyatt pulled the tray the rest of the way across the table and immediately put a handful of fries into his mouth. "Then tell her that. She waited almost eighteen years to do this. You have every right to take as much time as you need."

I knew he was right, but there was still a part of me that wondered if Ariana would get tired of waiting and decide to skip town again. But why should I care? I absolutely hated the fact that I did. It was also more proof that I needed to tread lightly.

"You're right," I finally said. I put my phone into my pocket making a mental note to answer that text later.

Just as I tucked my phone away, Wyatt's began to vibrate on the table. He quickly picked it up as if he didn't want me to see who was texting him.

I lifted my eyebrow. "Who's that?" I asked suspiciously.

"No one important," Wyatt answered, but he quickly typed back a reply to this unimportant person. When he looked up from his phone and found me still staring at him, he groaned. "Fine. It's Emma. Please don't kill me. She just really needs to talk to someone who understands what it feels like—" Wyatt cut himself off.

"What it feels like to what, Wyatt?"

"To come out," he said so quietly I almost couldn't hear him.

"Come out?" *What the hell was he talking about?*

"Emma came out to her parents and their reaction wasn't great. She told me not to tell you because she didn't want you to worry about her."

Of course I was worried about her. We might not have spoken since New Year's Eve but I still cared about her, much more than I probably should have at this point. "Oh God, Wyatt, is she okay?"

"Honestly, not really. She's really struggling right now. She feels like they'll never accept her for who she truly is."

I felt sick. I hated to think of Emma going through this. "I need to talk to her. I don't care if she wants to talk to me right now. I need her to know that I'll be there for her no matter what."

"Obvi. So, when are you going to do it?"

"If I can catch her before she leaves, then right after school."

Wyatt's smile widened. "She's parked in the third row right in front of the flagpole."

\*\*\*

My heart dropped as I briskly walked up to the flag pole and found an empty parking spot. Emma had somehow beat me out of school, which was crazy since I practically sprinted there as soon as the bell rang. I would have to settle for calling her once I got home. I obviously couldn't just stop by her house since I didn't know if she had told her parents anything about us. If she had, I was sure I was the last person they wanted to see.

I felt defeated throughout my drive home. Sure, I could call Emma, but the thought of talking to her in person admittedly had me excited and now I only felt disappointment. I didn't even know if she would answer her phone if I called.

As I pulled onto my street, I could see a car in my driveway that didn't belong to anyone in my family. As I got closer, I realized it was a car I knew really well. My heartbeat picked up as I continued to stare at the car—a red Jeep

Renegade with a dent on the passenger door—and confirmed that it was Emma's. But how? Why?

I practically ran up my driveway and across the sidewalk. I still couldn't believe that was Emma's car and had myself half-convinced that I must be dreaming or hallucinating.

As soon as I pushed the door open, Sophia called my name, then I heard her little footsteps coming in my direction. "Bailey! Bailey! Emma's here. She hasn't been here in so long. It's so exciting."

Sophia ran down the hallway and jumped into my arms, but I was too stunned to react. As I held her, my eyes drifted down the hallway to where Emma was hesitantly walking toward me.

"Emma," I said breathlessly, unable to push out any other words.

She stopped in front of me and smiled nervously as she stared down at her own feet. My heart was beating so rapidly I swore she could probably hear it.

Sophia wiggled out of my arms and landed on the ground with a loud thud. "I'm going to tell moms you're home and see if Emma can stay for dinner."

I was still so overwhelmed by Emma's presence that I barely let her words register and didn't try to fight her on them. I just stared at Emma who was now looking up at me. We both just stood there, close enough to touch, yet miles apart. What was I supposed to say? Where did I even start?

"I heard you—"

"I heard about—" Emma's words filled the air at the exact same time as mine.

We both laughed and briefly looked away from each other. I chanced another step closer to her and was satisfied when she didn't move away. "Did Wyatt talk to you? It seems he has an issue with keeping his mouth shut."

Emma shook her head. "It was Elijah." She reached her hand out like she was about to take my hand then quickly retracted it. "You could have texted or called me. This is huge. I hate that I wasn't there for you to talk to."

"Could I have though? Ever since New Year's Eve, it felt like you wanted nothing to do with me."

"That's not true at all," Emma answered quickly. "I… I was scared after everything that happened and talking to you… well, it seemed like it would just make everything harder. But not talking to you was the hardest thing I've ever done. These past few months have been awful."

"You came out to your parents." The words were out of my mouth before I could think of something more elegant or heartfelt to say.

Emma cleared her throat and closed her eyes, taking a deep breath as if she was trying not to cry. "I did."

Before I could say anything else, Sophia came running back into the hallway. "Moms said you could stay for dinner if you want, Emma. Want to play until it's time to eat? They said I shouldn't bug you guys but I told them Emma wouldn't mind. We're friends. Practically sisters." She smiled between the two of us, blissfully unaware of the tension and heavy air.

I gave Emma an apologetic smile then opened my mouth to tell Sophia that wouldn't be happening. But before I could, Emma knelt down beside her and took her hand. "I would love to do that if your sister and my parents say it's okay."

I was completely shocked. It was strange enough that Emma was in my house right now. Was she really going to just hang out here as if these past few months hadn't even happened? Weirdly enough, I didn't care. I wanted her here. I *needed* her here. With that text from Ariana that I still hadn't answered burning a hole in my pocket, spending time with Emma was exactly what I needed. "I would really like that."

Emma excused herself to call her parents and from the other room, I could hear her ask if she could eat dinner at a *friend's* house. It didn't escape me that she didn't use my name, and that made me wonder just how much she had come out to her parents about.

I didn't have a chance to ask because Sophia dragged both of us into the living room as soon as she was off the phone. She monopolized all of our time and attention for the next hour and a half until dinner was ready.

"It's so nice of you to join us, Emma," my mama said as we joined them at the dinner table, subtly lifting one eyebrow for just me to see.

I shrugged my shoulders because I was honestly just as confused as she was. Dinner passed as normally as it possibly could with the girl who broke my heart sitting beside me shooting the shit with my moms as if nothing had happened.

Once we were done, my mama somehow convinced Sophia to give me and Emma time alone, so we snuck away to my room before she could change her mind. As soon as my bedroom door was closed, Emma smiled nervously at me. "I'm really sorry about that. I know this is all very weird. I just felt bad saying no to Sophia. Plus, it felt good that someone actually seemed to want me around."

I could tell the last part was in reference to her parents and it took everything in me not to reach out and take her hand. "I'm really sorry coming out didn't go well for you. Do you want to talk about it?"

Much to my surprise, Emma shook her head. "No. That's not why I'm here. I came to talk to you about Ariana. When Elijah told me, I knew I had to talk to you."

"I tried to find you after school," I said in reply. "When Wyatt told me about your parents, I knew *I* had to talk to *you*."

A small smile parted Emma's lips as she took a step closer to me. "It's nice to know you still care. God knows I don't deserve it."

This time, I was the one to close the gap between us a little bit more. I was close enough to touch her, so I reached out and grabbed her hand. All of the feelings I had tried, and failed, to suppress, came rushing back with that one simple touch. I ignored the voice inside my head begging for more. That wasn't what this was about. Tonight was about us being there for each other. What we both needed right now was a friend, no matter how much I wanted so much more than that. "You shouldn't be so hard on yourself. I get it, Em. It's scary to have feelings for anyone, let alone someone that other people won't accept. But please tell me what happened with your parents. I'm here because I want to be. Because you deserve to be happy."

Emma looked away from me and shook her head once again. When she looked back up at me, there were tears in her eyes, and all I wanted to do was wrap her in my arms and never let go. "I'm just so scared. What if they never accept me? What if things never go back to the way they used to be?"

I wished I had answers to her questions. I wanted to say just the right words, but I didn't know what those were at the moment. The truth was, I didn't know what the future held. No one did. I squeezed her hand and took one step closer so we were practically toe to toe. "Then I guess you adapt to a new normal. A normal where you get to be exactly the person you were meant to be—the most genuine, real Emma you've ever been."

Emma's eyes were wide and she appeared to be contemplative and unsure. "What if I don't know exactly who I am?"

An unintentional soft laugh slipped out as I shrugged in reply to her question. "Honestly, I don't think anyone does. But being true to yourself is what really matters in the end."

"You're very wise for someone who isn't even eighteen yet."

"My moms say I'm an old soul. I think the first few years of my life just helped me to grow up fast."

Even though I wasn't saying that for sympathy, Emma's lips dipped into a slight frown and her eyebrows furrowed as if my words concerned her. "Speaking of which, tell me what's going on with Ariana."

I lifted an eyebrow at her, wondering if she was trying to avoid the topic of her parents or if she was more worried about me than herself. Knowing Emma, it was probably a little bit of both. "I asked you about your parents first."

Emma looked toward the carpet, then back up at me, her eyes clearly showing how much pain she was in. "There's not much to say. I told them, and they weren't very happy about it. There wasn't any yelling or anything. They weren't overly cruel. They didn't kick me out. I know I should be appreciative of all of that. But it's just weird. It was weird enough when we didn't address what happened in Texas, but the way they are trying to avoid it all over again after I told them the truth is so frustrating. I feel like I'm walking on eggshells all the time because I'm not sure what to say or do." Emma shook her head and stared down at her feet once again. "They don't look at me the same since I told them. It's almost as if I'm a stranger to them. They're cordial, but that's just how my parents are. The best way I can think of to describe it is that they are nice, but not loving. I don't know. I guess I shouldn't complain."

I shook my head. "You have every right to complain. You opened yourself up to them. That's a scary thing to do. If someone reacts with anything other than total acceptance, it's hurtful."

"Thanks for making me feel like I'm not crazy." Emma squeezed my hand that was still entwined with hers and shared the smallest smile with me; a smile that was still enough to put my stomach into knots. "Enough about me though. *I* came to *your* house. I want to know how you're doing."

How was I doing? That was the million dollar question. "Ariana wants to get dinner with me."

Emma's eyebrows shot up as if she was surprised. "Oh, wow. So, have you guys—"

I shook my head, sure that my answer would be no to whatever she was about to ask. "We've only texted. I don't know how to feel about any of this. Right now, I'd say we are acquaintances at best. She'll never be my mom. I have two moms. Mama may not have always been in my life, but she loved and protected me from the moment we met. *That's* what makes a mom. But, you know, if everything she says is true, I think I could eventually come around to accepting her as family. We have a long way to go though. I don't even think I'm ready to go to dinner with her. I saw her for a minute when she first stopped by and it was so strange. It's crazy to see an absolute stranger, but feel like you're looking in a mirror. I have her eyes, her nose…" I cut myself off by shaking my head. "I don't know if I like that. I always loved when people told me I looked like my mom. Even though I've always known that she didn't give birth to me, I guess I just liked the idea that I took after her, not some stranger who didn't want me."

Emma reached out the hand that wasn't holding onto mine and ran a finger along my cheek, causing a chill to run down my spine. "But you do take after her. You take after both of your moms. Even though you're super outgoing like your mama, you have this cool mysteriousness to you that I know you got from your mom. You said your mama was loving toward you from the moment you moved to town. You... welcomed... me to town as soon as I got here. What you got from both of your moms runs so much more than skin deep."

"Who's the wise one now?" I asked, trying not to cry from just how sweet her words were. I pulled my phone out of my pocket that still had an unanswered text from Ariana. "So, I'm not ready to have dinner with her, but you being here has made me feel more brave. Do you mind if I call her while you're here? It would be easier with your support."

"Of course." Emma pulled me over to my bed and motioned for me to sit down beside her. When we were both sitting, she ran her thumb along the back of my hand. "I'm right here."

She really was. I studied her face where her lips were curved into the sweetest smile, and it all felt so surreal. I couldn't believe she was sitting right here with me, the months we were apart suddenly feeling like a distant memory. Sure, I wasn't naive enough to believe this meant we were getting back together. We both had other things to worry about. Plus, depending where Emma decided to go to college, we could be hours apart. I wondered if she had made any decisions yet and was about to ask her when I remembered the task at hand.

I took a deep breath before clicking on Ariana's name. I held that breath while I listened to the phone ring. I wasn't sure what sounded louder—the ringing or the rapid beating of my heart. *Ring. Beat, beat. Ring. Beat, beat.* The pattern continued much too long and I was about to hang up when the ringing suddenly stopped.

There was silence for a few agonizing seconds until a soft voice came through the phone. "Bailey? Hi."

Ariana sounded surprised, almost bewildered, and as a silence hung between us once again, I realized I hadn't thought about what I was going to say. What did I say? There was so much that I could say, but so little that felt right.

"Hey." Not earth-shattering, but it was a start. I cleared my throat as I thought about what to say next. The feeling of Emma's continued touch gave me the confidence I needed to continue. "I'm not ready to get dinner. I'm sorry."

"You don't need to apologize, Bailey. You don't owe me anything."

"I'd like to though eventually. Just not yet."

Emma squeezed my hand and gave me a reassuring smile, encouraging me to keep going.

"I'm going to be honest. This is all very strange to me and I'm not sure how to feel."

Ariana laughed lightly. "I don't blame you. It's strange for me too. I never thought I would be doing this, but I've had a few eye opening things happen to me these past few years. I had to hit rock bottom to realize just how lost I was. When I finally found myself, all I could think about was making things right with you and your moms. Even if you don't want anything to do with me, getting your forgiveness would be wonderful. But, trust me, I understand if you don't want to forgive me."

I shook my head even though she couldn't see me. "I don't need to forgive you because I've never been mad at you. I can't be upset at you for giving me up because I've had a really good life. My moms have made sure of that. They're amazing." I hoped my words weren't hurtful. I was just trying to be honest with her.

"I'm really happy to hear that. Truly. Your mom tells me you're pretty amazing yourself. Homecoming Queen. Class president. Star athlete. I have a lot of regrets, especially when it comes to you, but I can't regret giving you up. Your moms gave you a life I never could."

I wasn't sure how to respond to that. She was saying all the right things, but what was I supposed to do with that? I had no idea how I was supposed to feel, but I couldn't help the smile that came to my face. "Thank you," I said finally. I focused my attention on Emma, my smile growing as our eyes met. "Well, I better go. I have a friend here right now. I just wanted to call and explain that."

"Thank you, Bailey. Feel free to call or text me anytime."

"I will."

I hung up the phone and blew out a long breath. Emma leaned in close, placing her forehead against mine. We were close enough to kiss and I found myself wishing she would, but instead she ran a finger along my cheek, a move that had me feeling just as much. "I'm really proud of you. That was huge."

"Thank you." I blinked my eyes, all of the emotions from the night putting me on the brink of tears. "Seriously. Thanks for being here."

Emma looked deep into my eyes and it was like everything she was feeling was passed from her to me. If I wasn't already sitting, the power of the moment would have knocked me over. "I just wish I had been here sooner. I really am sorry about how I've acted since New Year's Eve."

I closed my eyes and breathed her in. "I don't want to think about that. You're here now. That's what matters."

"And what about after tonight? Do you think I could be part of your life again?"

I didn't know how much of my life she wanted to be part of, but I was willing to take whatever she could give me. A part of me that was missing was finally back, and I didn't want to lose that again. "Please." I chuckled, trying to lighten the mood. "I don't really think we could have avoided each other much longer anyway with practice starting on Monday."

Emma laughed along with me, as she pulled away from me. "Yeah. That would have been awkward." She stopped laughing and became serious again. "So, we're okay?"

"We're better than okay."

And just like that, everything in my life seemed to be better than okay.

# Chapter 16: Emma

I took a few deep breaths as I ran through my warm ups and prepared for my first race of the season. My eyes scanned the stands until they landed on my parents. They both smiled at me, and my dad gave me a thumbs up, but there was something strained about the whole scene. To anyone else it would have looked completely normal, but I knew better. Maybe that was just because I knew what it was like behind closed doors. How my parents only seemed to speak to me in niceties. How they couldn't even really look at me. How I now felt like a stranger in my own house.

"At least they're here, right? That has to mean something," Bailey said as she walked up beside me, clearly reading my mind.

I shrugged. "I guess so."

I looked back up toward my parents where my dad was acting like he was interested in something on the other side of the track and my mom was rooting through her purse. I knew them well enough to know that wasn't actually the case. They didn't want to see me with Bailey since they knew about our previous relationship. Seeing us together would be too real for them. It would make it harder to avoid the reality in front of them.

Bailey gave me a knowing smile and squeezed my shoulder. "I know it's easier said than done, but try to forget about them and just focus on your race. You're going to kill it."

I nodded my head and shook out all the tension in my body. She was right. Even when my life seemed to be spiraling, track was the one thing I had control over. Track was the reason I would be at Bellman next year with a group of ready-made friends; *family* if what Coach Hopkins said was true. What made it even better was that Bailey and I would be there together, a fact that I had yet to share with her. I wasn't sure why I hadn't told her I was going to Bellman. I figured she would probably be happy about it, but part of me worried it came off a little stalkerish—the fact that I decided to go to the same school as her when we weren't even speaking.

I jumped up and down to shake the tension out of my body once more. Why did I keep letting my mind wander away from track? I needed to focus on the task at hand and forget about everything else.

When I finally allowed myself to do that, the meet went by in a breeze. I took first in the four hundred meter and second to Bailey in the two hundred. Bailey also took first in the one hundred and led our 4x100 relay team to a victory. I ended out the meet with a win for our 4x400 relay team as well.

As exciting as the meet was, nothing was as good as the sweaty hug Bailey wrapped me in as soon as the meet was over.

"Sorry," she said as she stepped back. "I got a little carried away. I'm just so happy to be back on the track, and you did awesome today."

"You really did," Bailey's mom said as her family walked over to greet us.

Before I could respond, Sophia ran up to me and jumped into my arms. "You are *so* fast. I didn't know *anyone* was as fast as Bailey, but you are! I hope I'm fast like you when I grow up."

A throat cleared beside me and I looked over to find Bailey with her arms crossed, raising an eyebrow at her sister. "And what about me? Did you forget all about your favorite big sister?"

"Nope," Sophia said as she reached her arms out to Bailey who grabbed her from me, our hands touching just enough during the exchange to put my whole body on high alert and leave me wishing for more. "I have *two* favorite big sisters. 'Member?"

"Hope we aren't interrupting," my dad's voice cut in. Even though he tried to keep it sounding light, I was pretty sure everyone, except maybe Sophia, could tell how forced it was.

Bailey's mama smiled and held her hand out toward my dad. "Never. I'm Kari, and this is my wife, Kacey. We're

Bailey's parents. It's very nice to finally meet you. You have a wonderful daughter."

"Thank you," my dad responded, his demeanor relaxing slightly. As if suddenly remembering his manners, he added, "You have raised a very nice young woman as well."

I felt awkward as introductions were exchanged between Bailey's moms and my mom and wondered if anyone else could feel the tension. I was relieved when my mom announced they needed to leave and gave me a quick kiss on the cheek before turning around.

As I watched my parents walk away, I felt a hand land on my shoulder. I looked over to find Bailey's mama smiling down at me.

"They'll come around," she said sweetly, a confidence to her voice that surprised me.

"How do you know?"

"They're here, and even though it might not seem like it to you, they *are* trying. That's a start. Just try not to lose faith, okay?"

I nodded. "I'll try my best."

***

Trying not to lose faith was getting harder and harder as the days passed by without any change. I sighed as I stepped onto the bus for our first away meet, the weight of all of this making me feel exhausted. That feeling slipped away as soon as I was on the bus and saw Bailey sitting in the front seat.

She scooted over and patted the spot next to her. "I saved our spot. Not that it was too hard. The front of the bus isn't in high demand."

She remembered. Even after all this time. Even after everything I had put us both through these past few months. I didn't even know if she would still want me as her bus partner anymore and here she was saving the front seat for us since she knew I got sick in the back. All I wanted to do was dive onto the seat, crawl on top of her, and kiss her senseless. At this point, I wasn't even sure what was stopping me. It's not like I had to worry about my parents finding out. All of the friends I really cared about in Bellman already knew, and I was sure it wouldn't be a big deal to anyone else. Then I reminded myself exactly what was stopping me. We weren't together. I had stupidly made sure of that on New Year's Eve. Now, Bailey needed a friend. She didn't need someone pining after her. I didn't even know if she still felt the same anymore. It seemed like it. I was sure we still had that same connection from before, and I didn't see how that could possibly be one sided.

Bailey tilted her head to one side, clearly confused by why I was suddenly frozen in place. "Are you going to join me or am I sitting in the front of the bus for nothing?"

I smiled as I walked the few steps to the seat and scooted in next to her, trying to ignore how good it felt when my leg pushed against hers.

"Are you doing okay?" Bailey asked, the concern on her face enough to bring back the urge to kiss her once again. She was constantly checking up on me, and it was so sweet I thought my heart might burst.

"I'm good. Much better now."

It seemed my smile wasn't enough to convince her because Bailey studied my face as if she was searching for something else; something I wasn't saying. "But how are you doing overall?"

I shrugged. She had no idea just how loaded that question was. "I'm okay. I feel like everything is the same, but at the same time I feel like nothing is the same. Does that even make sense?"

Bailey laughed. "More than you know. That's how I feel with Ariana too. My life is still going pretty much exactly as it was before, but her presence just makes everything feel so different. Are your parents still acting just as strange?"

I groaned as I thought about just *how* strange things were at my house. "Yes. There's a big giant gay elephant in the room, and they refuse to acknowledge it. Instead, they try to act like everything is normal, but they're failing miserably. They're acting the way they would act around someone from the church they barely know, which is obviously nice, but it's so different from how they used to act.

My dad doesn't randomly beg me to help him with something on the computer and my mom doesn't ask me to go to the mall with her. We just kind of coexist."

"What if you tried talking to them again?"

I cringed at the thought. "I know I probably should. I just don't know what to say. I put it out there. Shouldn't *they* be the ones to say something now?"

"They absolutely should. You've done all the heavy lifting so far. You don't owe them anymore of an explanation than you've already given." Bailey took my hand in hers like it was the most natural thing in the world. "I can tell how much this is eating away at you though. I'm not sticking up for them in any way whatsoever. I think their response to your coming out was super shitty. But maybe they don't realize just how much they're hurting you. Maybe they need to hear you say it to help get their heads out of their asses."

"I'm not used to you swearing," I said with a laugh, trying to lighten the heavy mood that was settling between us.

"I only swear when I feel really passionate about something."

"So, you're really passionate about coming out?"

Bailey looked deep into my eyes and everything else disappeared. The chatter of our teammates. The rocking of the bus. The nerves over the upcoming meet. All that remained was her and I and the strong current pulsating between us. "I'm passionate about you," she said breathlessly.

Oh, this definitely wasn't one-sided. Now the question was what I was going to do about that.

*** 

"Hey, Mom, can I talk to you?" I asked as I walked into my parents' bedroom a few nights after my talk on the track bus with Bailey.

My mom sat her book down on her nightstand and patted a spot next to her on the bed. "Of course, sweetie. You can talk to me about anything."

*Could I though?* I sat down on the bed and looked around the room, suddenly unsure what to say. How did I put into words how I had been feeling since coming out to them? How did I express just how hurt I was? How much this was tearing me up inside? Before I could say anything, tears streamed down my face.

"What's wrong?"

The concern in my mom's voice shocked me. Why would she even ask that? How didn't she know?

"It's so hard. It's just so hard," I said through my tears.

"What's hard, sweetie?"

I scoffed and motioned between the two of us. "*This.* Whatever it is that's going on around here ever since I came out. I hate it."

My mom looked genuinely confused as she stared down at me. "I feel as though your father and I have been very nice as we work through this."

I shook my head. "I don't need nice, Mom. I need my parents back."

"I'm sorry, but I'm not sure what you mean by that."

I stared across the room, my focus settling on a tiny spot on the wall that my parents apparently missed while painting and the tiniest bit of white snuck out between the gray. "Did you know that you haven't said I love you since I came out to you?"

"That can't be true. I'm sure we've said it."

"Nope. Not once."

"Well, even if we didn't say it, you should know you never have to question that. You're our daughter. Of course we love you."

I finally forced my eyes away from the wall and looked back at my mom. "Before I came out, you guys said it every morning before I left for school and each night before bed. Most days you said it even more than that." I sniffled as more tears fell from my eyes. "Do you know how it feels when that just stops? You obviously don't, because just for the record, I did question it. I've questioned every single day if I lost you; if you stopped loving me because of who I am. That happens, you know. Some parents just can't accept it and... and... they just..." I couldn't even finish my sentence because the tears had turned into sobs, I could barely breathe. Even saying those words made my heart feel like it was being ripped from my chest.

"Oh, honey." Much to my surprise, my mom wrapped her arms around me and pulled me tightly against her. "You never, ever have to question whether your father and I love you. We love you more than anything in the world, and nothing will ever change that."

"Nothing?" I asked, my voice muffled as I dropped my head onto my mom's shoulder.

"Absolutely nothing." My mom placed a kiss on my forehead and pulled me even tighter against her. "Randy, will you come here?" she yelled to my dad.

I didn't know how long it took, but at some point, the bed rocked from someone else sitting down on it.

"Could you tell Emma that you love her?" my mom said to my dad.

"Love her?" A strong hand landed on my back. "Of course I love you. How could you even question that? I tell you everyday."

I pulled away from my mom and wiped at my eyes. "Not anymore. You haven't said it since I told you... since the day we visited Bellman."

I watched as my parents exchanged a prolonged look as if they were having a silent conversation. After a very long minute, my mom subtly nodded her head then looked back at me. "I'm sorry about that. We just don't know how to react to any of this. We worry about you. We worry about all of the people who will judge you; all of the people who won't accept you."

"But that's the thing. I don't care if other people judge me or don't accept me. I care if *you guys* judge me. I care if *you guys* don't accept me."

My dad rubbed my back with the hand that had been resting there. "We're trying, honey. It might not seem like it, but we really are. My whole life I've been taught that being gay is a sin. It's going to take a lot of rewiring to change that belief."

"You could talk to Mrs. Green," I answered softly.

"The youth pastor? She knows?"

I couldn't tell if my dad's voice was confused or angry and I hoped I wouldn't get Mrs. Green in trouble by sharing this information.

"Yeah, I told her. She doesn't think it's a sin to be gay. She supports me."

My dad moved his hand from my back and rubbed it across his forehead, the way he always did when he was deep in thought. "She told you that?"

"Yes." My voice was so soft, I wasn't sure he could even hear me.

He sighed and moved his hand. "Well, I'm just happy she had a better reaction than that jerk back in Texas."

*Jerk?* My dad prided himself on finding the good in everyone and not speaking ill on anyone. So, even though jerk was far from being a stinging insult, it still sounded out of place coming from my dad.

"You didn't like Missy?" I asked, assuming he must have been talking about the youth pastor.

"I did until she tried to turn a whole congregation against my daughter." My dad's voice shook and it got louder as he spoke. A patchy redness that had started on his neck made its way up to his face. *Now* he was angry.

"Are you mad at me for what happened in Texas?" I swallowed hard. I had always wondered, but was too scared to ask until now.

My dad's eyebrows furrowed as he focused his attention on me. "No. Not at all. I don't blame you one bit. No matter what I believe about homosexuality, I think what the members of that church did was absolutely disgusting. It was the most ungodly, most hypocritical response I've ever seen in all of my time as a pastor. I'm happy we're not there anymore. I don't want to be the leader of a congregation that thinks it's okay to treat people that way."

"But this is why we worry," my mom added in. "If that's how people act over rumors, how will they act if they know it's true?"

"That's not your battle to fight. It's mine. And I've decided that it's worth it if it means I get to be who I am and love who I love." I lifted my head slightly, trying to exude confidence and not show how just saying the word love affected me. My mind immediately flashed to Bailey as soon as the words were out and my heart felt like it was soaring and breaking all at once. I had never been in love, but something told me that's exactly how I felt about Bailey, and I wasn't sure if that should make me happy or sad.

My internal struggle was interrupted by the sound of my mom laughing. When I looked at her, the smile on her face was the first genuine one I had seen from her in weeks. "Oh, sweetie, that's where you're wrong. I'm your mom. Any battle of yours is a battle of mine whether I agree with you or not."

I breathed a sigh of relief, releasing a breath that I didn't realize I had been holding since coming out to my parents. Heck, probably even before that. Things might not be perfect yet, and maybe they never would be, but I knew they would be okay.

My dad squeezed my knee. "I agree. We love you, honey. Sorry if we haven't done a very good job of showing that."

"It's okay. I'm really glad we could talk." I yawned and stretched as I stood from the bed. It wasn't late, but that conversation had been exhausting and now all I wanted to do was curl up under my covers. I stopped once I was at the doorway and turned around. There was one more thing I had to say. "Just so you know, this is who I am. That's not going to change. I'm glad you guys are willing to try to accept it because this part of me isn't going away."

I didn't wait to see how my parents would respond. I said what I needed to say and that was it. Bailey was right, and as soon as I lay down in my bed I texted her to let her know that. It didn't take long before my phone chimed with a text from her.

*Yay! I'm so proud of you! How are you feeling?*

I couldn't help the smile that bloomed across my face as I texted her back. *I'm good. Tired, but good. I might just go to sleep right now.*

*Aw, man. I was going to ask if you wanted to come over and watch a movie.*

Suddenly, sleep didn't seem so important. *A movie sounds great. I just can't guarantee I'll stay awake.*
*You never have ;)*

***

"Emma!" Sophia yelled excitedly as she opened the front door for me.

Before I could respond she wrapped her arms around my legs so hard that I almost lost my balance. As if that wasn't enough to throw off my equilibrium, the sight of Bailey coming around the corner almost knocked me off my feet. She was wearing baggy sweatpants and a Bellman Track T-shirt, and her hair was pulled up in a messy bun. Her dark eyes somehow looked even darker than usual, and I quickly became lost in them.

"Hey," she said softly as she stopped in front of me, her eyes never straying from mine.

"Hi," I said even more quietly. I could barely speak because my mouth felt so dry. Words were useless anyway. All I wanted was to stay lost in those eyes. I wanted to drown in them. Who needed air when you had Bailey Caldwell?

"Are you going to come in or are you guys going to just stare at each other all night?"

I jumped at the sound of Sophia's voice, her words ripping both me and Bailey from the moment we were sharing.

"Come in," Bailey said as she moved to the side to make space for me.

"Are you guys watching a movie?" Sophia asked as she jumped up and down like my presence was the most exciting thing in the world. "Can I watch it with you?"

Bailey patted her little sister on the top of her head. "Not tonight, kiddo. We're going to watch a grown up movie."

Sophia pushed out her bottom lip and crossed her arms in front of her chest. "No fair."

"It's time for *you* to get a bath and get ready for bed anyway, young lady," Bailey's mama said as she joined us in the hallway.

Sophia put her head down and walked toward the stairs. "Fine."

Much to my surprise, Bailey grabbed my hand and started to drag me toward the stairs as well.

"And where are you two going?" Bailey's mama asked when we were halfway up.

"To my room," Bailey answered quickly. "To watch a movie."

Bailey's mama lifted an eyebrow as her eyes focused on our hands and our interlocked fingers. Instinctively, I almost let go, but Bailey grabbed my hand even tighter.

"Door open," her mama said with a firmness that was far from intimidating due to the smile on her face.

"But we're not—"

Bailey's mama looked at our hands once again. "Door open."

"Yes, ma'am," Bailey said with a sigh, her pout looking hilariously similar to Sophia's.

Once we were in her room, Bailey threw most of the pillows off of her bed, then motioned for me to sit down. As soon as I was situated, she plopped down beside me, close enough that our arms just barely brushed against each other. I wanted to grab her hand again. It would have been so easy to. But that would be weird, right? The only reason she held my hand before was to pull me upstairs. Holding her hand now would mean something more.

I was so focused on our closeness, that I almost missed Bailey asking me what movie I wanted to watch as she scrolled through Netflix. I told her to surprise me, and I honestly wasn't even sure what she ended up choosing. All I knew was it was some high school drama and that Bailey smelled intoxicatingly good and the way her T-shirt was sliding up just the tiniest bit revealing a small part of her stomach had my own stomach doing somersaults.

I tried to turn my focus toward the movie, but it was useless. I kept stealing glances at Bailey instead. When the two characters kissed for the first time, I chanced another look at her, but this time our eyes met since she was already staring at me. I wondered if she was thinking the same thing I was—how easy it would be to lean over and kiss the same way the characters on the screen were. I didn't have to wonder for long because as soon as I licked my lips, Bailey closed the space between us and connected her lips with mine.

It was everything I remembered, plus so much more. It was so natural with Bailey. So easy. So addicting. As her tongue slid into my mouth, I tried not to moan since her door was open, but I couldn't stifle it completely. That only seemed to encourage Bailey more. She put a hand on my cheek as she pushed into me, placing her body partially on top of mine and moving against me.

My body was on fire and all I wanted to do was continue with everything I had missed so much. Unfortunately, one of us had to think with our brain instead of other parts and it seemed that was going to have to be me.

I pulled back just slightly and whispered against her lips. "Your door is open."

Bailey groaned and rolled away from me. She quickly returned to her previous position and turned her focus back toward the TV screen.

For the next few minutes silence hung between us before Bailey finally spoke. "I think…" She cleared her throat. "I think I'm ready to get dinner with Ariana."

My head snapped over to look at Bailey. I wasn't sure what I expected her to say, but it definitely wasn't that. "That's great," I said as convincingly as possible.

"Yeah." Bailey bobbed her head up and down as if she was nervous. "Will you come with me?"

Again, not what I expected, but somehow that question was even better than addressing our kiss. Bailey wanted *me* to be the person to share this huge moment with her. Instead of answering with words, I pulled her in for another kiss.

# Chapter 17: Bailey

"Maybe this isn't a good idea," I said as soon as I put my car in park in front of the restaurant we were meeting Ariana at. I chose a place in the town she was living in that I had never been before. That way, I didn't have to worry about one of my favorite restaurants being tainted if the night went terribly wrong.

Emma squeezed my hand. "I think you're just nervous. You've been saying how anxiously excited you were for this all week."

I nodded my head. "You're right."

"I know I am," Emma joked, then squeezed my hand once again.

I smiled down at our joined hands. Emma had grabbed my hand as soon as she got in my car and hadn't let go once. She knew exactly what I needed and was the perfect support person.

I had no idea what was going on between us, especially after our make out session in my bed just a week earlier. Since then, we hadn't kissed again. Neither of us even mentioned what happened. It was almost as if the kiss never happened. *Almost.* I knew it did because I could still feel it on my lips. When I thought about it, I could feel it throughout my whole body. I wanted to get lost in that feeling forever. I never wanted to forget what it felt like to be connected to Emma like that. What I also wanted was more. I wanted all of her. I wanted *us.* The problem was I had no idea what she wanted and was too nervous about this impending dinner date with Ariana to ask.

"We should head in," Emma said, her voice interrupting my spiraling thoughts, which was probably for the best. "It's past our reservation time."

I looked at the clock in my car that read 7:05. *Shit.* She was right. It was now or never. I turned off the car and took a deep breath before getting out. Before Emma could open her door, I hurried around to her side of the car and opened it for her. Even though she was just wearing jeans and a sweatshirt, she looked absolutely breathtaking, and my whole body tingled as she took my hand.

As soon as we walked into the restaurant, I heard someone calling my name and turned to see Ariana sitting at one of the nearby tables. I took in the restaurant as we walked over. It was cute; exactly what you would expect from a family-owned Italian restaurant. The room was dimly lit with candles on the tables providing most of the lighting. It smelled of fresh baked bread and spaghetti. It had the ambiance of romance. I made a mental note to myself to bring Emma back here on a date sometime. That is, if she wanted to. I was getting ahead of myself assuming she wanted to be with me too.

I was so lost in my own thoughts once again I didn't even realize we had made it to our table until Ariana stood up to greet us. Now that I was standing next to her, I could see that we were just about the same height. Her frame was more petite than mine, most likely what my body would be like if I didn't do track. She was wearing a neon yellow sweater and salmon colored pants. It was the type of outfit my mom wouldn't be caught dead in. But that was where the differences ended. All of her features were so similar to me and my mom it was almost scary. I knew absolutely nothing about the man that got Ariana pregnant, but I had to assume he didn't contribute much to my genetics.

I removed my hand from Emma's and moved it onto the small of her back. "Ariana, this is my friend, Emma."

I stumbled over the word friend because it didn't sound right. What was between us went so far beyond friendship.

"It's really nice to meet you, Emma." Ariana settled her dark eyes on me. "And it's great to see you again, Bailey." She shook her head as if she was flustered and pointed to the table. "Sorry. Let's sit."

As soon as we were all seated, a waiter rushed over to our table with three large menus. "And would you be interested in seeing our drink menu?" he asked Ariana.

"No thank you. I don't drink."

Given her history, I knew that comment was directed toward me more than the waiter. I smiled to acknowledge that I understood, and even that one smile seemed to make Ariana's body relax.

After returning my smile, Ariana moved her eyes from me over to Emma. "So, Emma, where are you going to school next year?"

I watched her intently, also interested in finding out. I needed to know just how far apart we were going to be. If she wanted to, I would find a way to make it work no matter what, but I wasn't kidding myself about how hard long distance would be.

Emma stared down at her menu as though it was suddenly imperative that she pick out her dinner at that very moment. Her eyes scanned the page as she chewed on her bottom lip. "Oh. Umm... I haven't decided yet."

She hadn't? The deadline for most colleges was just around the corner and at this point, it was probably too late to get any sort of track scholarship.

"That's okay," Ariana answered cheerfully. "I'm sure it's a really tough choice. I wish I had gone to college. At least I'm able to take online classes now."

Emma perked up. "Oh yeah? What are you studying?"

"Psychology. I'm hoping to become a counselor. I want to help people who are struggling so they don't go down the path I did." She laughed and shook her head. "Although, I don't think anyone could have stopped me from taking that path. I was too damn headstrong."

Emma placed a hand on my knee and gave Ariana a warm smile. "Well, you're turning over a new leaf now. That's what's important, right? It's never too late to start over."

The smile that took over Ariana's face was enough to light up the dark restaurant. "Thank you for saying that. Seriously."

After that moment, we easily fell into more small talk. I couldn't believe it when I looked at my phone after we had finished dessert and realized we had been at the restaurant for over two hours.

The waiter handed us the check, which Ariana swiftly grabbed. "Tonight is on me."

I reached into my pocket and put my hand on the credit card my mom had handed to me before I left the house. "Are you sure? My mom gave me her card. I can—"

Ariana cut me off by shaking her head. "Absolutely not. Having you two here is payment enough. I had a wonderful night."

I removed my hand from my pocket and instinctively grabbed Emma's, ignoring the fact that my body was begging me to get her alone. "Well, thank you. I really appreciate it."

Ariana looked between me and Emma and smirked, giving me the impression that she could feel the tension between us. "We should probably get going so they can seat someone else here."

Once we were outside, Ariana said goodbye to Emma, then turned toward me. She rocked back and forth on the balls of her feet as if she was nervous. "Would it be okay if I gave you a hug?"

When I nodded, she stopped rocking and took a step toward me before pulling me into a tight hug. Instead of letting go after a few seconds, she pulled me even tighter against her. "Thank you so much for tonight," she said as she continued to hold onto me.

"You too," I said as I pulled away. I could tell Ariana was waiting for something more, so I added, "I'll call you sometime this week. We can maybe figure out a time to get together again. Maybe you could come to one of our track meets. You know, if you wanted to."

Ariana's eyes lit up as if I had just told her she won the lottery. "Really? Wow. I would love that."

"Cool." I nodded my head and turned in the direction of my car. "Well, we'll see you later."

"Of course. Thanks again for coming. Enjoy the rest of your night. And Bailey, please text me to let me know you guys made it home safely." She took a few steps away from us, then hesitantly turned around. "Goodbye! I love you!"

I lifted my hand in some sort of awkward half wave. "Um, yeah. See ya."

As we walked to the car, I could feel Emma's eyes on me. Once we were inside, she turned to look at me once again.

"I hope you don't think I'm a jerk," I said quietly.

"Why would I think you're a jerk?" Emma asked, sounding genuinely confused.

"Since I didn't say I love you back. She's said it to me a few times now, but it's not a word that I just throw around. It's not like I don't say it. I tell my moms and sister that I love them all the time, but I'm not going to say it unless I really feel it, and I'm just not there with Ariana."

Emma reached across the center console and grabbed my hand. "I think that makes perfect sense. You're not a jerk at all."

We were both quiet as I drove. I needed time to decompress from dinner and it seemed like Emma understood that, making me appreciate her even more. As we pulled into town, I knew I wasn't ready for the night to end and I hoped she wasn't either.

As if reading my mind, Emma looked over at me at that exact moment. "The stars are really pretty tonight. Any chance you would want to sit out on your back porch swing and stargaze together?"

I couldn't think of anything I wanted more. "That sounds great. My moms took Sophia to dinner and a late movie, so we'll have the house to ourselves." I swallowed hard as I thought about the implications of what I just said. "You know, without Sophia bugging you the whole time."

I quickly drove us the rest of the way to my house. Once we arrived, I grabbed a blanket and we headed out back. When we sat down, I draped the blanket over both of us and was happy when Emma pushed herself tightly up against me, linking her arm with mine as she stared up at the stars. "They're really beautiful, aren't they?"

"Have you noticed a difference in the stars with living in different places?" I asked as I laid my head on her shoulder.

"Not really. I've only ever lived in small towns, so there were never the city lights to drown them out. My response to them is different though."

"What do you mean?"

"When I was younger growing up in California, the universe seemed so endless, and that made me excited. It was like anything I dreamed of was possible. Then after everything happened in Texas, I used to look up at the sky and feel so small. So insignificant. But right now, this is the most beautiful night sky I've ever seen. And that's because I'm here with you. You make everything more beautiful."

When she looked over at me, I could see the stars shining in her eyes and my feelings rushed over me. I was hit with everything I tried to deny when I first met her; everything that scared me while we were together; everything I spent the months following our breakup trying to forget. It all came flooding back. It all culminated in one word. One word that I couldn't deny. One word that I couldn't hold in anymore.

"You know how we were talking about Ariana and how I don't just throw the word *love* around. Well... I..." *Just say it you coward*. Emma watched me with anticipation and her deep longing eyes were all the encouragement I needed. "I love you."

Emma opened her mouth, but no words came out, and a sick feeling came over me. I had taken it too far. What was I thinking? Why would I tell her I loved her when we weren't even together? It was absolutely crazy.

This time when Emma opened her mouth, her words came out in a breathy whisper. "Can we go to your room?"

I didn't have to ask her why. The desire in her eyes told me everything. So, I grabbed her hand and ran into the house and up the stairs to my bedroom, pulling her with me. As soon as I shut the door, Emma nodded her head toward my bed, and then she was the one taking the lead. She walked us over to the bed and once we were right beside it, she pushed me down onto it. She wasted no time falling onto the bed as well and crawling on top of me.

It was mere seconds before our mouths met in a searing kiss, so different than any of our kisses from the past. It was slow, yet there was something more to it. Almost like we could both feel that this kiss was only the beginning.

I knew I was right when Emma began to run her hand up my shirt and under my bra. It wasn't the first time someone had touched me there, but this was different. It was so much different. The two guys who had actually gotten under my shirt mostly just fumbled around for a few minutes until I told them to stop before we could get carried away. Just like with everything else she did, Emma was meticulous. She gauged my reactions to figure out how and where to touch me. When I moaned in response to one especially tantalizing touch, Emma looked at me with so much desire I thought I might catch on fire. I wanted to ask her what we were doing, but I didn't want to ruin the moment. I didn't want anything to stop what was happening right now.

"Is it… is it okay if I take off your shirt?" Emma asked hesitantly.

"Please."

Emma pulled my shirt over my head, then moved her hands to the back of my bra and looked at me as if she was asking permission. When I nodded, she unsnapped it and slowly slipped it off of me, her eyes staring at me in a way no one else had ever looked at me before. It was like I was truly being seen for the first time, and it was the most amazing, yet scariest feeling all at once.

As if seeing this much of me had given her more confidence, Emma's hand migrated down my body until it landed on the button of my jeans. "I… I want my first time to be with you. Tonight. If… if that's what you want."

Oh God, if she only knew how much I wanted that. I was pretty sure I had never wanted anything more in my entire life. "It is. I want my first time to be with you too." Truthfully, I wanted *every* time to be with her. I couldn't admit that though. It was already crazy enough that I had told her I loved her. I didn't need her to think I was completely insane.

This was all Emma needed to hear, and she quickly removed the rest of my clothes. I followed her lead and removed hers as well, removing layer after layer until there was nothing between us but bare skin. I relished the feeling of Emma's naked body against mine. Her skin was like gas fanning the flames of the fire already burning inside of me.

First, she let her hands explore my body, followed by her mouth. Kisses were peppered across my jaw and neck, then up and down my arms. As her mouth moved back up my arms and over my chest, her hand slipped between my legs. Before I could fathom exactly what was happening, two of her fingers slid inside of me.

I knew it wouldn't be long before I lost all control, so I moved my hand between her legs as well, mimicking her motions in the hope that we could let go together.

And that's exactly how it happened. After a few well-timed thrusts, our bodies shook as a current of heat, lust, and love shot through me. It felt like nothing I had ever experienced in my entire life, and I wanted to bottle up that feeling and keep it forever, wrapping myself in it whenever I was lonely. But as our bodies became rigid before we both collapsed onto the bed completely exhausted, I had to wonder if I would ever feel lonely again. As long as I had Emma, I didn't know how that would ever be the case.

But there I was getting ahead of myself again. We hadn't even defined what all this meant. For all I knew, this didn't actually mean she wanted to be with me. I couldn't take it anymore. I had to know where we stood. "So, I'm not sure how you feel, but if you feel even half as much as I feel I really hope you want to find a way to make this work. I know this is still all so new to both of us, and depending where you go to college next year, we could be hours apart, but I don't care. I'll put in the work. I'll do whatever it takes to be with you. That is, if you want to be with me too. We don't have to define it if you don't want to. It can be whatever you want it to be. I just want to be with you, Emma. More than I've ever wanted anything in my entire life." I knew I was rambling, but I didn't care at this point. I had kept so much bottled up inside, all I wanted to do now was let it all out. I had to stop myself though. If I kept talking, I would never know how Emma was feeling.

Emma ran a finger over my cheek as she smiled the sweetest smile. "First of all, I love you too. I'm so *in love* with you. Second of all, I lied at dinner when I said I didn't know where I was going to college. I just wanted to make sure it was just us the first time I told you. I'm going to Bellman. I had a meeting with Coach Hopkins when we were broken up, and she convinced me it was the best fit for me."

"Wait. Really?" This all felt too good to be true. It felt like I was living in a dream.

"Really. I get to experience college with my girlfriend."

I swallowed hard. "Girlfriend?"

"Yes. Well, that is, if you'll still have me. I want to do things right this time." She cupped one of my hands with both of hers. "So, Bailey Caldwell, will you be my girlfriend?"

"Emma West—I thought you'd never ask."

### **Two months later**

"Okay, you two. Get together," my mom said to me and Emma as we stood next to each other in our caps and gowns.

"What about me?" Sophia asked with a pout.

I held my arms out toward her. "You too, kiddo. Get over here."

Sophia skipped over to us, but instead of jumping into my arms, stopped in front of Emma. "I want Emma to hold me."

I smiled at Emma as she scooped Sophia into her arms. "I guess the princess has spoken."

I heard a throat clear and turned to see Wyatt and Elijah walking toward us. Wyatt put his arms out in mock annoyance. "And what about us?"

I motioned to an empty spot beside me. "What are you waiting for? Get in here."

Wyatt stood beside me in his cap and gown while Elijah, who was wearing a button up shirt and khakis, joined on the other side of Emma. As my mom struggled to take the picture through her tears, Emma's parents hesitantly walked up to join us.

Things weren't perfect with them yet, but they were trying. Emma told them I was her girlfriend and although they had yet to refer to me as such, they did have me over at their house every Sunday night for family dinner. A few times they even had my moms and Sophia join us.

"You must be Emma's parents," Ariana said as she reached a hand out toward Emma's mom. "I'm…"

"This is my Aunt Ariana," I finished for her.

The wide smile that spread across her face told me she was more than satisfied with this title.

As our families became distracted talking to each other, I snuck a quick kiss onto Emma's lips. "Happy graduation, babe. I love you."

Emma pulled back just enough to rub her nose against mine. "I love you too. Thanks for the best year ever."

I grinned from ear to ear because I knew the truth. "Oh, babe, the best is yet to come."